OCT 15 2003

*Death at St James's Palace*

*Death at St James's Palace*

DERYN LAKE

First published in Great Britain in 2002 by
Allison & Busby Limited
Bon Marche Centre
241-251 Ferndale Road
Brixton, London SW9 8BJ
*http://www.allisonandbusby.com*

A catalogue record for this book is available from the British Library

ISBN 0 7490 0583 I

Printed and bound in Ebbw Vale,
by Creative Print & Design

*For Nick and Jane Ray - to celebrate ten years of friendship.*
*It all started on the Nile!*

# Acknowledgments

First and foremost I would like to thank all the staff at St. James's Palace for their charm, courtesy and general informal good humour when they showed me and my editor round on our own personal conducted tour. Particularly I would like to single out Alun Spencer who entered into the spirit of the occasion and even offered to stand where the victim did in order that I might push him. He was a total delight and I shall never forget what a great day he gave us, to say nothing of the ghost stories and mugs of tea that were thrown in. Next on the list comes my editor himself, David Shelley, the wunderkind, whose perception and ability are only matched by his glorious sense of humour. Without my agent, Vanessa Holt, I would never have found David and had such fun, so an enormous thank you to her as well. Also on the list are Geoffrey Bailey of Crime In Store Bookshop, the most discreet puller of strings around, and Rolf Stricker of Back-in-Print Books, who made sure that John Rawlings never disappeared. I must also mention Tony Fennymore, who gave me a truly unforgettable holiday in Crete. I learned so much from him - in every way. Finally, a huge thank you to all the people who keep me laughing when the going gets tough: Anoushka Ainsley, Fiona Brown, Mark Newington Butts, Charles Purle and the ever-cheerful editor of SHOTS magazine, Mike Stotter. Last but very far from least, I thank my companion in many adventures, past and future, John Elnaugh.

# Chapter 1

They were, considered John Rawlings, standing on tiptoe to get a better look, one of the finest rows of cabbages he had ever seen. Large and proud, green as gems and glistening still with the dew of an autumn morning, the vegetables by their very splendour seemed to boast of their royal connections as they spread their lustrous fronds towards the early sun. Stalks and leaves and juicy hearts, all begging to be crunched, could well have borne the royal coat of arms, John thought, as he briefly considered vaulting over the wall and plucking one from the rich earth of the King's Kitchen Garden, and hiding it beneath the skirts of his walking coat. In fact one particular cabbage that had immediately caught his eye and held most temptation for him, was so royal that it closely resembled the small and ugly new Queen of England, Charlotte herself.

Good sense and sobriety held sway and the Apothecary lowered himself to ground level and continued his walk along Church Lane, Kensington, the track running between the High Street and the road to the gravel pits. At the end of the lane, standing in its own field and garden, was the Parsonage House, occupied by the Reverend Waller, who was presently out of doors, breathing in the crisp September air. A typical country parson in every way, round of feature and rubicund of cheek, he exuded goodwill and benevolence.

"Good morning, Mr. Rawlings," he called out cheerily, doffing his hat towards heaven.

"Good morning," John replied, suddenly full of guilt at his earlier temptation and so glad that he had resisted the forbidden fruit or, in this case, vegetable.

"Lovely weather; a golden September, indeed."

"Yes, for sure."

"His Majesty is in residence at the Palace."

"When did he arrive?"

"Last night, quite late. It is a surprise visit."

"I thought he had no great love for Kensington since his marriage."

"I believe it is Her Majesty who has taken against the place," answered the parson, and looked wicked and saintly simultaneously, an attribute that John very much admired.

"I am not altogether surprised at that," the Apothecary answered meaningfully, then with a further exchange of greeting went on his way, turning in at the door of the house on the end of the row, the home in which his father Sir Gabriel Kent now lived permanently.

A great deal had happened in the three years that had pased since the winter of 1758, when that beau of fashion, now seventy-seven years old but for all that as spry and arresting as ever - and still famous for his dazzling rig-outs of black and white - had moved to Kensington, the country village much favoured by the *beau monde* as a rural retreat. Nationally, there had been a change of monarch. On the 25th October, 1760, the old King, George II, had died in the water closet, after checking to see if all his money was in his purse, according to the waspish Horace Walpole. He had been succeeded by his grandson, twenty-two years old and a bachelor. And though there had been a short-lived hope that there might at long last be an English Queen - for the young King's passionate attachment to Lady Sarah Lennox of Holland House, Kensington, had been glaringly obvious to all - these had been dashed when the new monarch, under orders from his adviser Lord Bute, had earlier this very month of September, married yet another German princess, this one uglier than most and dim into the bargain.

On the domestic front, John had also taken a bride, though two years earlier than the King, having eventually tired of his mistress, the wayward Coralie Clive, now the toast of London, having achieved even greater fame as an actress than her sister, Kitty. The charming Emilia Alleyn had been his choice, and the couple had set up house together in John's London home, number two, Nassau Street, Soho, in 1759. It had all been very delightful and it had also all been very dull, for no adventures had come the Apothecary's way since his honeymoon, when he had found himself involved in the hunt for a particularly vicious murderer. But for the last two years he had led a totally uneventful life and was presently finding it irksome in the extreme.

"Ha," said Sir Gabriel, looking up from the breakfast table as John came into the morning room, "how was your walk, my boy?"

"Very pleasant. I nearly stole a cabbage but my better nature prevailed."

"I'm glad to hear it."

"Is Emilia about?"

"No, she's resting. She got up but seemed rather listless and has retired once more. Pray sit down and eat."

"With pleasure. Is there anything of interest in the paper?"

"There most certainly is. It has happened at last, and not a second before time I might add."

"What?"

Sir Gabriel's golden eyes flashed over the newsprint. "A certain someone is to be given an honour."

John tucked into a slice of ham. "Father, you are being annoyingly coy. What is it you are trying to tell me?"

"Mr. Fielding is to receive a knighthood."

The Apothecary's fork clattered to his plate. "Really? How wonderful. If anyone ever deserved to be knighted, it is he."

"Utterly so."

"Does it say when this is to happen?"

"Sometime soon; it does not specify the actual date."

"I've a mind to call to congratulate him," said John, momentarily losing his appetite in his enthusiasm.

"Is he in Kensington this weekend?"

"I don't know but not a great deal will be lost in finding out."

"I think," said Sir Gabriel, wiping his mouth on a fine white linen napkin, "that I will accompany you. This occasion really is deserving of a celebration. I believe we should issue an invitation to dine."

"An excellent idea. When?"

"Tomorrow perhaps, before he returns to town."

"I was planning to go back myself before nightfall but if Mr. Fielding accepts - how strange it will be to call him Sir John - I shall delay my return till Monday morning."

"Will you leave Emilia behind?"

The Apothecary lowered his fork once more. "No. Why should I?"

"Because, my dear, I do not think she is in the best of health and might well benefit from the fresh country air. London's too full of stinks for anyone poorly."

"But Emilia isn't poorly," his adopted son argued. "She may be small but she is perfectly robust, I assure you."

"Ah," said Sir Gabriel, and returned to his reading.

"I shall visit her professionally immediately after breakfast," John announced to the newspaper."

"Good," replied his father from within its depths, and refused to be drawn further.


She *was* very pale; John had to admit it. In fact she looked almost as white as the pillowcase on which she was resting her head. The Apothecary halted in the doorway, cursing himself for being so unobservant, thinking that it was always the wives of physicians and herbalists who were the least well attended.

"Sweetheart," he said contritely.

She opened her eyes and looked at him in a flash of blue. "I'm sorry, I felt fit for nothing when I got up and now I've just been sick. The maid has taken the pail away so I hope the smell has gone."

He crossed to the bed and felt her pulse. "That seems

regular. Has anyone ever told you that you are absolutely beautiful, even when you're ill?"

"Only you."

John sat down and Emilia moved over to make room for him, her body a little slow, he noticed. "Tell me, what are your symptoms?"

"Are you being my husband or an apothecary?"

"Both. Describe to me what you feel."

"Fat," she answered.

"I beg your pardon?"

"Well, swollen. Puffed up."

"What else?"

"Nauseated. My appetite has gone."

"I can't say I've noticed."

"That's because you're too busy attacking your own victuals."

"Don't be rude. Anything else?"

"No, not really, other than a general lassitude."

John stroked his chin. "And your courses? How are they?"

Emilia looked aggrieved. "Need you be quite so frank?"

"Yes, I need. I am speaking to you in a purely professional manner."

"Well, then, the last I had was somewhat weak."

"I see." The Apothecary sat in silence, then very suddenly stood upright, an extremely bright grin on his face. "Let me look at your abdomen."

"You see it every time I undress."

"But I want to examine it specially. Come on, Emilia, don't be shy at this stage."

"What stage."

"Oh, never mind. Come on."

Reluctantly, his wife wriggled outside the covers.

"Would you be so good as to raise your shift."

She opened her mouth to object but the Apothecary did it for her, his fingers probing but delicate for all that. Then he threw his head back and laughed, then shed a tear, then kissed her exuberantly. "Mama," he said.

Emilia's colour restored itself and she went very pink. "Are you sure?"

"As sure as anyone could be at this stage. There's a tiny something there. Oh, my dear, let me go to my compounding room at once."

"How romantic of you."

John hung his head. "I'm sorry, the herbalist spoke, not the husband. My darling, this is the proudest day of my life. I thank you for the gift that you are giving me."

Emilia got to her feet and flung herself into his arms. "I am so excited and pleased. I wondered if it was ever going to happen."

He smiled. "I think the timing is just right. Two years wed, so we're ready for a newcomer."

"I suppose you planned all that."

John's crooked smile appeared. "I'm not an apothecary for nothing, my dear."

"Oh you!" said Emilia, and gave him a luscious kiss.

"I think I will drink a little champagne," John announced, walking back into the morning room.

The newspaper rustled. "A little early, is it not? But then I suppose it is not every day that we hear of Mr. Fielding's advancement."

"No, Grandfather, it certainly isn't." John rang a bell set upon the table and said to the girl who appeared, "Fetch a bottle of champagne from the cellar, if you please, Molly. And bring two glasses while you're at it."

"I don't think I'll join you. I am still drinking tea."

"Surely not too old for a toast, Grandfather?" John continued.

The newspaper rustled once more, then lowered slightly. "Are you referring to my extreme longevity or are you merely being cheeky, my dear? For to tell the truth I do not care to be addressed by that name."

"Well, you're going to have to get used to it," the Apothecary answered cheerfully, spreading marmalade on toast and crunching noisily.

"What do you mean?"

"Precisely what I say, Sir. From now on, Grandfather it is."

The paper hit the table fast. "John, what are you saying? Is Emilia ...?"

His son stood up and danced round the room, ending by Sir Gabriel's chair and kissing him soundly on both cheeks. "Yes, yes, yes. I'm certain of it. Of course she must see a doctor as soon as we get home ..."

"No, she shall see one this very day," put in his father. "Every care must be taken of my daughter-in-law and her child."

"Well said, Grandpapa," Emilia commented from the doorway.

"Oh, Madam, should I fetch another glass?" asked Molly, returning from the kitchen.

"No," Sir Gabriel announced grandly, "fetch one for every member of the household. I am to be a grandfather. Everyone shall drink to my grandchild."

Why, thought John Rawlings, quiet for just a second, should this be the moment when he experienced that frisson of fear which always told him trouble lay ahead? Why now after two years of peace and tranquility?

"John?" said his wife, giving him a strange look.

"My darling," he answered, pushing the feeling away with every ounce of his will and very gently picking her up in his arms till her feet no longer touched the floor.

"I saw you grow still," she whispered into his ear. "And I've seen that look before, just once, when we were on honeymoon in Devon. Is something going to go wrong with me - or the baby?"

"No," he answered seriously. "I shall make it my business to care for you both to the limit of my skill."

"Then what?"

"I don't know."

"Is murder afoot?"

"I don't know that either." Yet inwardly, somewhat to John's shame, he felt the first thrill of excitement.

Two hours later Sir Gabriel Kent's household was ready to go calling on Mr. John Fielding at his country retreat. A year earlier, in 1760, the Blind Beak had decided to take a place away from the stress and turmoil of the heaving city and had settled on Grove House, a spacious and elegant mansion, situated between highly fashionable Kensington Gore, where stood the homes of the monied and the mighty, and Brompton, a quiet hamlet regarded as very healthy by those who lived there.

Dressed to the whisker, Sir Gabriel in black and silver to mark festivity, Emilia wearing a bright blue open robe with embroidered white petticoat beneath, John striking in purple, the three were just entering Sir Gabriel's coach when there was a great cry of "Tallyho" and a thunder of hooves coming from the direction of Church Lane. They stared aghast as a large and familiar figure astride a sweating black horse came into view.

"Damme, but it's Samuel Swann," said Sir Gabriel, entering the coach. "Now here's good sport."

The Apothecary's childhood friend drew alongside and heaved himself off his mount, which snorted with obvious relief. "My dear," he said, wringing John's hand enthusiastically, "what wonderful news. I rode from town immediately hoping to catch you in. I thought there might be a celebration"

John gaped at him incredulously. "But how did you know?"

"Why, it was in the paper, of course."

"Oh, that's not possible. We've only just found out ourselves. Even now we're not absolutely certain."

Samuel stared. "Are you being humorous?"

"No, I'm not. It's early days."

Sir Gabriel put his head through the carriage window. "We're on our way to see Mr. Fielding now. Would you care to join us? We can wait ten minutes while you remove the stains of your journey."

"I would love to accompany you, Sir. That was the purpose of my visit."

"Oh, dear Samuel," said John, "I believe we have been at cross purposes. I thought you were referring to something else."

The large young man who, when excited and flailing his arms, could closely resemble a windmill, looked puzzled. "I was talking about the Blind Beak's impending knighthood. Is there some other news afoot?"

It was the turn of Emilia, who had accompanied her father-in-law within, to join in. Her head, topped by a very smart hat with the brim raised at both the front and the back and the crown almost totally concealed by a large blue bow, appeared at the coach's window.

"Samuel, how nice to see you. Take no notice of my husband, his mind is on other things. Now hurry about your toilette, do. We're impatient to visit Mr. Fielding, that is if he's in residence."

Samuel blew her a gallant kiss. "I shall be five minutes only, mark me." And with that he hurried indoors to change into something more suitable for a social call. He emerged fairly rapidly, his sturdy frame crammed into what was obviously his best suit, a daring attempt at the new fashion of English 'country' clothes, the skirts of his coat cut away in front as if for ease on horseback. John, who preferred a great deal of embroidery on his clothes, was not sure that he liked the style, though he had to admit that it suited his well-built friend.

Samuel squeezed into the coach. "So what was this other cause for celebration, then?"

Nobody spoke, everyone looking at everyone else.

"Let me apply my mind," John's friend continued. "You've only just found out, you're not absolutely certain. So what can it be?" He grinned round jovially, the perpetual innocent, as ingenuous and lovely as an overgrown school-boy.

"I am with child," said Emilia. "At least so my husband tells me."

Samuel swallowed noisily. "Well, he should know," he said, and looked wonderingly when the other three members of the party burst out laughing.

In view of the various delays encountered that morning, it was noon by the time Sir Gabriel's coach clattered down Church Lane, turned left down Kensington High Street, continued down the length of Hyde Park Wall, passing Mr. Mitchell's house and the Brompton Park nursery gardens on their right, then turned into the tree-lined lane that joined Kensington and the hamlet of Brompton together. At the junction of this lane with another, smaller, track, and surrounded by its own large garden, stood Grove House. Not as tall as Mr. Fielding's Bow Street residence, it was for all that wider and more generously supplied with windows, presenting a gracious facade to the coach which pulled up outside its front door. Carrying no postillion that day, it was the coachman's task to descend from his box and pull down the step for Sir Gabriel to alight. This, with much use of his great stick, John's father did, refusing all help from the younger members of the party.

A manservant who worked for Mr. Fielding at his Bow Street residence and who had obviously travelled to the country to be with his master at this time of celebration, answered the door.

He bowed. "Sir Gabriel Kent, is it not?"

"Indeed, it is, my good fellow. Is Mr. Fielding within?"

"No, Sir. Miss Chudleigh called in her coach and insisted that the family accompany her to her house for an informal levee. She had, of course, read the announcement in the newspapers. She did also say, Sir, that anyone who presented their card at Mr. Fielding's door, provided they were a person of *bon ton*, should make their way to her home to join the festivities."

"Good gracious!" said Sir Gabriel, clearly both surprised and delighted, for Miss Chudleigh was a woman of vast reputation and someone to whom he had been particularly anxious to be introduced.

From the coach came a shout of laughter, an interruption greeted by John's father with a severe look and a raised eyebrow.

"We shall be delighted to join Miss Chudleigh," he said crisply.

The servant bowed. "Very good, Sir. You know where the lady lives?"

"I have passed her house many times, a fine place indeed."

"Indeed, Sir." And with that the man bowed again and closed the front door.

"Well," said John as his father rejoined the company, "we've been invited into the hornet's nest, it seems."

"I would hardly have described Miss Chudleigh in those terms."

Samuel rolled his eyes. "She is much spoken of, Sir, you must admit."

"I feel nervous," said Emilia. "She is the sort of woman that makes other females totally terrified."

"Why?" asked her father-in-law. "She is unconventional, it's true, cares nothing for what the world says about her, has used her beauty to lure and entrap men, but I do not believe her to be actually cruel."

"Is it a fact," asked Samuel, "that she once appeared at a ball at Somerset House stark naked but for three fig leaves?"

"So they say."

"I wonder what she will be wearing today," John said, laughing.

"I wonder too," Emilia echoed nervously.


With that heady mix of high spirits and apprehension which sets pulses racing, the coach party went off once more, turning back towards Kensington and proceeding up Brompton Park Lane, then bearing right to Miss Chudleigh's house, presently quite modest but clearly still under construction. Yet for all its moderate size, it stood in extensive grounds and was obviously one day destined to be a mansion, the home of a woman who had made her way in the world - by whatever means. Greeted at the door by a fancifully liveried footman, Sir Gabriel presented his card. But there formality ended. From some inner room, the sounds of gaiety clearly audible as soon as she had flung open the door, Elizabeth Chudleigh herself emerged.

"Ah, the most elegant man in Kensington," she cried, going directly to Sir Gabriel and giving a deep curtsey. "I had intended to call on you one day. Sir Gabriel Kent, is it not?"

He was utterly charmed, his son could see that. "Madam, you are even more beautiful than your portraits would have us believe. It is a pleasure to meet you at last."

Miss Chudleigh turned, as politeness decreed, towards Emilia, then she gave a greeting that was a masterpiece of hidden messages, managing to convey simultaneously a hostess's welcome, a smile that did not extend to the eyes, and a sweeping glance at Emilia's ensemble together with a look that dismissed it as boring, John felt a definite flush of annoyance and only wished that he could have thought the same about his hostess's appearance. But this was not possible. It was a rig fit to daunt a queen, which, so the world said, Miss Chudleigh's appearance did to the new mouse who occupied the throne beside young George III.

The hoops of the lady's gown, in a deliberate snub to the fashion of wearing English country clothes, were as wide as the style of some ten years previously, at least fifteen feet in all and stretched over rods of osier. The black petticoat visible through the wide gap in her skirt was encrusted with rows of drop pearls, the gown itself was flauntingly crimson. But it was to Miss Chudleigh's face and hair that John's eye was drawn. For she wore the very latest coiffure, beginning to rise in height, plastered with pomatum and covered with white powder, the edifice topped with swaying black feathers of enormous size. This was a trend in fashion that the Apothecary had read about but not yet seen, a daring move away from the natural ringleted style that Emilia still wore. He noticed with slight anguish that his wife's attention was riveted on Miss Chudleigh and hoped that she was not feeling too much the pregnant little frump.

The Apothecary's gaze moved down from the formidable hair creation to the face below. It was beautiful, there was no denying that, though the passing years had added the lines of experience here and there and given a slightly wrinkled look to the petulant drooping mouth. But the large wide eyes, a difficult colour to pinpoint, clear as a stream and with the same liquid intensity, showed little signs of the excessive living of which Miss Chudleigh was accused. Yet even while they gave him a frank stare, in the depths of which flickered a definite appraisal, John had a strong sense of something else about the woman, something that he could not quite pinpoint.

"Miss Chudleigh," he said, and gave an unenthusiastic bow, still angry that she had snubbed Emilia.

She gave him the full beam of her attention, rather alarmingly so. "And you are, Sir?"

"John Rawlings, Madam, Sir Gabriel's son. And this is my friend of many years standing, Samuel Swann."

Oh how that woman could curtsey! A polite bob for

Samuel, a somewhat deeper salute for John, indicating respect for his father's status. The Apothecary decided that he definitely didn't like her, though he was still unable to find the word that described this daring and difficult socialite.

She was leading them into an inner saloon glittering with crystal chandeliers and rich furnishings. Within, a positive throng had already gathered, many of whom were local to the neighbourhood. John recognised Benedict Mitchell, who lived nearby, close to the Brompton Park Boarding School, and the Duke of Rutland, whose property bordered on to that of Miss Chudleigh. To add the royal seal of approval - though the Apothecary surmised that most of these people had probably come out of curiosity rather than to pay their respects to the blind magistrate - John saw that the old King's mistress, Amalia Walmoden, Countess of Yarmouth, whose grounds were adjacent to the Duke's, was sitting in a high-backed chair close to the fire. He turned to his father.

"I had not expected anything quite like this."

"Mr. Fielding is always a big attraction," Sir Gabriel answered cynically.

And indeed it was perfectly true. The court at Bow Street was perpetually packed to the doors by those idle people with nothing better to do with their time; come to see a sightless man dispensing justice to the criminal classes.

"But where is the great fellow?"

Sir Gabriel raised his quizzer. "Not in the room, though I do spy Mrs. Fielding over there."

"Together with that bundle of trouble, Mary Ann."

"Yes," said Samuel enthusiastically, revealing that his interest in the Magistrate's sixteen year old adopted daughter had not waned since he had last seen her. John, who had known the girl since she was a child, gave his friend a slightly amused stare which Samuel stoically ignored. Yet it was certainly true that she had developed into a stunning beauty for all her mischievous ways and the trouble in which she had been involved in the past. And she was presently surrounded by men of all ages, gazing at her midnight hair and sparkling eyes.

"Oh for heaven's sake go and talk to her," said John, bursting into laughter, "your tongue is hanging clean out your mouth."

"What a hideous description. But I shall not do so. I know you think I am far too old for her."

"A touch mature, perhaps. But, my dear friend, I cannot tell you how to conduct your life. She is now of an age. If you wish to pay court to her, you must do so."

Samuel, his cheeks rathered reddened, opened his mouth to reply, but the entrance of the Blind Beak into the room brought about a sudden hush. John, who had been his friend for so many years, stood in silent admiration, reappraising the man whom he respected nearly as much as his own father.

John Fielding, soon to be Sir John, stood a vast six feet in height, tallness being a characteristic shared with his famous half-brother, Henry. And not only was he tall but broad, a big powerful lion of a man at the height of his powers. His long wig flowed to his shoulders, his handsome face with its prominent nose seemed to personify strength. Only his eyes, hidden from the world by the black bandage that he always wore, revealed the flaw in the diamond, the one thing that made this colossus vulnerable. Yet he strode in with dignity, his clerk, Joe Jago, barely seeming to touch his elbow as he guided him.

Elizabeth Chudleigh hurried forward. "My dear Sir, there are more friends arrived to greet you."

Sir Gabriel led his party towards the Magistrate but before he could speak Mr. Fielding said, Mr. Rawlings is here I believe."

He had done it before, many times, but still John marvelled at the uncanniness of it. It was just as if the man could see.

"My essence?" he said.

"Just so. People have their own particular perfume; yours is quite distinctive."

John laughed. "I trust it is not of the kind that you would go out of your way to avoid."

A melodious rumble came from the Magistrate's chest. "Not at all. Those are the sort that confront me each day in court."

Miss Chudleigh interrupted and it occurred to John that she was not the sort who would remain silent a moment longer than she had to. "Is it true, Sir, that you can recognise over two thousand villains by their voices alone?"

"I believe claims of such a nature are made about me. Though the accounts do differ."

"In what way?"

"Why, Madam, sometimes it is one thousand, sometimes three."

"And which is true?"

Mr. Fielding smiled, his full, rather sensual, mouth curving. "I have no idea, Miss Chudleigh. I have never kept a record. You would have to ask Mr. Jago."

Elizabeth turned a ravishing smile on the Magistrate's clerk, that craggy faced, foxy haired individual who not only acted as John Fielding's eyes but who was sent to assist in investigating crime when the need arose. Somewhat to the Apothecary's surprise he noticed the colour suffuse Joe's neck as that wide-open limpid gaze fixed on him.

"Well, Sir."

The clerk bowed stylishly. "Madam, it would be indecorous of me to reveal the secrets of the courtroom."

Miss Chudleigh tapped him lightly with her fan and this time the man coloured violently. If John hadn't been so astonished, he would have felt sorry for Joe. But now it was his turn to receive the gaze.

"Mr. Rawlings - and Mrs. Rawlings, of course ..." Her eyes swept over Emilia who had been standing silently all this while. " ... come with me. There are people here that I want you to meet."

John turned to his wife. "My dear?"

Not looking too happy about it, Emilia said, "A pleasure."

But Miss Chudleigh had already swept on. Glancing back, the Apothecary saw that Samuel had given in to temptation and joined the buzzing group of males surrounding Mary Ann, while Sir Gabriel was deep in conversation with the Magistrate and his wife. Once more he observed with astonishment that Joe Jago, just as if he were being pulled by an invisible string, was tagging along behind Miss Chudleigh despite the fact that she hadn't even noticed him.

"Are you all right?" the Apothecary mouthed at his wife.

She pulled a face. "I feel so drab."

"But you're beautiful."

"I look an old-fashioned frump. And soon I shall be fat into the bargain. Oh dear!"

"I thought you were happy to be with child."

"I am. It's just that I have no *amour propre* today."

"You need some champagne," the Apothecary answered firmly, and taking two glasses from a passing footman handed one to his wife and watched while she took a sip. "Better?"

"A little."

"Good. Now brace up, we're about to be presented."

Miss Chudleigh was already in full flow.

"Lady Mary, may I introduce to you Mr. and Mrs. Rawlings, kinfolk of Sir Gabriel Kent?"

A fat woman with an even higher coiffure than her hostess's and a pale plump face, much rouged on the cheeks, nodded graciously. "Oh certainly," she said in a high, childish voice which did not fit at all with her roly-poly appearance.

Emilia curtsied low and John gave his second-best bow. "Your servant, Ma'am," they chorused.

"Lady Mary Goward," Miss Chudleigh continued. She

turned to the woman's escort. "Mr. Goward, Mr. and Mrs. Rawlings."

Further salutations were made and Mr. Goward proclaimed himself as "Chawmed." He was an absolute ass, the Apothecary felt sure of it, but clearly believed himself tremendously clever for having married into the aristocracy.

"Do you live in Kensington, Sir?" John asked politely.

Mr. Goward neighed a laugh. "No, I prefer Islington, more to do, you know. We have a country place there. But I like town life, never been one for buccolic chawms myself."

Lady Mary chimed in in her little-girl voice. "My son spends his days at the Brompton Park Boarding School. We are here on a visit to him."

"How old is he?" asked Emilia, desperately trying to look interested.

"Twelve," answered Lady Mary. She turned to her husband, "Frederick is twelve, isn't he?"

Mr. Goward shrugged. "I believe so. Something like that."

Emilia raised her eyebrows and he continued, "Not my child, you see. The lady wife was married very young. Frederick is the fruit of that early union."

"My first husband passed to his rest as the result of a riding accident," she added by way of explanation.

Leaving a rich widow ready for the plucking, thought John uncharitably, shooting a covert glance at her husband, who was devouring both Emilia and Miss Chudleigh with his eyes, the rogue.

"Do you have any other children?" Emilia was gallantly attempting to keep the conversation flowing.

Lady Mary appeared to get short of breath, her plump pale hands flying to her fluttering bosom. "No, fate did not decree that to happen." She rolled an anguished eye. "Do you find it very warm in here, Mrs. Rawlings?"

"Not particularly."

Lady Mary turned to her hostess. "Miss Chudleigh, I

would take a turn in the fresh air. Could you show me to the garden door?"

"Certainly, it's this ..."

But Miss Chudleigh got no further. Lady Mary's hands went up to her enormous hairstyle, she swayed giddily, then, turning in a large spiral, crashed to the floor, taking poor Emilia down with her.

"I say," said Mr. Goward, looking to where she lay, very white and very still, " I do believe the lady wife has fainted."

# Chapter 2

Just for a moment the Apothecary battled a strong desire not to get involved, certain that whatever move he made, the Gowards, husband and wife, would find fault with it. Then his professional training got the better of him but not before he had tended to Emilia, who was lying conscious but squashed beneath Lady Mary's billowing form. Rolling the fainted woman to one side, not the easiest of tasks, John helped his wife to her feet.

"Sweetheart, are you all right? Are you hurt in any way?"

"I don't think so." Her nose wrinkled mischievously and Emilia lowered her voice. She's damnable heavy though."

"You had no blow to the abdomen?"

"No. She simply knocked me flying then crashed on top of me." Her face changed. "You don't think the baby has been damaged?"

"No, but I will take you to a physician as soon as we leave here. Meanwhile, go and sit down. Let me just restore Lady Mary to consciousness and then we can make our excuses."

He knelt over the prostrate form.

"Have a care," said Mr. Goward protestingly.

"It is all right, Sir. I am an apothecary. I have been trained to tend the sick."

"Oh. I see. Very well."

John applied salts, a bottle of which was permanently in his pocket. Lady Mary's plump cheeks quivered but there was no other reaction. Looking up at the small crowd that had gathered round them, his gaze met Miss Chudleigh's.

"Madam, can you organise your footmen to carry Lady Mary upstairs?"

She looked astonished. "Why? Is she seriously ill?"

"No, the fact of the matter is that her stays are impeding her breathing and should be loosened immediately."

"And who will do that, pray?"

"I thought perhaps one of your maids."

"Very well, but I insist that you accompany her. I would not like a friend of mine to be left without medical attention when she is in distress."

"Terrible affair," said Goward suddenly. "Poor Mary. Not men's business though. Good luck, Rawlings."

By this time four stout footmen had been called and were heaving the unfortunate woman shoulder high. Very solemnly and walking extremely slowly beneath their burden, they started in procession up the staircase, John following like a mourner behind a coffin. The hilarious side of the situation suddenly struck him and it was all the Apothecary could do to stop himself laughing aloud. Unfortunately at that moment he looked down the stair well and caught the eye of Emilia, sitting meekly on a sofa. Her lips twitched and he was forced to cough to disguise the fact that his lopsided grin had broken out.

The footmen proceeded along a short passageway, then a door was opened by yet another servant and Lady Mary was deposited on a bed in the fashionably furnished room revealed. Miss Chudleigh appeared in the doorway.

"Mr. Rawlings, I shall send a maid directly. But now I must return to my guests. I'm sure you understand."

In her faint, Lady Mary was groaning in distress, and the Apothecary called over his shoulder, "If she is not here in a moment I will loosen these stays myself. The poor woman has been unconscious too long."

"Oh la!" answered his hostess roundly. "What would you know about corsetry? Here, give her to me." With that she heaved up poor Mary's petticoats, thrust her hoops into the air, and began to attack the formidable garment that lay beneath.

Several layers of stout canvas had been stiffened with paste and stitched together, these supported by lengths of whalebone inserted into hollow casings set at regular intervals round the stays. To add to the support, a wooden busk had been placed in a centre front pocket. Normally stays were laced at the back and front, but in the case of the very stout or the pregnant, side lacing was used. Ruthlessly, Miss Chudleigh produced a pair of scissors and cut through the strings on either side. Lady Mary's figure bloomed outwards and she heaved a deep, deep sigh. John once more applied his smelling salts and at long last his patient's eyes opened. She stared about her.

"Where am I? What has happened? Oh, Miss Chudleigh, my undergarments are in disarray."

"And so were you, Madam," her hostess stated firmly. "You'd laced too tightly and had swooned."

Mary's eyes fixed on John. "What is this young man doing in the room?"

"There's no need to be affronted, my Lady. I am an apothecary and was attending you in my professional capacity. Now, may I suggest that you rest for a half hour before returning home. And I would also recommend that, in future, you loosen your stays permanently."

The silly face clouded with annoyance. "I don't care for your effrontery, young man."

"Whether you do or whether you don't, he's right, Lady Mary," put in Miss Chudleigh. She rose from the bed. "Now, Mr. Rawlings, do come downstairs and meet some more of my visitors."

John bowed. "I'm afraid that I must take my leave. My wife sustained rather a bad fall. I would like a physician to take a look at her."

The wide-open eyes stared into his and once again the Apothecary saw that wicked little flicker in their depths. "Then I insist that you come to dine the next time you visit your father. To be honest I have taken a liking to both you and him ..." John noticed that she did not mention Emilia. "... and would very much like to pursue our acquaintance. I will not take no for an answer." And she linked her arm through his in the most familiar manner as they walked down the stairs. Horribly aware that Emilia was watching from her vantage point below, John tried to look nonchalant.

"How kind of you, Madam. I will consult with Sir Gabriel."

"Yes, do so. I am interested in people and am always looking to widen the circle of my acquaintance."

"Thank you again. Now I really must seek out Mr. Goward and report on Lady Mary's progress. But first I shall fetch my wife."

Emilia's eyes were very slightly narrowed. "I see that you and Miss Chudleigh have become well acquainted."

"She assisted me in bringing Lady Mary round, that is all."

"How nice of her."

"Sarcasm does not become you. Sweetheart, I am not interested in Miss Chudleigh. She is a shade too mature for my taste."

"I believe she has scarce turned forty, not a great age by anyone's reckoning."

"Enough," said John firmly. "Let me just find Mr. Goward ..."

"His name is George, so he told me."

"Well then, let me find George and after that we can go. I'm taking you straight to a physician and I shall tell him that my wife is most likely with child and must be cherished as no mother has ever been before."

Emilia laughed. "A little excessive surely." Her face changed. "But why do you say that? You don't think I'm going to have a difficult time, do you?"

"Certainly not. You are the sort who will blossom like a rose. Now, why did Miss Chudleigh put you out of countenance?"

"She has such a fierce reputation with men. They say she was the old King's mistress and that he gave her a watch worth thirty-five guineas which he paid for himself, not from the privy purse."

"Quite true that," said a voice at their elbow, and they looked up from their conversation to see that George Goward had joined them.

He really was a strange looking individual, very ginger beneath his flowing white wig. Indeed, his skin was so freckled that he appeared almost to be mottled orange, John thought, and what facial hair there was, where the razor had presented a blunted edge, was sandy. Further he had a very odd profile, there being scant division between his nose and brow, which except for a bump over the eyebrows continued in one long line. However the chin receded beneath his full, loose lips so that the entire countenance seemed to consist of one enormous beak. In fact, with the front of his wig slightly curled outwards in fashionable style, George Goward looked incredibly like a vulture.

"How's the lady wife?" he asked now.

"Resting, Sir. She has regained consciousness."

"What caused her to faint like that?"

John hesitated, then said, "I believe she was too tightly laced."

George looked knowing. "She does that to hide her corpulence, you know."

Not succesfully, John thought, but did not say so.

"She was the Countess of Lomond, when I first met her," Goward continued, taking champagne from a passing footman and digging in for a story. "However, she had a far older title than that in her own right. She was born Lady Mary Milland, daughter of the Earl of Grimsby. She married Lomond when she was quite young, you know, and gave birth to a son a year later. Her husband was a drunken wastrel ..." George drained his glass and took another. and fell off his horse while hunting. Broke his neck, of course. They tried to pretend it was an accident but the man was a piss-maker, nothing more nor less. Now, how could one regard a woman left alone like that and not feel pity? I met her at a ridotto and married her in a three month."

John's earlier uncharitable thoughts about a fortune returned.

Emilia asked the unaskable. "Was Lady Mary fat then?" Then realised what she had done and went very pink indeed.

"Huge," said George comfortably. "But she slimmed down under my tutelage quite considerably. I think fat runs in the family, though. Old Grimsby was vast and riddled with gout. While the boy, little Frederick, grew more and more obese, like a barrel of lard. Well, there you have it, these hereditary tendencies cannot be denied. So, Rawlings ..." He patted his pocket. "... how much do I owe you for your services."

"Nothing, Sir. I acted as a guest of Miss Chudleigh's." John looked round. "Now, if you will forgive me ..."

But he was interrupted. A familiar voice said, "I believe I hear Mr. Goward in conversation with Mr. and Mrs. Rawlings," and there stood the Blind Beak, his arm linked through his wife Elizabeth's.

"You do indeed, Sir," answered George, bowing as did John, while Emilia curtseyed and smiled, clearly glad to be rescued by another female.

From his considerable height, John Fielding held out his hand. "Then let me congratulate you, Sir."

George took it and pumped warmly. "As I you, Sir."

The Apothecary's mobile eyebrows rose and Mrs. Fielding said by way of explanation, "Mr. Goward is to receive a knighthood on the same day as John."

George's slack lips parted in a smile. "Charitable work, you know. I have done much to support the Foundling Hospital."

Emilia said, with a secret smile at John, "I don't know how women can abandon their babies so. Were I to have a child I would love and cherish it."

At that moment Miss Chudleigh floated past with Joe Jago in attendance, again to John's intense amazement.

"Not all women are of like mind with you," said George, waving his fingers at his hostess. "Why, there's many who put newborn infants out to cruel guardians and there let them die."

"I know of it," Emilia answered, "and it sickens me."

There was a sudden burst of laughter and Mary Ann, complete with four men including Samuel, erupted into the group. She turned to John, glancing a smile at Emilia, but no more.

"Is it not wonderful news about my uncle, Mr. Rawlings? But not before time I am sure you will agree."

"I certainly do. It is an honour he should have received years ago," John answered, giving her a small bow, knowing that anything more might be misconstrued by the minx.

The vulture George spread his wings. "Will you not introduce me," he said in a glutinous voice.

The Blind Beak, whose hearing had sharpened to a fine degree, said, "My niece, Mary Ann, now my adopted daughter. She has been in my care since she was six and is growing more of a handful with each passing year. Mary Ann, this is Mr. George Goward, soon to be Sir George."

She dropped a flirtatious curtsey and John realised to his horror that the little beast would trifle with any male, however old and unattractive. She was, in short, a born coquette and simply couldn't help herself. A surreptitious glance at Emilia told him that she had realised it too and was now quite definitely growing tired of the whole gathering.

"Of course, I am young to receive such an honour," George continued, lying through his teeth, "being but eight and thirty."

"John," said Elizabeth Fielding, rather pointedly, "has just celebrated his fortieth birthday, this very month in fact."

As always, the Apothecary was slightly shocked, even though he knew that the Magistrate was much younger than he looked. Probably because of his height and powerful build, to say nothing of the strong features of his face, he thought of the Blind Beak as being permanently fifty years old, or thereabouts.

"And you have already achieved, Sir, more than most do in a lifetime," John said, then bowed. "Now, ladies and gentlemen, if you will forgive me, my wife and I will bid you farewell. We have another appointment."

Emilia gave him a rather dark look, "Yes, we do," she said, but as they left the group, muttered, "Really, John, I am quite capable of speaking for myself. I may be with child but I have not lost my tongue."

The Apothecary rolled his eyes and sighed silently. He had the most uncomfortable feeling that this was going to turn into one of those days when he could do little right.

Despite his fears, the evening brought a wonderful calm. Emilia, contented with the fact that Dr. Grant of Kensington also believed her to be pregnant and had confirmed that her fall had brought about no damage, had retired early to bed. So, as they had done so often in the past, the Apothecary and his father sat on either side of the fire, listening to the melodious chimes of Sir Gabriel's longcase clock, which had been brought by cart from Nassau Street, along with his most precious possessions, the best beloved of which was a portrait of Phyllida Kent, John's mother, who had once begged on the streets of London with her bastard child before Sir Gabriel had taken her into his home and married her. It hung over the fireplace of the room in which they sat and John looked at it now.

"I wonder if the baby will take after her."

"It would be a gift from God if it did. She was, after all, one of the most beautiful women I have ever seen."

"Throw Emilia's good looks in, to say nothing of your distinguished features, and the child should be the handsomest creature on earth," John added without thinking.

Sir Gabriel laughed softly. "My appearance will have

nothing to do with it, my dear. You forget that I am not really your father."

The Apothecary's smile vanished and a look of great sincerity came in its place. "Yes, I forget because you mean far more to me than he, whoever he was, could ever have done. But because the baby will be Phyllida's grandchild it will be part of you, please remember that."

"I already consider it my flesh and blood. Yet how strange it is to think that a little person is growing, quite unknown to any of us, who is destined to play a major role in all our lives. Will it be a boy or girl, I wonder?"

John shook his head. "A matter for delightful conjecture until the moment comes."

The clock, which played a rousing military tune on the hours and quarters, struck eight and harmoniously burst forth. The Apothecary, listening to it with the pleasure it always gave him, became vaguely aware of another sound beneath its charming chimes. Somewhere, out in the quiet street, somebody was shouting.

"What the devil's that commotion?" said Sir Gabriel, cupping his ear.

"A fight? A theft? I've no idea. I'd best go and look." John reluctantly heaved himself from his chair.

"Be careful."

"I'll take a cudgel," and picking up a stout stick from a niche near the front door, the Apothecary stepped outside.

At first he could see nothing, then he became aware of a figure struggling to its feet, waving an umbrella aloft to aid its ascent and closely resembling a beetle in distress.

John hurried forward, slipping an arm beneath the struggling form. "My dear Sir, what happened? Did you slip?"

"Slip?" gasped the other. "Slip be damned. I was pushed over."

"Have you been robbed?"

"No, I don't think they would go that far, the little beasts."

"Who? What little beasts?"

"The stinking young fellows who attend the Brompton Park Boarding School. It was three of them. Knocking older citizens down for sport, that's their idea of amusement."

"But surely they should be shut up in school by this hour."

"They should but they're not. They creep out through windows, then over the garden wall in a trice."

"Here, let me help you up." And John heaved with a will as the angry gentleman he was assisting finally managed to struggle upright and dust himself down.

"My thanks to you, Sir."

"Anything bruised or cut? I am an apothecary and can tend your wounds should you have any."

"Well, that's mighty kind of you, Sir. I do believe that my knee is bleeding."

"Then pray step instead. That is my house behind and I have a small compounding room at the back."

"Obliged to you, Sir. I will."

In the light of the candlelit hall, John realised that the newcomer was known to him by sight, a neighbour from somewhere close by. Short and stocky, his face strong-featured and florid, his clothes made of sensible work-a-day material, he was every inch ordinary. The sort of man that one could see about the streets in any small town.

"Digby Turnbull," he said, bowing.

"John Rawlings. Follow me, Sir. My compounding room lies at the end of this passage."

They passed through the house quietly, John putting his head round the parlour door to tell Sir Gabriel what had taken place, then leading the visitor to the small sanctuary he had made for himself in what had once been an old outhouse. The familiar paraphenalia of compounding was everywhere and the Apothecary felt the comfort of customary things about him. Moving carefully, he rolled down Mr. Turnbull's stockings and eased the breeches upwards, to see that both knees were lacerated and one was indeed oozing blood.

John applied warm water, boiled in a little kettle over an oil lamp, with bruised red archangel within. This he finally applied to the wounded knee together with a little vinegar.

"Tell me," the Apothecary said as he worked, "why do these boys roam the streets at night? Are they just intent on mischief or are they heading for some place of amusement?"

Mr. Turnbull snorted. "In rural Kensington? Though I wouldn't put it past them to be visiting the brothel. They're all the sons of rich folk with more money than sense."

"The brothel? How old are they, then?"

"The Brompton Park school takes lads from the age of ten upwards but this particular bunch of hooligans are aged between twelve and fifteen. There are usually about six of them, a dozen at the most. They like rampaging about, making catcalls and throwing stones."

"Is the headmaster aware?"

"Mr. Sebastian? He has been written to, of course, but I think he can't - or won't - identify the boys concerned."

"What do you mean, won't?"

"As I said, Mr. Rawlings, there is a lot of money at stake. Some of these boys have titles, others are heir to them. It would not be in his best interestes to come down too hard on the guilty, therefore it is easier to remain vague as to exactly who they are."

"I see. Well, I do hope that you will register your protest."

"You can be certain of that, Sir," Mr. Turnbull replied, rolling up his stockings and fastening the silver buckle of his breeches over them. "I shall visit said Sebastian in the morning."

"If you would like me to bear witness I shall be only too happy to do so, though it will have to wait a while. I return to town early."

"Oh, you do not live here?"

"This is my country retreat though my father is permanently in residence. You may know of him: Sir Gabriel Kent?"

"I have certainly heard the name. I believe he is a master of whist."

"I am sure he would like to hear himself described thus."

"So where is your home?"

"In Nassau Street, in Soho. Though my shop is in Shug Lane."

"I shall make a point of visiting it when I am next in town. Now, how much do I owe you?"

"I cannot charge when I act as a Samaritan."

"Then I shall certainly call at your shop and make some purchases. You see, I also live in London," he added surprisingly.

"Really?"

"Yes, I am attached to the Court in a very minor way. Nothing grand I'll have you know. I'm a type of steward. I oversee other servants."

"It still sounds very responsible."

"Believe me, I am a little cog in a vast wheel."

"Are you connected with the palace at Kensington at all?"

"I have a room there, that is why I am seen around these parts from time to time. Of course I do not generally broadcast the fact that I am connected with the royal household, it is considered more discreet not to advertise these things. But this time, when I call upon Mr. Sebastian to voice my complaint, I intend to tell him."

His patient, now respectably garbed but walking with a definite limp and leaning hard on his umbrella, made his way back to the street. In the doorway he raised his hat, somewhat muddied from its sojourn on the ground.

"Well goodnight to you, Mr. Rawlings. Shug Lane, you say?"

"Yes, I am the only apothecary there. You can't miss me. If I should be out, my apprentice, Nicholas Dawkins, will look after you."

But as he closed the door on his visitor and made his way back to the parlour, where Sir Gabriel sat snoozing, John realised with a shock that the period of Nicholas's indentures was drawing to its close. He had taken the young man, older than customary because of his difficult and chequered past, to be his apprentice in 1755, at the time of the strange incident in The Devil's Tavern. Next year, in 1762, the seven years would be up.

How quickly life goes by, considered John, and thought of the child that was coming in to the world, probably in April of the year that lay ahead, and felt for the first time the full weight of his thirty years.

"Glum face," said Sir Gabriel, opening a gleaming eye.

"I'm old, Father."

His adopted parent sat upright, straight as a whip and just as incisive. "That word is now allowed in this house, my dear. You are as old as you damnably well feel." He tapped his forehead. "Here's the key to it all. If you're old inside there, then, by God, you are. But cheat that and you can be as bright as a button all the days of your life. So I'll hear no more of such talk, is that understood?"

John smiled. "Perfectly," he said, and kissed Sir Gabriel on the cheek.

# Chapter 3

The next morning, John departed for town, leaving his wife behind to enjoy the country air and to make a leisurely visit to her mother, who still had a home in Chelsea even though in far smaller premises now that she was a widow living alone. With no woman aboard, Irish Tom, John's coachman, decided to go at a good speed and by half past seven on a sharp September morning, the sky so clear that you could see a leaf fall at half a mile, he had passed The Swan, the last building in Kensington Parish adjoining the City of Westminster. Slowing down for a moment to allow the stage coach to draw out from the yard, John, staring out of the window, found himself witnessing the most pathetic sight. The stage, with much hornblowing and noise to indicate its departure, set off at a reasonable pace, only to leave a passenger stranded. A small figure, clutching a bag, rushed into the yard as hard as it could, just in time to see that the coach had gone too far to turn back. Staring disconsolately after it, the figure then sat on its luggage and burst into tears.

It looked to John, from the very way it wept and moved its head, like a girl, but it was most certainly dressed as a boy. Sensing something sadly odd, the Apothecary called to his coachman to stop. Opening the door, he pulled down the step and got out.

"Now, my lad," he said, approaching the weeping child, "what's your trouble? I take it you have missed the coach."

It looked up at him through waves of tears. "Yes, Sir."

It was a girl all right. The guinea bright hair might be cut short, the garb be totally masculine, but nobody could deny the stamp of the features. What game could possibly be being played here, the Apothecary wondered. He blanked his features.

"Where are you heading for, my lad?"

43

"London, Sir."

"Whereabouts exactly?"

The poor thing thought wildly, obviously having no clear idea about its destination. If ever John had seen a case of a runaway, this was it.

"Do your parents know you're on your own?" he asked quietly.

The girl paled. "I only have a mother alive, Sir. I'm on my way to see her."

"And where can she be found?"

"In Soho, Sir."

"I see." John fingered his chin. "Look, let me be blunt with you. I don't believe your story. I think you are trying to escape from something. Now, would you care to step inside the inn and tell me your troubles over breakfast? I have had none myself and neither has my coachman."

A terrified look appeared in the girl's eyes. "I do not know you," she said. "It would not be seemly."

John smiled. "I am a married man, my boy, and I can assure you that young fellows are not to my taste."

She could hardly betray herself by protesting that she was a girl and that it was her virtue she must protect. The poor little thing stood opening and shutting her mouth, shifting from one foot to the other - John noted with amusement that her boy's buckled shoes were the smallest he had ever seen - unable to say a word. And it was at that moment that Irish Tom, beckoned by, decided to leap down from his coachman's box, and arrived at her side, his cape flapping round him, landing like a flying bat.

She shrieked, very startled, and the coachman made everything much, much worse by saying, "There, there, little lady, I won't hurt you."

She lowered her voice an octave and said gruffly, "Gentlemen, allow me to introduce myself. I am Lucas Drummond."

"Lucas, is it?" said Irish Tom, peering into her face intently.

"Tom," said the Apothecary, with just the hint of a laugh in his voice, "leave the young gentleman in peace. He has missed the stagecoach and I am just about to buy him breakfast. And you as well. Now shall we all step inside."

Tom let out a bellow of merriment. "I take your point, Mr. Rawlings, so I do. You and the young fellow enjoy your repast. I'll make my way to the coachmen's parlour." And he strode off, still chuckling.

Wondering how he was going to manage this potentially disastrous situation, John ushered his young companion into the dining parlour, and it was not until a great plate of ham and herrings and a steaming pot of tea had been placed before them, that he asked his first question.

"How old are you, Lucas?"

The girl looked up, her mouth full. "Sixteen, Sir," she said after a moment.

"Have you left school? Are you an apprentice?"

She shook her head. "No, Sir. I attend the Brompton Park Boarding School."

"That place again," John muttered. "Why is it always coming into the conversation?"

"What did you say?"

"Nothing. How long have you been there?"

"Since I was eleven."

"Eleven. That's well young to be put out to board."

She blushed wildly. "I've got no father and my mother has other interests. It was more convenient that I go to school."

Oh God's mercy, thought John, poor devil, thrust in with a load of boys - and mischievous boys at that if Mr. Turnbull is to be believed - with her breasts sprouting and her courses started. He looked at her with enormous pity.

"Why does your mother want you to masquerade as a boy? What advantage is there in it?"

The poor child looked utterly wretched, tears welling in her eyes again. "I *am* a boy," she protested miserably.

"No," said John, "you are not. You are an attractive female

45

and your life must be one of pure agony surrounded by all those eager young males."

She exploded into sobs, so violently that John was forced to leave the table, ignoring the curious eyes cast in his direction by his fellow breakfasters.

"Landlord," he called, "can you show me to a private room. My niece is indisposed." He lowered his voice. "Her age, you know."

In the past, the Apothecary had found that any mention of women's complaints always drew instant results, and now it happened again. They were ushered into The Lamb, a private snug set aside for discerning travellers.

Settling Lucas by an extremely sickly fire, but better than nothing, John thought, he waited for the weeping to subside which, eventually, it did.

"Now," said the Apothecary, "let me explain something to you. I am an apothecary by trade which means that I am entitled to treat the sick even though I am not a physician. Many people ask me for physick to cure nervous disorders so I am very used to hearing sad and sorrowful stories. Why not tell me yours, in the strictest confidence. I promise that nothing you say to me will go further than these four walls."

Lucas looked tortured and opened her mouth, however no sound came out.

"For a start, your name cannot really be Lucas. What is it actually?"

"Lucinda."

"And is your other name Drummond, or did you make that up?"

Lucinda wiped her face with her sleeve. "No, that is what I am called. So may I know your name, Sir?"

"John Rawlings." The Apothecary decided that formality might be the keynote. "Allow me to present you with my card."

He withdrew one from an inner pocket and she read it slowly, then raised her pretty wisteria-coloured eyes to his face.

"Mr. Rawlings, there is one thing I have to say to you."

"And what is that?"

"I cannot, indeed I will not, reveal to you the identity of my mother. She is quite famous in her way and I would do her great damage if I were to tell anyone, anyone at all, who she is. So please accept that and ask no further questions about her."

Twitching with curiosity, the Apothecary nodded.

"That understood, I'll tell you my tale." Lucinda drew breath, then said in a small, sad voice, "I was born to her when she was very young and I was put out to a family to be raised from babyhood. Then her circumstances changed and she gave birth to another child, this time a boy, my half-brother."

"Was he also put out to be reared?"

Lucinda paused, then said, "Yes, after a while."

"Were you both bastards?"

She shook her head violently. "I can't and won't say. You must draw your own conclusions."

John looked contrite. "I'm sorry. I shouldn't have asked that. It was wrong of me. Am I forgiven?"

She drew her youthful dignity round her, a heart-wrenching sight. "Yes, I forgive you. Anyway, my brother was sent to school when he was eight but shortly after that he got ill. My mother particularly wanted me to look after him, he was so very fragile. Anyway, Brompton Park only took boys, so it was then that she got the idea of disguising me. I was very small at that time. It was quite clever, don't you think?"

She said this with an air almost of pride and John felt he could weep that any mother should so betray her offspring.

He cleared his throat. "You speak of your brother in the past tense. Is he dead?"

"No. I meant he was frail at that time."

"And now?"

Once more she shook her head and small bright curls flew

around. "He's a little better these days, I suppose. It's hard to say."

"But now you have decided to leave him."

"He is twelve and has other friends - and I cannot stand the strain of it any longer."

"Can I deal honestly with you?" asked John. "As a doctor would his patient?"

"Ye - es," she answered uncertainly.

"I would hazard a guess that a boy, or boys, has discovered that you are a girl and wants to get into your bed."

The tears started once more and she nodded dumbly. "It has already happened. He came to me silently in the night. It was so painful, so violent, but I did not dare call out. I could not bear it to take place again. That's why I'm running away."

"By God," said the Apothecary, jumping to his feet. "Your school has much to answer for. The principal must have seen what we can all see. He should be publicly shamed - and so he shall be."

"Oh no," said Lucinda, suddenly pale with fear. "It would all be so dreadful. The boy will say I was willing, he's just the wretched sort that would. And my poor brother might be shocked to death. As for my mother ..." Her voice trailed away.

Resisting the comment that Lucinda's parent should have more on her conscience than even the headmaster, John sat silently, wondering what he should do next. The unwritten rule for anyone who discovered a runaway was to take them back to their place of education and let those in authority sort the matter out, dealing with the miscreant as they saw fit. But this terrible story, provided it were true, was something entirely different. Wishing that Sir Gabriel were present to advise him, the Apothecary stared into space.

Lucinda broke the moment. "You don't believe me, do you?"

"I find it hard to credit that any mother could abandon her daughter to such a fate, yes."

Again came that odd note of pride. "Mama has had a great deal to put up with. She did what she thought was best."

It was impossible to argue with such blind faith and John simply gazed into the fire. Finally he said, "Were you on your way to see her? Does she really live in Soho?"

Lucinda looked a little ashamed. "No, that was a lie. I had thought to get work as a maidservant in some house. To earn my keep and have a roof over my head."

The Apothecary shuddered, knowing what the poor creature did not. That every stagecoach was met by harpies from the whorehouses, their purpose to pick up pretty and innocent young girls from the country and take them to work in the brothels. Lucinda, with her bright hair and lovely eyes, would be a target from the minute she set her foot upon the carriage step.

He turned to her, a note of appeal in his voice. "Lucinda, I beg you to let me call upon your mother. She must be told what is happening."

"No she must *not*," the girl answered vehemently. "She has made a new life for herself. I will not have it ruined."

"You are very loyal." He did not add 'in view of what you have had to bear.'

Lucinda made no comment but instead said, "So you see that it would be best for me to head for London and make my own way in the world."

John shook his head fiercely. "No that you must not do. The city is riven with vice and viciousness, a trap into which any young girl might fall. Let me offer you instead a post as maid to my wife. Her own maid came with her after her marriage and a second girl has been taken on. But now that Emilia is expecting a child, another pair of hands would come in useful."

"But I could not live in Kensington, Sir. I might be seen and forcibly dragged school."

"Our home is actually in Nassau Street in Soho. And that is

where I am going now. Do you trust me enough to accompany me?"

The small face seemed to shrink before his eyes and all the colour drained out of it. "My life has not been filled with good fortune but perhaps that is changing. I must trust somebody, sometime. Mr. Rawlings, I will come with you," Lucinda said.

He nodded but said nothing, making a silent vow that those responsible for the poor child's predicament would one day be called to answer for it.


It was very late when he walked into his shop, after noon in fact, but the place was fairly full, a strong female element being present, no doubt attracted by the pale, dramatic looks of John's apprentice, Nicholas. As he had grown older, so had the young man's slightly melancholy air been enhanced. And this, much to his Master's astonishment, had caused the ladies to clamour after him, presumably wanting to mother him as well as get him into their beds. Apprentices, of course, were forbidden from fornication but John had long ago turned a blind eye to this regulation. Nicholas was older than most, twenty-four by now, and to enforce such a ruling would have been ridiculous. He looked up as John came in, his blue black hair, tied in a queue by a tidy ribbon, enhancing his exotic appearance.

"Master, I was expecting you early," he said.

"I was waylaid by a most extraordinary event". And drawing his apprentice into the compounding room during a temporary lull in custom, John told Nicholas the whole pathetic story.

"And where is the girl now?"

"At home. I left her in the hands of the head footman, Dorcas being away with Emilia. Thank God he is old and kindly, for I fear for her safety with some of the younger men. She's a beautiful little thing."

"You'll have to give strict orders, Sir."

John grinned. "For the notice they'll take of me, I certainly will."

The door bell clanged and both returned to the shop.

"Good day to you, Mr. Rawlings," said a cheerful voice, and the Apothecary gaped in amazement.

"Mr. Turnbull! Why, I was only thinking of you this morning."

"Were you now. And why might that be?"

"I apprehended a runaway from Brompton Park School."

"Oh that place! Well, I'm hardly surprised. What did you do with the young absconder?"

"I did not return him, I can tell you that. Sir, can you spare me ten minutes? I would very much appreciate your advice."

"By all means," said Digby jovially, and allowed himself to be shown into the compounding room where John brewed tea while Nicholas saw to the customers.

The Apothecary, uncertain whether to tell all the truth, found himself greatly encouraged to do so by Turnbull's honest, ordinary countenance, which reacted with horror as the terrible tale unfolded.

"And you say that this girl's callous mother inflicted such a plight on her own flesh and blood?"

"Yes. But the headmaster, Sebastian, can be little better. He must have known full well that he had a girl in his midst and deliberately chose to do nothing about it."

"As ever. As I told you I have written to him on numerous ocasions regarding the behaviour of his rowdies but he declines to take any action."

"Do you think a visit might be in order?"

Mr. Turnbull looked delighted. "I would say it is essential. No doubt he'll raise a hue and cry for poor Lucinda as soon as he realises she's gone. So best we"And no doubt I'll be accused of abduction when the truth emerges."

Digby looked thoughtful. "I doubt you could be. The girl is

over the age of consent and is free to enter service or an appren-ticeship of any other arrangement for that matter. It is probably only the mysterious mother who could legally object."

"I rather think she would prefer to remain silent than draw attention to herself."

"But who is she? Do you have any idea?"

John looked thoughtful. "It has to be somebody highly placed in society. Nobody else would go to such lengths to hide the fact that she has children."

Digby Turnbull pushed out his lower lip. "Could be any-body. They're all at it, farming out their bastards and unwanteds to any unscrupulous woman who'll take 'em."

John sighed. "You're right. But in any case, the sooner I tell the wretched headmaster what has happened the better it will be for the girl."

"So do you plan to return to Kensington tomorrow?"

"It seems as if I will have to."

Digby looked stolid. "Then I'll accompany you. I have come back to town to prepare the servants for the investiture but another day without me will make little difference."

"Is that the ceremony at which John Fielding is to be knighted?"

"The very same. It takes place at the end of the month. Will you be present? Three guests are allowed."

"No. Those three will be his wife, niece and clerk, I imagine."

"Which is quite right and proper."

"Indeed, Sir. Now will you do me the honour of coming to dine? It will be an all male gathering I fear but I would be delighted if you would agree. We shall eat at four o'clock."

"I should be honoured," said Digby Turnbull, and having made several purchases and taken John's personal card, he bowed several times and sauntered from the shop.


The next day brought yet another early start, but not before John had given some money to the resourceful Nicholas

Dawkins and told him to buy Lucinda a dress and apron suitable for a girl in service. Then he had watched as the two of them had left the house together, heading for a dressmaker who ran up clothes in a matter of hours. Something about Lucinda's small stature and Nicholas's tall spareness as they walked side by side, she still garbed as a boy, touched his heart and he was pleased when his apprentice extended a hand to guide her across the road.

He had arranged to meet Digby Turnbull, who seemed to have rooms in several royal palaces, at the junction of St. James's Street and Piccadilly, and for them then to proceed to Kensington via Knight's Bridge. Fortunately, there being not a great deal of other traffic on the highway, this journey was achieved in excellent time and so John and his companion found themselves deposited outside the Brompton Park Boarding School by Irish Tom at just after ten o'clock in the morning.

It was a magnificent building with a half-moon carriage sweep leading to it, yet the house itself was the other way round, the sweep leading to the back of the place and the central wing and the two adjoining pavilions facing the extensive garden. Yet though the house was wide, nine windows - all large - gracing its facade, it was only two storeys high, there being dormer windows in the roof where the domestics, no doubt, were housed.

A man servant, dressed soberly, answered the door. "I have come to see Mr. Sebastian," announced Digby Turnbull grandly.

"Do you have an appointment, Sir?"

"No, but you may tell him that I wish to see him regarding Lucas Drummond."

For a very ordinary looking man, John thought, Mr. Turnbull certainly had an impressive way with him.

"I will discover if he can receive you, Sir."

"You may tell him from me that if he does not do so I shall place this matter before Mr. John Fielding of Bow Street."

A voice called from the top of the staircase leading from the round entrance hall. "Show the gentlemen up, Jenkins."

The Apothecary and his companion exchanged a glance and with a dignified gait started to ascend the stairs.

Mr. Sebastian, who was everything that John disliked, being heavily wigged, heavily jowled and heavily stomached, stood awaiting them at the top, fiddling with his watch chain. Well?" he said.

Digby came straight to the point. "You, Sir, are a jackanapes. A young girl was raped beneath your roof and you have done nothing whatsoever about it."

The red complexion deepened to purple. "Simply because I don't know what you're talking about, Sir. How dare you come here uninvited and make false accusations against me."

John spoke up. "You recently had a pupil called Lucas Drummond in your charge. Is that not so, Sir?"

Mr. Sebastian frowned, pretending, not very convincingly, to be deep in thought.

"Drummond? Drummond? The name's familiar. I think you'd best step into my study, gentlemen." He produced a book from his desk. "Ah, yes, here he is. There are two of them, of course. Lucas and Frederick."

"I rather think you mean *were*. Lucas - or shall we call him by his real name, Lucinda - ran away yesterday and has put herself under my protection."

Sebastian went from purple to deep violet. "Under your protection? What rubbish is this? And why are you calling the boy by a girl's name?"

"For the simple reason he is a girl and you damn well know it."

He was a good actor, John had to give him that. "Girl! Girl! We do not have girls in this establishment, Sir."

Digby came in furiously. "You not only had a girl here but you deliberately turned a blind eye to the fact. So much so that the poor creature was raped in her bed the other night by one of your older pupils and was so terrified that she has run away."

"Now I know who you're talking about," Sebastian snarled. "A snotty little fellow, very effeminate looking. Yes, it's true, he went missing yesterday. I have informed his parents."

The Apothecary was lost for words. Was it remotely possible, he wondered, that Mr. Sebastian had actually been deceived about Lucinda's gender? He caught Digby Turnbull's eye and saw that he was thinking the same thing.

The headmaster continued to speak. "So you say you have the boy in your care?" His voice took on a nasty edge. "And what do you intend doing with him might I ask?"

"If you are hinting what I believe you may be," John answered, "you can cease to do so forthwith, or the consequences will not be pleasant for you. The creature in my charge is a girl, and before your mind goes down that path as well, I have engaged her as a servant for my wife."

"For the last time," growled the headmaster, his cheeks so discoloured he looked fit to have a stroke at any moment, "there are no girls at the Brompton Park Boarding School."

He had won, there was no doubt about it. By the simple means of denying everything and refusing to budge, Sebastian had silenced them. Inwardly John seethed with rage but there was absolutely nothing he could do about it.

Mr. Turnbull tried one last thrust. "You say you have informed Lucinda's parents. May I know who they are so that we may write and assure them that all is well with the child."

"Certainly not," said the headmaster, rising to his feet to indicate that the interview was at an end. "All such information is strictly confidential. How dare you even ask it, Sir. Now to the practicalities. I want Lucas Drummond handed back into my care within the next twelve hours."

"That, Sir," said John, also standing up, "you can sing in the street for. There is no Lucas and as you deny the existance of Lucinda you cannot demand her return. Besides the child is of an age to speak for herself. You can pursue me through the courts if you want to claim her. And then what a pretty can of worms shall be opened. I promise you that I would spare you nothing."

Mr. Sebastian glared at him. "You have not heard the end of this affair, young man."

"Neither have you," said John, "nor has Lucinda's mother when I finally discover her actual identity."

# Chapter 4

They drove back to town in gloomy silence, both wondering whether they had completely wasted their time. So much so that when they reached The Hercules Pillars, the coaching inn at Hyde Park Corner, its odd name deriving from the fact that it was situated at London's western limit, as were the rocks guarding the entrance to the Mediterranean, the two men alighted to take refreshment. The hostelry had already been made famous in a novel, *Tom Jones*, written by Mr. Fielding's half-brother, Henry. Consequently, sightseers frequently visited the place, some half-believing that Squire Western and his entourage were real people and had actually stayed there. Now, as Digby Turnbull and John Rawlings shouldered their way into the taproom, they found it was as crowded as ever.

There were no seats to be had except for two at the very end of the room, close to a long, low window overlooking Hyde Park. The reason why these had not been taken, John discovered as they drew close, was that a dog, apparently dead, lay beneath, legs aloft, mouth agape, its tongue lolling.

"Dear me!" said Mr. Turnbull mildly.

"It's here or nowhere," John answered, looking around.

"Whose is it?"

"Probably wandered in off the street to die, like a wise creature. At least its last moments would have been spent in the warm."

At that moment, the dog, without moving, voided wind. The Apothecary raised a svelte brow. "So that's why nobody's sitting here. It plays dead, then lets rip at all comers."

"I'll take my chance with it," answered Digby. "To stand in this crush would be too much after a morning such as ours."

A pot boy, sweating profusely and pale with exhaustion,

was summoned and went away with their order, glancing miserably at all the other customers demanding his attention.

"I doubt he'll be back within a half hour."

"Was it even worth coming in here?"

"Yes, Mr. Rawlings, it was. We were routed this morning, we may as well admit it, so it was necessary for us to withdraw and regroup. And what better place than a warm and cosy inn?"

"If by cosy you mean heaving with humanity, then you're right. But Sebastian did best us, didn't he?"

Digby Turnbull had never looked more ordinary or more honest than when he answered, "I have heard it said that to deny all knowledge of an event is an excellent defence. And I can truly say that I, personally, have never seen it better employed. But it is, when all's said and done, an ostrich's way."

"Your meaning, Sir?"

"That the truth will emerge one day; it almost always does. And then he will be worsted for his lies and evasions."

"I hope you're right. Do you think he will take this matter further?"

"No, Sir, I don't. By the way, did you notice that he referred to Lucas/Lucinda's parents, not just her mother?"

"Yes, but I thought that was a bluff."

"I wonder," said Digby thoughtfully.

"Yes," John answered slowly, "now that you come to mention it, so do I."

There was a silence during which the dog voided wind again, still without moving. And then the Apothecary's attention was drawn by two voices, known yet not identifiable, speaking in urgent tones quite close at hand.

" ... think I didn't hear," said one, female, "then you are mistaken. To anyone with the remotest idea, the innuendo was obvious."

"But who *has* the remotest idea?" answered the man. "You are letting your imagination run away with you."

"Far from it. I'll swear that one or two members of the company looked at me knowingly."

"Guilty conscience and guilty conscience alone," the male voice drawled in reply.

There was a hiss. "You bastard! Never forget that you are not without guilt."

"But you would never name it."

"Would I not if I were driven."

It was at that most interesting moment that the pot boy reappeared, kicking the dog accidentally as he set down two glasses and a jug. The animal, thus disturbed, began to bark furiously, drowning out all other sound. Cursing, John stood up to discover who it was who had been speaking. But he was too late. All he saw was the skirt of a woman's cloak as she went out of the taproom to the street, and the backview of a man, vaguely familiar.

Digby looked up from pouring the wine. "Was that someone you knew?"

"Yes, but though I recognised their voices I could not place them. Do you know they almost seemed to be blackmailing one another about revealing some terrible truth."

John's stolid companion sighed. "That could be virtually anyone in the *beau monde*. They're all riddled with corruption. I fear for society, I truly do."

"You're right," the Apothecary answered, taking a draught. "Recent events do not encourage one to have a great deal of faith in human nature."

"I suppose Lucinda really *is* a girl," said Digby ruminatively.

"She certainly is. I particularly noticed her breasts," John answered thoughtlessly, then pulled himself up short for being just as base and basic as all the rest.


By the time they left The Hercules Pillars, neither man was feeling as fraught as they had earlier. In fact the glow of good wine was about them as they clambered into the coach. It would seem that Irish Tom had also had the benefit of ale because he set off at a brisk pace and reached Piccadilly in record time, dropping Digby off so that he could walk the short distance to St. James's Palace.

"When is the investiture?" John asked, as his companion alighted.

"On the 30th September."

"It should be most impressive."

"It is a colourful ceremony indeed. Tell me, how will Mr. Fielding manage? I mean regarding his blindness."

"His wife, Elizabeth, will walk with him, arm in arm. That is what he does in a place he doesn't know. Of course he has memorised his home and the courtroom. In those he has only a switch or cane to guide him."

"He could have been knighted privately, you know."

"I somehow think that he would not have wanted that. He is a very proud man, is John Fielding."

"So I have gathered." Mr. Turnbull paused. "You know him quite well, I believe."

"Yes."

"Do you intend to mention the Brompton Park School affair?"

"Yes, I think I will, just in case there are any repercussions. I may as well state my side of the case."

Digby looked thoughtful. "I wonder just who Lucinda's mother is."

"We'll know one day," John answered, but did not feel the confidence that his cheerful manner implied.


It seemed that everybody had returned to town, for several letters awaited the Apothecary as he walked into his hall, where they were handed to him before he made his way to the library to read their contents. The first, in flowery hand, was from Miss Chudleigh, announcing that she had returned to court to resume her duties as maid of honour to the Princess of Wales, the young King's mother. She hoped very much to see him again and entertain him in her apartments. No mention whatsoever was made of Emilia. The Apothecary smiled wryly and threw it on one side, then picked it up again with a thoughtful expression on his face.

The second was from the Blind Beak himself, inviting him to dinner that very day. Suddenly realising that if he was going to accept he had little time in which to prepare, John rang a bell and when a lower footman replied asked him to fetch the head man.

The staff had changed enormously since John's marriage and Sir Gabriel's departure to Kensington. Three of the older servants, including the cook, had gone with him, and the arrival of Emilia, complete with her personal maid and a newly employed housemaid to assist, had altered the entire balance of the household, which had once been all male and dominated by footmen. Sir Gabriel, who had never considered his establishment grand enough to employ a steward, had left behind the head footman, Axford, to make sure that the newlyweds' domestic life ran without a hitch.

"You sent for me, Sir?" Axford asked now.

"Yes, I've several things to discuss. First of all, how is Lucinda settling down?"

"Very well. She has been kitted out in suitable clothes and has been doing her chores quite competently."

"What position have you given her?"

"An undermaid. I felt that when Mrs. Rawlings returned with Dorcas and Hannah there would be trouble indeed if they found that anyone of equal status to themselves had been employed in their absence. Household politics, Sir." He sighed.

"Very wise. Anyway, I must hurry. I have been invited to dine with Mr. Fielding. Can some hot water be brought to my bedroom immediately. That and a glass of pale sherry."

"I'll send Lucinda up with the tray and Gregg with the ewer. Is there anything else, Sir?"

"Yes, Axford. You meet a lot of other servants when you are out and about, tell me what is said about Miss Chudleigh. Is it true that she is the mistress of the Duke of Kingston?"

To have talked so freely with a footman would have been frowned upon by that doyen of good taste, Sir Gabriel. But John had known Axford for years and had long ago realised his value as a source of London gossip.

"It is indeed, Sir. She met him about eighteen months ago and, if you'll forgive the phrase, he has been in her clutches ever since."

"He was not at her levee for Mr. Fielding the other day."

Axford looked very knowing but said nothing.

"You are wearing a mysterious face, Axford. What is it you want to say to me?"

"That the Duke is kin to Mr. Fielding; they are connected in some way, I believe through cousinage to the Earl of Denbigh. Whatever the case, that is why Miss Chudleigh is so well disposed towards the Magistrate. Her carriage is often seen outside the court, where she has gone as a visitor of course."

"How interesting. Tell me, is not the Duke quite an elderly and scholarly man?"

"He is indeed. No ripsnorter rakehell he."

"But she is so beautiful and so outrageous. The attraction of opposites I suppose." The Apothecary looked pensive. "Does Miss Chudleigh have a bastard child, I wonder."

"Rumour has suggested it, Sir."

"That proves nothing."

"Indeed not. Yet if she has she would merely be like many a great lady before her."

"Yes." John got to his feet. "No doubt I shall learn more of her this evening. But first I must get ready. Send Lucinda and Gregg up as soon as you can."

"Yes, Mr. Rawlings."

As soon as they had returned from honeymoon, John and Emilia had moved into the largest bedroom in Nassau Street, the room once occupied by Sir Gabriel and the Apothecary's mother, Phyllida. Situated at the back of the house, the room overlooked the long thin garden, a fact that Phyllida had preferred to a view of the street, though convention decreed that the master bedroom should always be in the front of the building. Now John stood there, staring out over the autumn borders, just one or two flowers still blooming, adding their colour to the bright flame of the leaves. He did not turn when the knock came at the door but saw Lucinda's blurred reflection in the glass of the window. She was quite definitely female, he thought, and rather too pretty for her own good.

"I brought your sherry, Sir."

He wheeled round. "Lucinda. How nice of you. How are you settling in?"

"I like it here very much, Sir. Everyone has been so kind. These are the clothes that the dressmaker made for me."

The dress was a light dove grey, adorned by a lilac collar and cuffs. To complete the outfit Lucinda wore a lilac apron.

"The trimmings are not too fanciful, are they, Sir?"

"They are but they match your eyes. You look very beautiful."

She blushed wildly and the Apothecary realised that he was going to have to be careful with her; that she was young and vulnerable and ready to fall in love. He put on his serious face.

"I saw Mr. Sebastian this morning."

Lucinda went pale. "What did he say?"

"That you were a boy. That he knew nothing of any girl at his school. That he claimed you back."

She looked positively ill. "Are you going to send me away?"

"No, you are of an age now."

"What does that mean?"

"That you are old enough to choose what you want to do

regarding certain things. The age of consent is twelve, you are sixteen. But for all that you do not come of legal age until you are twenty-one. Therefore if your mother wanted you to return to school, she could force you to do so, though I truly believe that Mr. Sebastian on his own could not demand it."

"My mother will let sleeping dogs lie," Lucinda answered firmly.

"How do you know that?"

"Because I will fight," said his new servant with sudden fire. "I shall threaten that if I am sent back I will make the fact of my birth public, that I will go to the newspapers. I will not return to that evil school, I will not."

John took the glass of sherry from the tray and sipped it. "I am delighted to hear it. But now I must prepare. I am dining with Mr. Fielding. Thank you, Lucinda."

She hovered in the doorway. "Before I leave can I just say thank you. You have rescued me from a life of hell."

"And will you tell your mother that if she should call?"

"She will not call," answered Lucinda with certainty, and left the room.


"So," said the Blind Beak, "it's damsels in distress now, is it?"

"I'm afraid so. Do you think I will be accused of abduction?"

"Technically you could be. But if what the girl says is true - and from what you have told me there seems no reason to disbelieve her - the school is too rum to court publicity and the mother sounds the usual hard-faced harpy that the upper eschelons of society are so very good at breeding."

John was silent, looking round Mr. Fielding's dining room, enjoying the cosiness of the autumn evening, of the rich red curtains, admiring the Magistrate's new acquisition, a mahogany sideboard with an inlay of satinwood, designed by Robert Adam. The flames were reflected in its dark gleaming wood, giving a glow and harmony to the room that the Apothecary found enormously relaxing. Worries about malevolent headmasters and uncaring mothers suddenly seemed a million miles away.

"Another port?" said Mr. Fielding and, as ever, poured with the dexterity of a sighted man.

John sighed with contentment. It had been a marvellous meal, just the two men together, the ladies having gone to the playhouse to see David Garrick as Shylock in *The Merchant of Venice*. The Apothecary presumed, though he had not actually asked, that the woman he had once loved with all his heart, the actress Coralie Clive, would be taking the part of Portia.

"I miss the theatre," said the Magistrate, slowly lighting a pipe.

"Could you not go and listen?"

John Fielding shook his head. "It isn't worth it. The difficulties of getting in and out of my seat are too great to justify the few hours of pleasure involved. Occasionally, though, as Garrick and I have been friends for years, he will bring some of his players here and I have a performance all to myself."

"Does Coralie come?" John asked before he could control the words.

"Yes, now and then."

"How is she?"

"Still beautiful, that is according to my wife and Mary Ann. Climbing high in the theatre since her sister's retirement last March. And with a string of admirers into the bargain," Mr. Fielding added, answering John's unasked question.

"I suppose she will finally marry into the aristocracy."

"I dare say," answered the Magistrate comfortably.

"Talking of the aristocracy, I thought it most kind of Miss Chudleigh to invite us the other day."

Mr. Fielding chuckled. "Ah, Elizabeth, yes. Of course she is not really a member of that social order, not yet that is."

John looked interested but said nothing, anxious to hear more.

"No, her father was merely Colonel Chudleigh and she was left very badly provided for when he died suddenly. Elizabeth was only six years old at the time. But she has always been a beautiful girl and has risen very high because of that. They say the Earl of Bath was much attracted to her and the Duke of Hamilton was on the point of marrying her, though some misunderstanding caused them to break up and he married one of the Misses Gunning instead. However, she is now much attached to my kinsman, the Duke of Kingston."

"Will she become his wife, do you think?"

"I don't see why not. There is nothing to stop either of them. In fact I am surprised she has not done it by now."

"Has she ever had a child?" asked John, out of the blue.

Mr. Fielding looked slightly startled. "Not that I know of. Though there was a rumour that some years ago she left court for a considerable length of time. But then there are rumours like that about all lovely and daring women."

John nodded, longing to ask when this was but not quite having the courage to do so. It was obvious by the way he spoke that the Magistrate was fond of the lady in question and there were other ways of finding such information. However, Mr. Fielding had not finished speaking.

"It is said that when she returned, one young woman commented that she had heard Miss Chudleigh had given birth to twins, and this to her face, mark you. Apparently, Lord Chesterfield was standing nearby and Elizabeth at once drew him into the conversation and asked if he could believe such gossip. 'Ah, Miss Chudleigh,' he answered, very straight-faced, "I make it a policy only to believe half of what I hear.'"

The Magistrate rumbled another melodious laugh, in which John joined him.

"Why is it that I can never think of witty ripostes until too late?"

"A fact common to most of us," John Fielding answered. He changed the subject. "The investiture is going to be quite an ordeal, I believe."

"Why so?"

"My dear friend, there is a great deal of walking involved. Apparently, we enter by one staircase, leave by another, and have endless rooms to process through until we reach the throne."

"But Mrs. Fielding will walk with you surely."

"Not only she. I have asked permission for Jago to take my other arm. He is as used to guiding me as my wife. They shall proceed on either side of me and Mary Ann will sit by herself to observe."

"How I wish I could be there," said the Apothecary. "It would be one of the great moments of my life to see you knighted." He meant every word.

"Alas Mr. Rawlings, we are limited to three guests. As it is there will be a mighty crush."

"Is the Queen to be present?"

"Not she. I have heard that she does not care too greatly for public show. She is formidably ugly you know, and I am sure that someone must have giggled this behind her back. I suppose one should feel sorry for the poor thing. Sometimes ..." He burst out laughing again and John came to the conclusion that the great man was very slightly the worse for liquor. "... one almost feels blessed that one cannot see her."

"Is it true that the King wears a blindfold at night?" asked the Apothecary. He, too, was feeling the effects of the port.

"If he doesn't, he soon will. The only thing the poor girl has on her side is youth and that will pass quickly enough."

"I am sure that half the people present at the ceremony will be disappointed not to get a close look at Her Majesty. It is the talk of town that wagers are being taken on exactly how plain she is."

"Well, she's not going to be there. Apparently it is not the thing for consorts to attend."

"Ah well," said John. There was a noise on the stairs and he looked at his watch. "I do believe that is the ladies returning. My dear sir, I have outstayed my welcome."

Mr. Fielding shook his head. "You could never do that, my friend. Remain to greet them and have another glass of port."

"In your company, Sir," answered the Apothecary, "I am always weak willed. I shall be only too happy to do so."


He had walked to Bow Street and now hailed a chair for the return journey. A link man was also summoned to light the way and the little party set off at a steady pace towards Nassau Street. The ways were empty and full of shadows and John, looking around him, thought that the *beau monde* were all at play and honest citizens were all abed, it was so unusually quiet.

It was as he was approaching his home that he caught his first sight of anyone tangible, though gloomy figures had been lurking in the denser patches of shade throughout the journey. Slipping along Gerard Street, coming from the direction of Nassau Street, was a cloaked figure, the hood pulled well forward to mask the face. It was a small, slight person, whoever it was, and they held a paper in their hand. John surmised that even at this late hour someone was on their way to the post. He peered more closely, raising his quizzing glass to his eye. And then the hood slipped back very slightly and he saw who it was braving the darkness of this chilly September night. His new servant Lucinda had not only left the house but had written to someone, no doubt to inform them precisely where she was now residing.

# Chapter 5

He had said nothing, though the incident had given him food for thought, For it seemed to John, the more he considered the matter, that Lucinda was still in her mother's thrall and might quite possibly write to that most undeserving of women to inform her of her whereabouts. Yet that didn't quite make sense. The girl had declared most emphatically that she would fight fire with fire rather than return to boarding school, and her mother was the one person with the legal right to make her do so. Eventually he concluded that the letter must have been intended for someone entirely different and decided in view of Lucinda's exemplary behaviour to let the matter drop.

Emilia returned home with her two maids and there was the usual rather cool reception of the new girl by the established servants, particularly as she was so very pretty and so very young and capable. Fortunately, Emilia took to her, even more sympathetically when Lucinda related the story of her ordeal at the Brompton Park Boarding School. So, the Apothecary thought, as the month of September drew to its close and his wife complained that her stays were getting too tight, that all was well with his little domestic world. And he sighed to himself that his adventuring days were over and the strange premonition he had experienced in Kensington had turned out to be false after all.

The weather remained fine and fair; leaves fell in the parks and squares, making a carpet of red and gold. With his feet crunching over them, the Apothecary made his way to Shug Lane on the morning of the penultimate day of the month, basking in the sunshine, thinking that Nicholas would be preparing tea at this very moment and that he would enjoy a cup before he started work for the day. But when he arrived in the lane it was to see his apprentice in a state of some agitation, anxiously peering down the street to discover if he was on his way and running to greet him as soon as he came into view.

"Oh, Master, thank heavens you are here."

"Why, what is wrong?"

"It's Mrs. Fielding. She has been taken ill and the Magistrate has requested that you go directly to Bow Street. Apparently she has pronounced that she has no faith in physicians since old Dr. Drake retired and she will see no one but yourself."

"What are her symptoms?" asked John, rushing into the shop to collect his medical bag.

"Nausea, vomiting, laxes. Apparently she is in a pitiable state and too weak to leave her bed."

"Call me a chair, Nicholas. I'd best get there straight away."

"They are all hoping you can work a miracle, Sir, for tomorrow is the day of the investiture."

The Apothecary groaned. "Oh dear God, I hate this sort of thing. A bad purging will not cure itself fast, as you well know, Nick. Whatever has caused it must pass from the system and though physick can ease the suffering it is not guaranteed to do so at once."

His apprentice, nicknamed the Muscovite because of an exotic ancestry linking him with the court of Tsar Peter the Great, nodded.

"What you say is completely true. I wish you luck, Sir. Anyway, let me find you some chairmen."

"Thanks," answered John, and began to pack his bag methodically, uneasily aware that a great deal depended on him.

Elizabeth Fielding looked terrible, pale as a cloud, her skin drawn so tightly over the bones of her face that she had an almost skeletal air.

"How long has she been like this?" John asked over his shoulder.

Mary Ann who, to give the silly flap her due, looked genuinely anxious and upset, said, "Since yesterday afternoon, Mr. Rawlings."

"Did she eat anything that upset her?"

"No, Sir, just what we all had."

"Then it is an evil disposition of the body caught from another. Infections tend to breed and fester in the warm weather. Mary Ann, you must hold your adopted mother up while I spoon some physick into her."

"Will she be better by tomorrow, Mr. Rawlings?"

"Realistically, no. Not unless there's a miracle."

"But my uncle is to receive his knighthood. It would break her heart to miss it."

"It would break her heart even more to be caught short before the King."

"Oh God's life!" said Mary Ann, and giggled despite the awfulness of the occasion.

John administered three different concoctions; the outer bark of black alder to bind the laxes, stalks of burnet in claret to staunch the castings, and the seeds of quince tree in boiling water. This mixture produced a soft mucilaginous substance similar to white of egg which he painstakingly fed to the patient on a spoon.

"What does that do?" Mary Ann whispered.

"There is nothing finer for soothing the intestines. Now, my girl, these doses are to be repeated every four hours without fail. I will call again this evening to see how the patient progresses and during the day I will send my apprentice, Nicholas, whom I am sure you remember well."

He looked at her beadily, recalling the time when she had driven the young man to his wits' end with love for her.

The girl had the good grace to blush, but then said slyly, "Don't worry that incident is closed. Besides, I have been replaced in his affections I believe."

71

John stared at her. "What do you mean?"

Mary Ann made much of sponging her aunt's fevered brow, looking at John over the top of Elizabeth Fielding's head. Then she whispered pointedly, "Nicholas has a new sweetheart. I have seen him walking out with her."

John, despite the fact he had long ago waived the strict rules regarding apprentices in view of the Muscovite's age, was interested. "Really? Who is she?"

"I don't know. I've never seen her before. But very pretty though."

A warning bell went off in the Apothecary's mind. "Small, bright headed, with eyes the colour of wisteria?"

"Yes, that's her. Who is she?"

"A new servant. Nicholas was probably showing her the way to a shop. She does not know this area."

Mary Ann's face went from sly to foxy. "Oh no doubt he was, but strange that they should be handfast as they walked."

Inwardly, John groaned as he wondered just what bundle of trouble he had let into his house. However, he put on his sweetest smile for the benefit of the inquisitive imp regarding him.

"She may well have felt nervous when she walked. I'm sure that Nicholas was doing no more than guide her along."

"Oh for certain," Mary Ann answered, and gave him the sort of pert grin that made him want to slap her.

John turned back to his patient. "Keep your aunt like this, utterly quiet and still, and do not attempt to give her any food. She can have sips of water and no more. Tell your uncle that I will see him tonight."

"Yes, Mr. Rawlings."

"And can you also tell him the facts. Namely, that Mrs. Fielding will most likely not be able to attend tomorrow's ceremony."

"He will be very upset."

"He probably will, but it is better that he should get used to the idea now."

"I'm sure he will refuse to go himself if she cannot be there."

"I do hope that he won't even consider anything so foolish."

It was a busy day in the shop, particularly with Nicholas out for an hour, and John was pleased when they finally closed for the night and he was able once more to take a chair to Bow Street. The court, which had been sitting that day, was no longer in session and as John turned into the tall thin house in which Mr. Fielding and his family lived, he passed Joe Jago, the Magistrate's clerk, making his way outwards, a determined expression on his craggy face.

"Joe," said John, delighted to see his old friend again, "where are you off to?"

"I've an appointment with my tailor, Mr. Rawlings."

"A new suit for tomorrow?"

"Indeed, Sir. I thought a rich dark blue with silver trimming might be dee rigour."

Joe had never got the hang of pronouncing *de rigueur* and the Apothecary grinned, though not mockingly.

"What time do you have to be at the palace?"

"The levee begins at eleven, so carriages will be arriving from an hour beforehand. Anyway, Sir, I must be off. The tailor has to make a final fitting then will be working through the night if all's not perfect."

"Good luck tomorrow," said John and went within.

He found Mr. Fielding sitting beside his wife, gently holding her hand. It looked to John, as he went quietly through the door, as if both of them were fast asleep, the Magistrate absolutely still, Elizabeth not moving, pale against her pillows. The Apothecary hardly liked to disturb them but even as he silently approached, John Fielding raised his head.

"Mr. Rawlings?"

"Yes."

73

"Thank you for what you've done. My wife has ceased to vomit and purge and is now sleeping quietly. I owe this to your rapid response to our call for help."

John felt his patient's brow. "Sir, I know that Mrs. Fielding has greatly improved but I do not think it would be prudent to disturb her tomorrow. It is my honest opinion that she should be allowed to rest for several days more. She is still very weak, believe me."

The Magistrate nodded. "Nothing would induce me to jeopardise her recovery. No, Mr. Rawlings, if you are agreeable it is you who will act as my second guide at the palace tomorrow."

"Me?"

"Yes, you Sir. I must take another person - I should die of shame were I to trip on my way to the throne - and I can think of no one I would prefer to accompany me. John, will you say yes?"

The Apothecary reeled, partly at being called by his first name, something that the Magistrate had done only once before in their entire acquaintanceship, and partly at the thought of attending an investiture at St James's Palace.

"Sir, I would be highly honoured," he answered breathlessly.

"Then, my friend, when you have tended your patient I suggest you make for home and bring forth your best clothes for your servants to sponge and press. I intend that we shall put on a goodly show, us representatives of the Public Office."

"And what are you wearing, Sir?"

"A new suit, dark damson in shade. I refuse to have anything too showy. It is Mary Ann who will outshine us all."

Like the devil she will, thought John, and mentally started going through his wardrobe as he took his leave and headed home in a flurry of excitement.


In the event he chose his green and gold wedding suit, the finest day-wear he had, and rose early to make sure that he was as clean and well-shaven as it was possible to be. The rest of the household rose with him, running about with alacrity and barely concealed enthusiasm for the fact that their master was to go to the palace that day.

"They are longing to stand outside St. James's and wave you in," said Emilia over their early breakfast.

"Indeed I shall let them," John answered, then promptly felt middle-aged and pompous because of his words and tone of voice.

"What about Nicholas?"

"He'll have to run the shop."

"Oh how could you? He's been your faithful creature all these years. How could you exclude him from the fun?"

"They're not going to see much; just me entering the palace that's all."

"What about everybody else going in? What about the clothes and the coaches and the cheering? If you leave Nicholas out of all that, may it be on your conscience for ever more."

Feeling more of a selfish wretch with every word his wife uttered, John swallowed noisily. "Oh very well. The shop will close today. But, sweetheart, somebody must stay and look after the house. I can't give everyone the morning off."

"Then let it be the two most recently joined, Lucinda and the lad. The rest can follow our carriage down." Emilia caught breath. "Oh John, I'm so excited. To think you will see Mr. Fielding kneel before the King."

"I wish you could come in."

"I shall be quite happy watching from the coach. Then afterwards we can drink champagne and you can tell me all about it."

The Apothecary got up from his place and going round the table, kissed her on the lips. "You are like a child, with that sweet ability to really enjoy an occasion. Promise me that you will never lose that."

"I promise."

"Now, let us go and put on finery. The greatest hat in your collection must be worn today, so that everyone staring in through the carriage windows can admire you."

"I hardly think that anybody will be looking at me with so many important people making their way within."

"A beautiful woman is always regarded," John answered gallantly as they left the room, calling for the servants to help them dress.

The coach made its way to St. James's Palace by turning out of Nassau Street, down Gerrard Street, then through Princes and Coventry Streets into Piccadilly. From there Irish Tom clipped the horses smartly to the junction with St. James's Street where, somewhat to John's astonishment, he saw that a crowd had begun to gather. It seemed that as this was the first investiture following the coronation there was still a certain amount of interest in the new young monarch and his recently acquired Queen.

The Apothecary had always thought that very old and very young sovereigns held a certain amount of popular appeal. It was merely the middle-aged who tended to bore, their very years making them stuffy and lacklustre. George II had been no exception. Short, strutting, charmless, Germanic, swaying of jowl and crimson of visage, the public at large had been thoroughly bored with him and were only too anxious for his grandson to ascend the throne. And now he had. Amiable, tall, good-looking, blue-eyed, and very proud of the fact that he had been born in England, young George was high in popularity and at the moment was cheered wherever he went. If he had married the beautiful Sarah Lennox his star would have blazed in the firmament, but instead he had wed Charlotte, German as they come and with a face like a squashed fig. She was not the glamorous consort that the public craved but, still, they liked the lad and now they had turned out to see the carriages full of grand personages proceed to the palace through that area of London known as St. James's.

Originally the Tudor building had stood in a rural setting, hunting and grazing grounds surrounding it on every side. Now urban development had caught up, but its earlier associations were reflected by the parks which adjoined it. Behind St. James's Palace lay St. James's Park, to its right as one faced the building, Green Park, while its own small but adequate gardens lay behind the state apartments.

As they entered St. James's Street, the Apothecary saw that a line of coaches was ahead, moving at slow speed down the road towards the junction with Pall Mall.

"Is that the way in, Sir?" called Irish Tom from the box.

"Mr. Fielding said that the carriages were to drop us by the walkway leading to the German Church. The doors going into the palace open off there."

Across the top of this walkway, which led from Pall Mall down to St. James's Park, were a pair of stout gates to keep unwanted visitors out. But today these stood open, allowing those descending from their conveyances to pass down the path and inside the building without hindrance. Further, at intervals along the way, a dozen or so little pageboys were stationed to assist people in and help with the disposal of travelling garments.

The crush in Pall Mall, even though there was still some time before the levee proper was due to begin, was considerable. Carriages moving at a snail's pace were edging forward to join the queue which had formed at the gates leading to the walkway. Postillions were leaping about, pulling down steps to allow passengers, all dressed to the zenith, to alight onto the specially swept cobbles. Huge feathered headdresses, quite the latest thing in high fashion, bobbed dangerously as ladies in mighty gowns minced forward on tottering heels. Gentlemen from the professional classes, looking uncomfortable in stiff new clothes, attempted to strike a note of decorum. Whereas the bucks and the blades vyed with each other as to the amount of gems stitched upon their waistcoats, the number of curls flouncing on their wigs and who could have the most fantastical shape of patch worn upon his face. One demi-rip, alighting with a look of disdain from his carriage, boasted a galleon, a coach and horses and a cupid upon one cheek, a sickle moon, several stars and an arrow on the other.

"Look at 'im," shouted an urchin in the crowd, at which the young man waved his beribboned great stick at the miscreant, tripped over the cobbles and nearly fell over, much to the delight of the onlookers.

A plain coach that John recognised drew to a halt, having finally reached the top of the queue, and Joe Jago, garbed to wonderment, jumped out and pulled down the steps. He was followed by Mary Ann, daintily shod and dressed like the little beauty she was, her dark hair not powdered but adorned with the brightest and cheekiest feathers that the Apothecary could remember seeing. And then, resplendent in a flowing cloak and truly mighty wig topped by a tricorne with flashing buckle fixed to the left cock, there stepped out John Fielding himself. Joe Jago guided him downwards, then offered his arm.

A cheer went up, for the onlookers knew who he was and that he delivered rough but fair justice, and there was a cry of, "There's the Blind Beak." In response, the Magistrate doffed his magnificent hat towards the crowd, and there was another cry of "Good fellow."

"I don't think I'll be able to watch from the coach after all," said Emilia. "They're all being directed onwards to make way."

"Well I don't want you on your own in the crowd."

"I'll be with Nicholas and the servants. Anyway, there's Samuel, look!"

And she pointed to where John's old friend, head and shoulders above the throng, was making his way towards the gates, cheering as he went.

Another coach, very fine indeed, drew to the head of the

line and Miss Chudleigh, fashionable from frills to feet, emerged, sauntering into the palace as if it were her rightful abode. Then eventually, after several more parties had made their way within, it was the Apothecary's turn. Nicholas, who had travelled with his master, jumped out and pulled down the steps personally, then made a low bow. John, very deeply honoured, stepped into the street and for the first time in his life felt something of what it must be like to be truly rich and famous, attending palaces and great functions, gaped at by a staring multitude. He turned back to look at Emilia who was waving to him out of the window. John raised his hat to her, then proceeded at a measured pace down the walkway to the entrance.

A pageboy stepped forward. "Your card, Sir."

"I do not have one. I am with Mr. John Fielding's party. He is just there ahead of me."

The boy bowed. "If you will wait a moment, Sir, I will go and check."

"Very well."

The page looked solemn and added apologetically, "We are instructed to monitor all visitors, Sir."

He was a very strange little chap, John thought, thin to the point of emaciation, with a hollow haggard face and listless eyes, not at all suitable for a child of his age. In fact there was something so haunting about the boy that John found himself studying him with more attention than he would normally have paid such a creature.

Walking rather slowly, the page made his way into the palace, into a long reception hall, lined on both sides with sofas on which several people had already taken seats. He obviously was not certain who John Fielding was, for the Apothecary observed him pluck at the sleeve of another boy and whisper something into his ear. The other page, dressed in livery and with a white wig, as were they all, glanced over. A fleeting impression that he had seen the larger, older boy before came over John strongly, but a second later when he looked again, both children had vanished into the throng.

The wizened little page finally reappeared. "Are you Mr. Rawlings, Sir?"

"Yes."

"Mr. Fielding is expecting you. I am so sorry for the inconvenience. Please to come in."

Handing him his cloak and hat, John entered St. James's Palace.

The reception hall, even though thronging with people, could be seen to have the most elegant lines, running as it did along the side of one of the old Tudor courts. John gazed with approval at mirrors and candlesticks and splendid furnishings as he made his way to where the Blind Beak sat on a sofa, waiting the moment when the levee would begin and they would be called upon to climb the stairs to the state apartments.

Joe Jago, standing guard over the Magistrate and keeping up a running commentary as to who was present while Mary Ann burbled on about the cutting fashions of the *beau monde*, turned at the Apothecary's approach.

"You look very splendid, Sir."

"As do you, Joe. I have never seen you in such a becoming rig-out. Did your tailor work all night?"

"No, Sir, only till eleven."

John bowed before Mr. Fielding. "I have arrived, Sir."

"Delighted to hear it. Tell me, Mr. Rawlings, do I look a fool in all this finery?"

"No, Sir. You look magnificent. You all do. The Public Office can be proud of its representatives this day."

Joe's eyes, a shade lighter than his suit, filled with tears, though none spilled on to his rugged cheek. "It is the finest hour in the Office's history, Sir. The Beak rewarded at long last for all his efforts."

"I saw Miss Chudleigh come in earlier. Is she here to honour you, Sir?"

"In part, perhaps. Though, of course, as maid-of-honour to the King's mother, she has the right of entree to all the royal palaces."

John stared about him. "Who are all these little pageboys? Are they royal servants?"

Mr. Fielding rumbled a chuckle. "Far from it. They are either peers of the realm in their own right or the sons of peers. However, they are on call for all state occasions."

"A funny little monkey-faced lad saw me in. He hardly had the strength to get about it seemed to me."

"We had a very handsome one," Mary Ann answered. "Pupils the colour of mauve flowers. I wonder if he has a peerage already."

"You are incorrigible," stated her uncle firmly. "You are to behave yourself, Miss."

"Oh, Papa," she cooed in response. "When do I not?"

John and Joe exchanged a glance and rolled their eyes but said not a word.

The reception room was now nearly packed to capacity and there had been no new arrivals for several minutes. Therefore it surprised no one when there came a stirring and a call for silence from the far end of the room.

"My lords, ladies and gentlemen," announced a major domo, "the levee will shortly begin. Will you make your way to the left hand staircase in the order that I call out. If you will then proceed through the state apartments and assemble in the Queen Anne room. Footmen and pages will be on hand to assist you."

"So," said Mr. Fielding, rising, "this is the moment, is it?"

John, looking the length of the great room, saw that everyone was now standing in expectancy, including, at some distance from them, the sandy-faced George Goward and his abundant wife, still tightly corseted despite the Apothecary's warning.

"I think it is, Sir," he answered.

"Take my arm, Beak," said Joe, using the word as a term of

endearment. "Mr. Rawlings, you latch on to the other side." He was starting to use cant phrases in his excitement.

"So do I walk behind?" asked Mary Ann petulantly.

"Yes you do," Joe answered firmly. "You'll mind your manners today, Miss Whittingham."

She looked at him, ready for confrontation, but withdrew at the steely look in the clerk's eye. "Oh, very well."

"Mr. Anthony Fifield and party," called the major domo, and the first three people, clearly a recipient and his guests, moved towards the staircase.

John, looking ahead, saw that the pageboys had formed a guard of honour on either side of the stairs, a footman on every other step between them  He gazed in wonderment, thinking that he had never seen quite so many servants gathered together in his entire life. Then he remembered that these boys were not servants at all, but young members of the nobility. Astonished that so many could be present at one time, he counted them, and was surprised to see that there were thirteen boys on the staircase an unlucky number for any occasion, he would have thought.

But it was time to move. As the name, "Mr. John Fielding," was called, Joe, John and the Magistrate stepped forward, and somewhat awestruck by the grandeur of it all, the two sighted men guided the blind one towards the great staircase.

# Chapter 6

It must have been how salmon felt when swimming to the spawn, John thought as he made his way, right arm linked through Mr. Fielding's left, up the staircase leading towards the state apartments. For on every side were people thronging happily upwards, the majority gazing about, quizzing glasses raised, to see the magnificence that surrounded them on every side. Moving more slowly as the Magistrate negotiated the stairs, John had a greater opportunity than most to study his surroundings.

There were in fact two staircases, connected by a long balustraded balcony, the right hand one leading to private apartments, the left to the state. These stairways, though both made of marble, were, however, different in shape. Whereas the left had a small landing in the middle, dividing the two flights, the right was steep and straight, not something to hurry down in the teetering heels of high fashion, John reckoned. From the staircase, he could see as he ascended, a great chamber lead off to the left, obviously the King's private place, but ahead lay the most ancient and historic suite of rooms in the entire building. With his heart pounding at the sheer excitement of it all, the Apothecary stared, trying to commit every detail to his pictorial memory.

The peacock crowd slowed as it entered the first room, gazing at the Tudor woodwork, somewhat hushed by the sense of the past, thinking, perhaps, as the Apothecary did, that the great hulk that was Henry VIII had once stalked his way through this very place. And there was further evidence of him in the next apartment. Over the Tudor fireplace, clearly visible on the left hand side, was the H & A monogram of that monarch and the woman for whom he had severed his connections with the Church of Rome, Anne Boleyn herself.

The skinny pageboy reappeared at John's side. "This is the Tapestry Room, Sir."

"But there's no tapestry," the Apothecary answered, somewhat amused.

"It was sold by Oliver Cromwell. He wasn't fond of beautiful things."

"No he wasn't, was he," John replied, thinking of the vandalistic destruction of graceful buildings, the closure of theatres, and the general darkening down of any aspect of life that was light-hearted and pleasure-giving.

"Some people are like that," said the boy and vanished into the throng once more.

"What was all that?" asked Mr. Fielding.

"A page was saying that there are no tapestries in the Tapestry Room."

The Blind Beak stopped dead in his tracks. "Is that where we are?"

"We certainly are, Sir," Joe Jago answered.

"Then we are indeed touching history," the Magistrate stated solemnly. "For it was from this room that Queen Elizabeth and her advisers received news of the Spanish Armada and planned the response."

"I can just imagine her," chimed in Mary Ann, "all orange hair and chalky face and a great ruff sticking round her neck."

"An unattractive word picture," answered her uncle, and laughed.

A voice spoke at the party's side. "Mr. Fielding, Sir, we meet again."

It was George Goward not looking unalike Mary Ann's description of the Tudor queen, though minus the neckpiece.

"La, but the press of people is intense," said his wife breathlessly. She was very flushed, the Apothecary noticed, and gasping as she walked. Indeed today she looked even sillier than she had when he first met her and her little-girl voice seemed more out of place than ever.

"I hope you don't feel faint, Madam," John stated cautiously.

"I feel as if I could pass clean away at any moment. I think I'll stay close to you, Mr. Rawlings."

"Oh brace up, Mary, do," said George, as the Apothecary wildly searched for an excuse to get away from her. He found one.

"Alas, Madam, today I walk with Mr. Fielding as his assistant. My first duty lies with him. I pray you seek another should ill befall."

"Indeed so," said Miss Chudleigh, joining them. "May I be your guide, my dear?" She spoke to the Magistrate but the effect on Joe Jago was astonishing. His ragged cheeks filled with colour and he even went so far as to let go of Mr. Fielding's arm as he bowed his very best bow. Observing, John felt quite certain that the clerk had a passion for her.

Without waiting for a reply, Miss Chudleigh continued to speak. "It is from the balcony outside the windows of this hall that the accession of the new monarch is announced."

They had walked out of the Tapestry Room and the throng was now heading down, pressed quite closely together, towards a huge and magnificent room that lay at the end of the suite. John, looking to his left, saw the stone balcony, used only recently when the young King had come to the throne. He also saw Lady Mary Goward start to wobble like a great jelly, her face a nasty shade of green. The Apothecary leant towards Mr. Fielding.

"I don't wish to hurry you, Sir - no, that's not true, I do - but I think Lady Mary is about to faint so I really must escape."

They marched forward at increased speed, Mary Ann fluttering to keep up, Miss Chudleigh slipping her arm through Joe Jago's right for support. Thus four abreast they made their way into the room especially designed for Queen Anne where, much to John's surprise, Mr. Digby Turnbull, very sharply dressed, was marshalling the crowd into two groups, guests and recipients.

The Apothecary gazed round at the resplendent interior, its late Baroque style quite stunning in its use of gold leaf and intricate moulding. He had never in his life been quite so overwhelmed by any room in any great house and he felt as if he could stay there for hours, soaking up the intense beauty surrounding him. And then he turned and gasped. The far door of the Queen Anne room was open and through it he could see out and beyond, in the manner of a Dutch painting. At the very end of his line of vision, dominating all, was the throne, canopied and raised, so impressive that it did not look real but like something from a stage presentation.

"Well?" said Miss Chudleigh. Then she turned to Mr. Fielding. "John, we are standing in the Queen Anne room. It is probably one of the finest and most beautifully decorated in the kingdom."

"I would say," Joe Jago answered, his head tilted to take in every detail of the ceiling, "that it is *the* finest."

But Digby Turnbull was calling for silence as the last of the assemblage swept in. By now the Apothecary reckoned there were about a hundred people present and even that great room was full. As he turned back to the speaker, he saw Lady Mary Goward, the front of her dress suspiciously damp as if it had been sponged down, hobble in on the arm of the larger of the two pages who had overseen his arrival.

"My lords, ladies and gentlemen," Digby was saying, "as you will see we are dividing into two groups, recipients of an honour and guests. I would ask the guests to go through to the Throne Room and take their seats on the chairs provided. Recipients will wait in the Entree Room from which they will be called individually. Once you have received your honour, kindly make your way into the Long Gallery and await the end of the levee. When His Majesty enters the throne room everyone must stand."

These instructions issued, Mr. Turnbull held up a gloved hand and said, "Follow me."

The throng trooped forward in solemn fashion, more

subdued now that the great moment was actually drawing near. Watching Mary Ann, the Apothecary saw her go through the Entree Room and into the Throne Room, taking her seat with a great show of adult composure. Then in the Long Gallery an orchestra, which had been tuning up while people processed, struck up a short selection of works by Mr. Handel played with a great deal of bravura. At the end of this rendition nobody applauded, as this would not have been considered seemly, and there was a moment's silence before the music of the national anthem. In both rooms everyone got to their feet as - from a chamber situated behind the throne - the young King, a bodyguard on either side, entered the Throne Room. There was a great deal of bowing and curtseying which George acknowledged with a grave nod of his head. The major domo who had first seen the company in appeared at his side and without any further fuss the ceremony began.

Names were called out and one by one the recipients made their way into the Throne Room, either standing or kneeling on a footstool to receive their honour. Seated as he was at the side of the Entree Room, John could only listen to what was going on, growing more anxious by the minute about the time it was going to take to get the Blind Beak across that empty space and kneeling before the throne. But there he had overlooked the court's excellent organisation. A hand touched his shoulder and Digby Turnbull murmured, "Mr. Fielding will be after the next man. If you would like to get ready, gentlemen."

Joe was on his feet and pulling his skirted coat straight almost before he had finished speaking. Then he turned to the Magistrate. "I'll just tidy you up, Sir, and then we'll be all ready when your name is called."

John stood and together he and Joe adjusted the Blind Beak's cravat and suit, checking that his long curling wig was straight. Then they linked their arms through his and waited.

"Mr. John Fielding," came the summons and the long walk began. Through the door of the Entree Room they proceeded, then down the length of the Throne Room towards the dais.

John Rawlings's thoughts flew, thinking that the King looked thoroughly pleasant, a modest fair-complexioned young man with steady, if slightly protruberant, blue eyes and a pleasing smile revealing strong white teeth. His Majesty smiled a lot in fact, and even though John Fielding not see him George seemed very touched by the picture of the great blind man making his way towards him and smiled all the more. The footstool was reached and Joe brought the Magistrate to a halt, then the three men bowed their heads before the two sighted helped the Blind Beak to kneel down.

The time-honoured words of ceremony were spoken, the sword flashed into the air and came down lightly on John Fielding's shoulders.

"Arise, Sir John," said the King, and then quite impulsively and most endearingly added, and may God bless you."

The Apothecary felt tears well in his eyes but knew that to reveal them would be out of the question, instead he took the new knight's arm and together they made their way back to the Queen Anne room and out into the Long Gallery. Here all formality ceased and Joe flung his arms round the Beak and said in a rather strange, somewhat hoarse voice, "Well, Sir John."

"Well, indeed," the Magistrate answered. "Recognition for the Public Office at long last."

"I think," said the Apothecary, "that it is more likely recognition for you, Sir."

Sir John shook his head. "No, it's for all of us. Everyone - and that includes you, Mr. Rawlings - who has given his time and effort to free our streets from criminals."

John and Joe blew their noses simultaneously, then laughed, and the emotional moment was over. In fact the atmosphere in the Long Gallery was now that of a jolly rout.

The orchestra was playing for all it was worth, the place was packed with people who had just received honours and were in the highest of spirits. All it needed, thought John, was for champagne to come round on trays and the party would be complete. However, that had to wait till later, when each individual would go home and celebrate with his family.

The Gallery, though very large, was filling with people as more and more recipients came through from the Throne Room. Finally, though, the crush was complete as the guests made their way in, rushing to their relatives and congratulating them. Mary Ann, with two high spots of colour in her cheeks, appeared and jumped on her uncle like a small cat.

"Oh Uncle, Papa, whoever you are, congratulations. I thought you looked mighty. I was so proud."

He laughed, very delightedly. "Oh you foolish girl. Is the levee over?"

"Yes."

But before anyone could say another word there was a stirring in the doorway and suddenly the King was there, passing from one end of the Gallery to the other, cutting a swathe through a hastily saluting crowd, heading for the private apartments.

"His Majesty?" asked Sir John.

"Indeed," said Mary Ann, "and handsome into the bargain. Pity he's married to such a monkey."

"Keep you voice down," hissed the Magistrate.

But nobody had heard her because the major domo had appeared in the far doorway, Digby Turnbull hovering behind. "My lord, ladies and gentlemen, the levee is at an end. If you would proceed out of this doorway and down the far staircase, then make your way out through the lower corridor. Congratulations to you all."

The throng was on the move once more, traversing the gallery, making its way along the balcony to start going down the steep staircase.

"Greetings, Sir John," said George Goward, immensely pleased with himself and grinning like a ginger cat.

"Greetings, Sir George. A remarkable day." The Magistrate turned to Lady Mary. "Did you enjoy the ceremony, Madam?"

She made a sickly moue. "Unfortunately, I am indisposed. I was forced to quit the room and find a closet so did not see my husband knighted."

"I saw him," said Mary Ann, "he knelt well."

Sir George turned to her and John could not help but notice the way that Goward put his arm round her waist, pretending that she was nothing but a child, yet with lechery oozing from his very pores.

"My dear, how sweet of you. You must allow me to buy you a doll."

"I am past the age of dolls, Sir."

He slowly ran his eyes over her. "So you are, my dear. So you are."

They had reached the top of the right hand staircase and John looked round. Once more, pageboys and footmen were stationed on each step to assist as heeled shoes started to clack over the marble. But as the procession began to make its way downstairs, all eyes were suddenly drawn upwards. >From out of the private apartments, proceeding along the balcony, by now quite free of people, and heading in the direction of the great room to the left of the entry stairs, came the King, leading by the hand the much talked-about, highly criticised, Queen Charlotte. Every head turned, every quizzer gleamed, as people craned to see if she was really as ugly as rumour had it. Poor thing, thought John, she truly *is*, just like a gloomy little gnome. And then a sudden terrible cry, quite close at hand, brought his attention back to his surroundings.

In order to see Charlotte, everyone had rushed to the side of the staircase, leaving a clear path from top to bottom down which someone might fall. And indeed somebody was falling.

The Apothecary watched in horror as a figure in salmon pink tumbled downwards, gaining momentum as it descended, the stairs too steep for anything to break its plunge. Time seemed frozen, everything was still, nobody moved. Then the figure crashed to the hallway below and its wig flew from its head as blood poured over the whiteness of the marble.

"My God!" exclaimed John, and began to hurry downwards as fast as his new heeled shoes would let him.

He reached the hall below, saw that footmen had already gathered round, that a pageboy was running down the reception corridor.

"I'm an apothecary," he gasped, and a servant stood aside to let him through. John knelt by the prostrate figure and raised its copiously bleeding head. Then knew by the very feel of the neck that it was shattered and that life was already extinct.

"My God," he said again, and turned the head to look into its face. Parodied by death, the eyes staring straight into his, a terrible smile still upon the lips, was the ginger feline countenance of the newly knighted George Goward.

# Chapter 7

Chaos erupted. Those ladies standing nearest started to scream and there was a shriek from above as the ample Lady Mary passed out yet again. In the midst of all this clamour, the Apothecary alone remained silent, unbelievably shaken by the terrible thing he had just witnessed. He had hardly known George Goward and what little he had seen of him, John had not liked, but to die in such a terrible way, to fall precipitate and break one's neck, was something that no man should have to suffer as an exit. Soberly, and with a hand that shook very slightly, John closed the staring eyes. Then there was the clatter of hurrying feet as a man hastened down and pushed him abruptly aside.

"Sir Danvers Roe, physician," he announced brusquely.

"John Rawlings, apothecary," John answered, not allowing himself to be unnerved.

"You may step away. I shall care for this man," Sir Danvers continued, kneeling down.

"Nobody will care for him now but God. He's dead. His neck has been broken by the fall." And with that John got to his feet, though refusing to move from his place.

Digby Turnbull hastened to join him. "What's happened?"

"It's George Goward, one of the new knights. As the Queen passed along the balcony he must have turned to look at her and lost his footing. The fall has killed him, I'm afraid."

Digby made a hissing noise through his teeth. "Good God, what a terrible thing." He thought on his feet, shouting to the major domo who still stood at the top of the stairs, "Henry, hold them on the staircase. Let nobody move until I give the word."

"Make way," the major domo responded, passing through the crowd, who actually parted for him, still in a state of shock, John realised.

Henry arrived at the bottom and took command, throwing a cordon of footmen across the top and base of the staircase so that people were actually trapped where they stood.

Sir Danvers stood up, declaring grandly. "This man is dead."

"I know," said Mr. Turnbull, giving short shrift. "The Apothecary has already told me." He turned to John. "Mr. Rawlings, stay by the dead man. I'm off to get a stretcher of some kind."

"Best get a cleaning woman too. We can't have the fine ladies stepping through that pool of blood."

"You're right." Mr. Turnbull bowed to the physician. "How kind of you to help us, Sir Danvers. If you would care to take a seat in the reception corridor until we have sorted this matter out."

"But ..."

"No buts I'm afraid. This is St. James's Palace, Sir, and nothing further must be allowed to disrupt the levee."

And with that Digby made a polite bow and watched while Sir Danvers very angrily walked off, then hurried away himself.

A voice called out from the staircase. "I must relieve myself. Allow me to pass."

"Go to the top, Sir," the major domo replied. "A page will direct you to a closet."

Staring upwards, John saw that the pages, all white-faced and shaking, mere children when all was said and done, still stood at their posts, disciplined to the last, heirs to mighty estates or already owners of them. He could also see his party; Mary Ann utterly pale, Sir John hugely tall and somehow ominous, Joe Jago seething with frustration that he could not be at the heart of the action.

Knowing that Digby Turnbull would be back at any moment, John briefly knelt once more at the body's side, again struck to the heart by the dramatic and frightful nature of Sir George's death. Then his professional training took over and he examined the crumpled corpse as Sir John

Fielding would have wished him to do, trying to keep a cool head as he did so.

The dead man told him nothing except that he had died unexpectedly, still smiling at whatever had amused him a second before, probably the sight of the dim dull characterless Queen herself. On a sudden instinct John looked at the heels of the body's shoes to see if one had scuffed as Sir George had caught it when he tripped, but there was nothing there. Like most of the people present, Goward wore a new pair, his footwear immaculate with lack of wear. Which made the Apothecary realise, as he stood up once more, that his feet were beginning to hurt.

Digby reappeared with two burly young men who hefted a plank between them. There was a great deal of screaming from the onlookers as they lifted the body high, placed it on the board and moved swiftly out of sight with it. At that, two women with pails and cloths and pained expressions on their faces, came forward and began to mop up the spilled blood of the dead man.

Five minutes later it was all over. "Let them go," Digby said to the major domo and the cordon of footmen parted so that people could leave at last.

It was a subdued crowd who came down the stairs, carefully stepping round the place where the body had lain, John noticed. Finally Sir John Fielding, Joe on one side, Mary Ann on the other, drew close to where the Apothecary stood. Elizabeth Chudleigh, John saw, was still making her way downwards but was heading towards them.

"What a terrible way for the morning to end, Sir," John said quietly.

The Magistrate shook his head. "There's something not right, Mr. Rawlings."

"What do you mean?"

Sir John lowered his voice. "I am unable to say more at present. Would you be good enough to accompany me to Bow Street so that we may speak in private."

"But Emilia and Samuel are waiting for me outside, to say nothing of the servants. I promised to go home and regale them with stories of the Palace."

Mary Ann spoke up. "Could we not all go to Mr. Rawlings's house? I can chat to Mr. Swann while you two talk."

The Magistrate was about to protest at her forwardness but was forced to silence by the arrival of Miss Chudleigh.

"Off to celebrate?" she asked brightly.

"Indeed," Sir John replied smoothly. "Mr. Rawlings has been kind enough to invite us all back."

"Then I wish you joy, that is if any joy is to be found in view of this tragedy."

But no answer could be made, for it was at this very moment that Lady Mary Goward was half-carried down the stairs by a team of sweating footmen. Her eyes rolled piteously in her head as she passed the group. "God help me," she moaned.

Digby Turnbull stepped forward. "Do you wish to see your husband, Madam?"

"No, no. I could not bear to look on him, so wounded and broken." She started to howl "That it should end like this" over and over again, then turned another nasty shade of green.

The Apothecary stepped rapidly to one side, mindful of his best suit. "Would you like salts, Lady Mary?"

"I shall have nothing, thank you. Why should my pain be dulled when George lies cold and dead?" She paused, then said, "I shall send a funeral coach to collect him."

"I think not, Madam," Sir John stated quietly.

"I beg your pardon?" she replied, her foolish face suddenly furious.

"I offer you my sincere condolences, of course, but I believe that Sir George should be taken to the mortuary and there examined by a physician."

"To what end? My husband is dead. No doctor can help him now."

"To establish exactly how he died, Lady Mary."

"But why? His neck was broken by the fall, that is what Sir Danvers Roe told me."

"Madam, there has been a sudden and violent death. The law must now take its course."

"I don't understand you, Sir John."

"I cannot allow the body to be released until the coroner has been informed and gives permission. You see, we cannot rule out foul play in this matter."

"How dare you?" the fat woman shouted, her voice amazingly loud for one who felt so faint. "What are you suggesting?"

"That Sir George's fall may not have been accidental, Madam."

"Preposterous! You are preposterous, Sir."

"That," answered John Fielding, "remains to be seen. I offer my sympathies in your hour of grief." So saying he took Joe Jago's arm and purposefully made his way outwards.


To locate everyone, to send the servants hurrying home to prepare a cold collation, to get Samuel out of the crowd and into the Apothecary's coach, then to get the coach itself home to Nassau Street through the hordes of carriages, had been a major effort. But it had finally been achieved and now Emilia was rushing round tending to her guests, trying to entertain Mary Ann - who was behaving pettishly because Samuel preferred to sit in on the men's conversation - and cursing the fact that the fires had not been lit in her absence.

John, meanwhile, had turned the library over to Sir John and after a glass of congratulatory champagne, he, Samuel and Joe Jago had made their way in there.

The Magistrate sat in the chair that had once been Sir Gabriel's favourite, his face very serious. "Gentlemen, are you all present?" he asked as the other three took seats.

"We are, Sir," Joe Jago answered. He came directly to the

point. "Sir John, what is it that makes you think Sir George's fall was not accidental?"

"I heard something," the Magistrate answered quietly, and the very tone of his voice sent a chill of unease over the Apothecary's body.

There was a silence, broken eventually by Joe asking, "What?"

"Somebody whispered something just before the scream and the fall. It was right beside me, almost at my elbow. Everyone else, all the world it seemed, had turned to look at the Queen, and I was the only one remaining where I had originally stood."

"My God!" said Samuel, awestruck.

"What was said?" enquired John.

"Nonsensical words. 'What price greatness now?' Then there was an exhalation of air, as if an effort had been made. Then Goring screamed and plunged to his death."

"The words aren't that nonsensical if they were uttered by someone jealous of his advancement. Was it a man or a woman who spoke?"

"That I can't tell. It was an unearthly voice, distorted by whispers. I believe it to have been disguised somehow."

There was another silence, then Joe said, "If someone did push him then it was not premeditated. It must have been a seizing of the moment, a grasping of opportunity as all heads were turned."

"Except for a blind man's," answered Sir John. "A man who had no interest in what the Queen looked like as he would never be able to see her."

"That eventuality the murderer would not have realised. The one twist of fate that he could not have taken into consideration."

"What price greatness now?" John repeated thoughtfully. "Someone who did not receive an honour venting their spleen on someone they disliked who had."

"The word greatness is the only one I'm not sure of," the

Magistrate answered. "There was a shriek from one of the ladies as the Queen passed by. It slightly drowned the beginning of the word. But it ended in ness, that's for sure."

"What a puzzle," said Joe. He took one of John Fielding's hands, grasping it in a most companionable manner. "Sir, you're absolutely sure of all this? There is no chance that you misinterpreted an entirely innocent remark and sound?"

Sir John sighed deeply. "Today I received an honour at the Palace and, supposedly, part of the skill for which I have been rewarded is the ability to recognise a great many of the criminal class by their voice alone. Joe, do you really think I made a mistake in this? The sounds I heard were a whispered message full of menace, followed by the exhalation of air as somebody made the effort of pushing. Next came a cry as George Goring fell."

"I'm sorry, Sir," Joe answered humbly. "It is just that so much depends on your being right. All the planning and man hours, the seeking of witnesses, the following of trails that go cold."

"If I did not know you better I would have thought you had lost your stomach for the fight, Joe."

"No, Sir, it's not that."

It was a fraught moment for all concerned, John half agreeing with the clerk's summation that so much depended on the merest shred of overheard evidence. Yet, by the same token, his respect for the abilities of the Magistrate was boundless and he found it hard to credit that Sir John Fielding himself might have made a mistake. Eventually, the Apothecary spoke.

"Look, we have two courses of action open to us. One is that we ignore Mr. Fielding - sorry, Sir John's - testimony and put George Goring's fall down to an accident. The other, is that we heed what he says. And it seems to me that we have no choice but to listen. How else will we ever know what really happened? Let us open an enquiry and, should we find nothing, close it again."

Joe nodded. "You're right, of course. I must be getting old and lazy."

Or have your thought diverted elsewhere by Miss Chudleigh, thought John.

The Magistrate shifted in his chair. "I am glad that you have come to this conclusion, gentlemen, but I can tell you now that I would have pulled rank and ordered an enquiry anyway, so certain am I about what I heard."

Joe Jago drained his glass, which John refilled. "Right. Then the first thing is to make a list of all those who were near George Goring on the stairs. Mr. Rawlings, you have a fine memory. Who were they?"

The Apothecary raised his eyes to the corner of the room, fingering his chin thoughtfully. "Well, there was his wife, of course. Then our party. Miss Chudleigh was near at hand and Digby Turnbull, I believe, though I couldn't swear to that. Then there was a woman whom I didn't know and also a man. I am not sure whether they were together. Then, I suppose, there was one of the most extraordinary characters of all." He stopped.

"Why was that? Why was he extraordinary?"

"He was black, somebody's slave I suppose. But beautiful-ly dressed and turned out, quite a blade in fact. The odd thing is that I don't remember seeing him at the investiture."

"He could have been sitting with the guests."

"Yes, he could. We must ask Mary Ann."

"How strange for someone to bring their slave with them."

"Not if he was highly regarded. And some are, you know."

"That's true enough. Now, was there anybody else?"

"No, not that I can recollect." He turned to Joe. "Did you see anyone further?"

"No, I think that account is fairly comprehensive, Sir."

"Well," said the Blind Beak, "that gives us a lot to be going on with. Joe, can you find out on my authority who the two strangers and the black man were. Mr. Rawlings, would you be so kind as to question Digby Turnbull ... who is he, by the way?"

"A servant of the crown. He describes himself as being in charge of the other servants. He was present at the investiture in his official capacity."

"Then he might be very useful. Miss Chudleigh, too, must be questioned."

Joe flushed a little, then said, "That should be Mr. Rawlings's task, I believe."

The Magistrate cleared his throat. "Yes, perhaps. But that leaves us with the most difficult witness of all - Lady Mary Goward herself."

"Perish the thought!" John exclaimed. "Surely you would be better with her, Sir."

"I'm quite prepared to quiz her but I shall want someone with me to note her every reaction. For as far as I am concerned she is probably the perpetrator of the crime."

"What? The widow?" asked Samuel incredulously.

"They mostly bear more grudges than anyone else. Did they have any children?"

John answered. "Not jointly, no. But she had a son by her first husband. I think she said his name was Frederick."

"Where is he?"

"At boarding school in Kensington, the Brompton Park strangely enough. I must ask Lucinda if she knew him."

"How is the girl settling down to her new life?"

"Very well. She is hard-working and conscientious."

"I've made a list, Sir," said Joe, who had been scribbling away on paper produced from an inside pocket. "Where would you like us to begin?"

"First we must trace the identity of the three strangers. But meanwhile, Mr. Rawlings, I think you should presume on your acquaintanceship with Mr. Turnbull and find out as much as you can. What went on behind the scenes at today's ceremony, if anything."

"Sir," said Samuel tremulously, "I know that I wasn't present when the murder took place but I would so love to help if I can."

A slight air of resigned despair crept into the atmosphere, for John's friend was not the most tactful of creatures and had been known in the past to frighten witnesses into silence.

"Of course," Sir John answered, over-heartily. "I think your opinions would be most welcome. May I just cogitate a little as to how you can best serve us."

"By all means," said Samuel, and drained his glass jollily.

Emilia appeared in the doorway. "Gentlemen, have you finished your discussion?"

Sir John rose and made a bow in the direction of her voice. "We have just concluded, Mrs. Rawlings."

"Then perhaps you would like to come to the table. A repast awaits you."

"I can think of nothing more delightful," said the Blind Beak, and slipped his arm through Joe's that he may guide him from the room.


"Damn that girl," said Emilia, undoing the last lace of her stays and throwing them across the room with a great sigh of relief.

"Who?" said John from the depths of their bed, where he had retired almost as soon as their guests had left, completely exhausted by the day's events.

"Lucinda, of course. Didn't I tell you what she did? Or rather didn't do?"

"Sweetheart, forgive me. My mind is still full of the many, varied things I saw today. All that pomp and beauty to be followed by such a starkly horrible death."

Emilia turned before the mirror. "My stomach is swelling."

"So it is. Come here and let me kiss it."

She did so, well pleased as he put his lips to the rounding. Then she looked contrite and said, "I'm sorry, it was selfish of me to talk about domestic things."

"Not at all. What was it you had to tell me?"

"The new girl is a little wretch."

"I thought you liked her."

"I thought I did too. But I'm furious with her after today's performance."

"What did she do?"

"She disobeyed my instructions and left the house. She must have gone down to the Palace to see the crowds."

"But she was here when we got back."

"Yes, and in fine disarray. Panting and dishevelled. None of the fires were lit as I had instructed."

"Did you have it out with her?"

"No, I thought you could do that as she is your protegee." The Apothecary groaned. "Are you sure she went out?"

"Yes, the boy told me. Slipped out of the house as soon as the coast was clear. Then came rushing in and went straight up to the attic, so he said."

"Well, she'll have to mend her ways or I'll put her out."

Emilia's angelically impish smile appeared. "You know perfectly well you'd do nothing of the sort. Nor would you take her back to the school. You're all bark, Mr. Rawlings, with not an ounce of bite in you."

John bared his teeth. "I could still sink these into your delightful little bum, my dear."

"I doubt you'll do anything of the kind."

"I wouldn't wager a fortune on that."

"You are taking advantage of a pregnant woman,"

"I'm glad you noticed."

"Oh John!" said Emilia, and giggled wildly as he blew out the candle and drew her down beside him in the darkness.

# *Chapter 8*

It would be impossible, thought John Rawlings as he dressed in sober clothes, the kind he wore when attempting to convince people that he was a fit person to ask questions about their lives, to track down Digby Turnbull without further details of his whereabouts. In fact the man who moved from palace to palace, organising servants for special events, would probably be the more difficult to contact of the two people Sir John Fielding wished him to see. This left Miss Chudleigh, possibly still in residence at St. James's Palace or, more likely, in Kensington, fled there to recover from the shock. Not knowing quite how to proceed, John went downstairs to breakfast, after kissing Emilia, who was still asleep.

Nicholas had already left for the shop and the house was quiet, the servants no doubt gossiping about the investiture and its terrible aftermath in their own quarters. This gave the Apothecary the opportunity he needed. Ringing a bell, he asked for Lucinda to be sent to him.

As soon as she came into the room she exuded a strange mixture of defiance and guilt, yet her amazing eyes refused to meet John's as he cleared his throat portentously.

"I am highly displeased with you," he said, leaning forward on the table and glaring at her. She opened her mouth to reply but before she could get a word out, the Apothecary continued, "Since your arrival in this house there have been nothing but bad reports of your behaviour. I personally saw you creeping out late to post a letter, long after the maids had gone to bed. Gossip has reached my ears that you are walking round London hand-in-hand with my apprentice, and now you defy my wife's instructions and leave the home when she particularly asked you to stay in and light the fires."

There was a long silence, then Lucinda said, "Are you giving me notice, Sir?"

"No I am not, though I am sorely tempted. But I would like an explanation."

She replied like a barrister, enumerating points. "The letter I posted late was for my brother, who is still at the Brompton Park school and far from well. And it is true that Nicholas has befriended me and sometimes takes my hand when we are walking out together. As to leaving the house yesterday, yes I confess that I did give in to temptation and run behind your coach to share the excitement. I had intended to be out only a few minutes but became distracted by all that occurred."

It was very difficult to be angry in the face of this artless account and John strove hard to maintain a stern manner.

"Lucinda, you must not go on like this if you wish to remain in this establishment. I agree that yesterday was a very special occasion but the fact remains that you flouted the orders of Mrs. Rawlings."

She hung her bright head. "I'm sorry. It won't happen again."

"Hardly likely, considering that investitures are not weekly occurrences. Now, prove your worth and bring me a decent breakfast. All the excitement of yesterday has given me an appetite. And Lucinda ..."

"Yes, Sir?"

"I would rather that Nicholas did not fall in love with you. His indentures do not come to an end for another year."

"I will do my best to discourage him," she replied with a slight edge to her voice, then left the room.

John picked up *The Daily Courant* which was lying on the table and saw that the sensational news of the death of Sir George Goward within the confines of St. James's Palace and immediately following the levee at which he had been knighted, had reached the ears of the gentlemen of the press. They referred to the murder as a 'fatal fall' and a 'tragic accident'. However, the story went on for pages, probably being one of the most extraordinary it had ever reported. The Apothecary read the whole thing through, tucking in to a robust repast as he did. Then, his plans laid, he left the house to walk to Bow Street.


Sir John Fielding had taken no time off to celebrate his new honour and John saw as he approached the Public Office, the building in which the Magistrate both lived and worked, that those butterflies of society, the *beau monde*, were flocking into the public galleries of the court in droves, probably titillated by the fact that Sir John had been present when George Goward had crashed to his death on the previous day. Hoping that he hadn't missed Joe Jago, who always sat in court with the Magistrate, John hurried inside and gave his name to the official at the desk.

But he was to be disappointed. "Mr. Jago has left, Sir. He and Mr. Fielding - I mean, Sir John - have just made their way inside."

"Damnation," said John forcibly, and behind him another voice, female, echoed the same sentiments. He turned and saw, somewhat to his surprise, that Elizabeth Chudleigh had followed him into the tall, thin house, third on the left as one entered Bow Street, and was now standing disconsolately, also wondering what to do.

The Apothecary bowed flamboyantly. "Miss Chudleigh, good morning to you."

"Oh, Mr. Rawlings. I did not recognise you in such dark clothes. It seems we are too late to see Sir John or Mr. Jago."

"So it appears. And I'm afraid I do not have the time to sit in court and await them. Therefore, dear Madam, may I accompany you to the shops or wherever you are bound?"

"No," she responded, "you may take me to Will's Coffee House. It is but a step from here and besides they know me."

"It is a very male preserve, Miss Chudleigh. You are certain you will be welcome?"

To this she snapped her fingers. "If they want me to leave

they will have to carry me out physically. Now come along, good Sir, I feel the need to talk."

And she stepped out of the building, walking briskly, with the Apothecary in hot pursuit.


Will's Coffee House, situated at the corner of Bow Street, was the establishment in which the wits and literary men of the day foregathered. Henry Fielding and William Wycherley had been regular visitors, together with an Admiralty secretary named Samuel Pepys. Indeed, it had the reputation of being the meeting place from which poetry emanated, for every coffee house in London had its own particular following. The *beau monde* went to White's in St. James's Street; intellectuals to the Grecian in Covent Garden; men of the church to Truby's or Child's; while financiers patronised Jonathan's in Exchange Alley. Merchants interested in shipping would go to the coffee house run by Edward Lloyd in Lombard Street, which had grown from a humble meeting place to premises in which ships were auctioned, as well as producing its own newletter of shipping intelligence.

There were also coffee house of a less materialistic nature. Theatre people, both audience and actors, poured into the Bedford, where every branch of literature and every performance at the various playhouses was weighed and determined. Further, Tom King's was notorious for its clientele of fashionable fops and noblemen, bloods, bucks and choice spirits of London. Even politicans bowed to the decree. The Whigs congregated at the St. James's or the Smyrna, Tories could be found at the Cocoa Tree or Ozinda's. But in none of these places were women expected to be present and so it was with a great deal of courage, in John's opinion, that Elizabeth Chudleigh swept into Will's and demanded a box.

Yet it was typical of her. She cared nothing for convention - her appearance virtually naked at a court ball gave evidence to that - and her liaison with the Duke of Kingston, scandalously discussed in the great salons of the land, was indiscretion gone wild. But her beauty, though slightly faded, was powerful and her arresting manner hard to resist. Despite all the many points against her, John found that he liked her more and more.

Now she looked at him very directly with those wide limpid eyes of hers and said, "Why were you calling on Mr. Fielding?"

He kissed her gloved fingers. "It's Sir John now. And why were you?"

"Because a strange rumour has reached my ears."

"Which is?"

"That George Goward's body was taken to the mortuary and will not be released until the coroner has been notified."

"The death was sudden and violent."

"But natural." She paused. "Wasn't it?"

John weighed up the odds and decided she would be of more help to him if she knew what was going on, though on the other hand wondering whether the Magistrate should be the one to inform her.

"Your silence tells me a great deal," said Miss Chudleigh, raising a cup of hot chocolate to her lips. "I can only presume there is suspicion of foul play."

"Sir John thinks so," the Apothecary answered slowly. "But I think I had better let him speak about that personally. But meanwhile you might answer a question or two for me."

A cloud appeared at the back of the sensational eyes but Miss Chudleigh continued to sip her chocolate, apparently unperturbed.

"Do you recall being on the staircase when Sir George fell?"

"Yes, I was standing quite close to him."

"Who else was there?"

The beauty frowned. "Let me see now. Sir John, of course, and dear Joe. Yourself and Mary Ann."

"Anyone else?"

"Mary Goward, naturally. One of the silliest women ever to see daylight in my view. Then there were the Witherspoons, brother and sister, close as book leaves and probably incestuous."

"Dear God!" exclaimed John, eyebrows flying.

Miss Chudleigh disregarded him and frowned in even deeper concentration. Then she smiled. "Jack Morocco was there as well. Large as life and perfumed like a lotus."

"Jack Morocco?" John repeated. "Who's he?"

"The Duchess of Arundel's little pet. He started off as her black boy but by the time he reached puberty she had grown so fond of him that she didn't follow custom and send him to the plantations. Instead she kept him on and treated him like a son. She dresses him as a fop, pays all his bills, bought him a horse and even fetched a dancing master to him. Can you credit it?"

"And is he a dutiful son to her?"

"Not he. He has a secret life that is the talk of the town, though she knows nothing of it."

"And are you going to tell me what that is?"

"The usual. A private apartment, a white mistress, scores of hangers-on, claret and champagne. Need I say more?"

John laughed. "No. I take it the Duchess has no natural sons of her own?"

"No children at all, fate did not curse her with any."

What an odd choice of word, thought John. Surely it should have been bless? But Miss Chudleigh was continuing to speak. "Anyway, he is quite the dandy man, though very pleasing in personality when one converses with him. In fact he has quite contributed to the clientele of Signor Luciano. All the young noblemen go there to learn fencing and horsemanship from friend Morocco."

"He sounds a character indeed. I wonder what he was doing at the investiture."

"One of his jolly friends receiving a knighthood I expect."

"I see. Was there anybody else standing near Sir George?"

"No, I don't think so."

"Who are the brother and sister you mentioned?"

"The Witherspoons? Oh just a strange couple who have always shared a home. I believe there was another sister who died. If my memory holds, there was talk of suicide."

"Surely it's not true they are incestuous?"

Elizabeth Chudleigh shrugged a careless shoulder. "Who knows? Nobody has been in their bedrooms, just as they haven't anyone else's. It's mere conjecture, after all."

"Do you know where they live?"

"Somewhere in Islington, close to George Goward, so I've heard."

"Ah."

"Do you think that is significant?"

It was John's turn to shrug. "It's possible I suppose." He finished his coffee, putting the cup down carefully in the saucer. "Tell me, how well do you know the Gowards?"

The wide eyes gave him a penetrating stare. "She more than him. When I first came to court she was married to Lomond, a drunken wastrel if ever there was one. George Goward was on the fringes of polite society then, but he was good with the ladies and spoke well, so managed to climb the ladder. Every rung a woman, of course."

And were you one of them? thought John.

"Culminating in Lady Mary?"

"Yes, though to marry that vapid fool must have been a sacrifice for him indeed."

"I wonder why they never had children," said John reflectively.

"Perhaps she wouldn't, perhaps he couldn't. She had a son when she went into the marriage. Not that George had much to do with the child, rumour has it that he couldn't abide the little fellow, teased him constantly about his porky appearance."

"He was fat?"

"Huge. Took after his mother in that, to say nothing of his

grandfather. Old Lord Grimsby was a veritable barrel of a man."

"I believe that Goward told me this himself."

"How cruel of him. But then how typical. He was not a kind person."

"Would you think that he had many enemies?"

"I would say," answered Miss Chudleigh, lowering her lids so that he could not see the expression in her eyes, "that he probably had dozens."

"Fascinating," said Sir John Fielding, "absolutely fascinating. Do you know, Mr. Rawlings we only received intelligence a few moments ago as to the identity of the other people standing in Sir George Goward's vicinity. You have done very well indeed."

"Miss Chudleigh was most forthcoming - at least about the others."

"What do you mean by that?"

"Sir, I know she is a friend of yours yet I could not help but get the feeling that it was really she who was in control of the entire conversation. She talked freely about anything that did not concern her but said little about her own self."

The Magistrate frowned. "Do you think she is hiding something?"

"More than likely, though what I cannot imagine."

Sir John looked thoughtful. "Perhaps she knew Goward better than she cares to admit. Could you follow that up, do you think?"

"I can try," John answered, none too hopefully.

Today the court had risen early, there being few cases to hear, and the Apothecary, who had spent far longer with Miss Chudleigh than he had intended, had returned to Bow Street to give the Blind Beak the names of the three unknown people on the stairs.

"Mr. and Miss Witherspoon and Jack Morocco," Sir John

said consideringly now. "I feel that if you would be so kind, Mr. Rawlings, it might be helpful if you saw them. Find out if any have past connections with George Goward."

"The Witherspoons live near him in Islington, I believe."

"And Jack Morocco?"

"No connection that I know of but then, according to Miss Chudleigh, Morocco lives wildly and has many friends. He was the Duchess of Arundel's black boy, incidentally, but she grew to adore him so much that she brought him up and educated him as a son."

"How lucky he was to be kept on. As you and I know full well, Mr. Rawlings, when the black boys approach manhood and are no longer sexless toys to accompany fine ladies, they are usually despatched to the West Indies and slavery."

"A few remain because their owners have grown fond of them."

"Sometimes too fond! Certain white women of rank and position have allowed their black servants familiarities that propriety would not tolerate."

"With tragic results if they are discovered. Anyhow that would not apply to the Duchess," John said with certainty. "Apparently she treats this young man as an indulged child and always has."

The Magistrate rumbled a laugh. "I would rather like to meet him. I've a mind to call him in to Bow Street on some pretext or other."

"But meanwhile do you want me to track him down?"

"Try and find him in one of his haunts. It could be very enlightening. Meanwhile I will attempt to make an appointment with Lady Mary and inform you of it should I be succesful."

"She will plead her grief as an excuse not to see you."

"Of course I could demand an interview."

"She'll throw a vapour if you do," the Apothecary warned.

"Then I shall have to have you on hand to revive her,"

answered Sir John, and laughed again, very much amused by the involuntary groan which escaped his visitor's lips.

A letter from Digby Turnbull awaited John on his return to Nassau Street:

Dear Sir,
I am Informed by Miss Chudleigh that Much is Spoken of Concerning the Demise of Sir George Goward. In view of the Circumstances I would be Obliged for the Opportunity to Converse with Your Self. If you Would Care to Call at St. James's Palace presenting at the Same Entrance, I will be Pleased to recive Your Good Person.
I remain, Sir, Your Humble Servant,
D. Turnbull.

"What is it?" asked Emilia, appearing in the hall and looking most charming in a slightly loose blue robe.

"I have been summoned to the palace."

"By His Majesty."

"There's no need to be frivolous. Now how has Lucinda behaved herself today?"

"Well enough. But John ..."

"Yes?"

"The girl's preoccupied. All's not well with her."

"I am hardly surprised. Her history, both recent and past, has not been without incident, to say the least of it."

"I wish I could feel more at ease with her."

"My darling," said the Apothecary, "if she is upsetting you in any way I will remove her. No, of course I wouldn't put her without doors but I would ask my father to give her a position - or at the very least, someone of his acquaintance."

"Let that rest for the moment." Emilia grinned at him. "Perhaps I am jealous because she is lissom and I am daily getting fatter."

"Which for once just doesn't matter. There - I'm a poet. Now let us dine in peace and you can tell me all that has befallen you."

"Nothing really, except that I went to the shops and was given a rose for my bodice by an ebony man of striking visage."

"An ebony man? Do you mean a servant?"

"No, I mean a handsome strutting dandy of a fellow, as well set up as you or I."

"Who was he?"

"He gave me his card as it happens. I'll fetch it for you." And she returned a moment later with a gilt-edged calling card which she handed to the Apothecary.

"Well, well," he said, reading it. "Here he is again."

"Who?"

"None other than the elusive Jack Morocco. Riding and fencing instructor to the nobility, and beloved pet of the Duchess of Arundel herself."

# Chapter 9

The palace, which by daylight had seemed so welcoming and regal, by night took on a very different aspect. Dimly lit courtyards became pits of shadow and the walkway leading to the German church was dark and somehow rather frightening. Further, the gates were closed and barred and a sentry - a tall, faceless figure with a gruff voice - had to allow the Apothecary entry, opening up with a clanking set of keys. However, halfway down the walk a door already stood open and John, after calling out several times, made his way within. He was quite alone in the deserted reception corridor which only so recently had been thronging with the great and the gaudy, dressed in the highest fashions London and Paris had to offer.

Inside, candles flickered in wall sconces but even they did not throw enough light and the Apothecary walked in the half dark, his feet inadvertently drawn towards the Grand Staircase and that fatal spot at the bottom where George Goward had crashed down onto the marble floor and died. Then in the shadows above a door opened and closed twice, very rapidly. John stood transfixed, looking upwards, but nothing moved and his entire body froze with fear.

"Who's there?" he called cautiously.

Nobody answered, but it seemed to him that in the darkness came a sigh which blew like a wind, flickering the candle flames and whispering in the corners. John turned, too frightened to take another step, and then a larger shadow detached itself from a lake of darkness and moved towards him. The Apothecary froze but a familiar voice said, "Mr. Rawlings, forgive me for being late," and Digby Turnbull came into view.

"Good God," John replied, "you frightened me. I had begun to think this place haunted."

"Oh it is," Digby answered cheerfully.

114

"And the palace seems deserted. Has everyone gone?"

"Their Majesties left this morning, very distressed by reports of the accident. The court departed with them so that just a few of us remain in residence to oversee matters. Now, Sir, would you like to step to my apartments where I can offer you refreshment and we can speak more freely."

John's courage had returned. "Before we go, would you mind if I took another look at the staircase?"

"By all means. But everything has been thoroughly cleaned. I doubt you will find anything."

"None the less, I would appreciate a quick glance. If I could have some more light perhaps."

"I'll bring a candle tree."

Digby picked up a substantial silver stick and together they walked to the stairs.

The place where the body had lain had by now been thoroughly scrubbed so there was nothing to show for the blood that had gushed from Goward's skull.

"Not a sign here."

"As I told you, the staircase has also been cleaned. Do you still want to look?" Digby asked.

"I think perhaps I should."

It was tremendously eerie, climbing through the dimness to the place where they had all stood such a very short while ago and watched the Queen walk along the balcony.

Digby Turnbull spoke in the darkness. "Miss Chudleigh tells me there is talk of foul play."

"Sir John Fielding certainly thinks so."

"May I ask what his contention is?"

"He believes that George Goward may have been pushed to his death."

Turnbull drew in breath but said nothing.

"Sir, would you do me the favour of standing exactly where you were that day."

"I was here," Digby answered, taking up a stance two stairs behind the place where John Rawlings had been.

"Who else was close to you?"

"Miss Chudleigh was on the step in front of me; there was nobody else with her, which was odd in view of the crush."

"And in front of her?"

"Sir John Fielding, his clerk, his niece and yourself. On the step beneath yours were Mr. and Miss Witherspoon and Jack Morocco. In front of them stood Lady Mary and Sir George Goward."

"Anybody else close by? Anybody at all?"

"There were footmen and pages-of-honour on alternate stairs, that is all."

"I see," said John.

He dropped to his knees and while Digby held the candelabra high, began examining the staircase with his fingertips. But whoever had cleaned had done an excellent job. There was nothing.

"Is Goward still in the mortuary, poor wretch?" Digby asked tentatively.

"Yes. I believe the coroner is about to release the body but leave the case open."

The older man cleared his throat. "Mr. Rawlings, have you seen enough? I would prefer that we continued this conversation in my quarters which are just across the courtyard, in an older part of the building."

"Very well," John answered, and at that moment a door on the landing above opened and shut twice again. "Is there anybody up there?" he asked Digby nervously.

The other shook his head. "No, it does it by itself. Come along, my friend, this is not a place to linger after nightfall."

"I totally agree with you, said the Apothecary, and hurried down the corridor without looking back.


True to his word, Digby Turnbull had provided an excellent cold collation and a good burgundy in his three roomed apartment in St. James's Palace. Further, a fire burned brightly, casting a glow on the heavily beamed and ancient room in which he was entertaining his guest.

"I can't help wondering if Sir John is right," he said, sipping his wine. "What do you think, Mr. Rawlings?"

"Over the years I have learned to trust the Magistrate's judgement. He has the hearing of a bat and swears something was muttered just before George Goward fell. That, together with the sound of exhaled breath - exhaled because of effort - led him to the conclusion that the man was pushed."

"But why didn't anybody see anything?"

"Because everyone had turned to stare at the Queen. She is still a novelty to the likes of us, you know." John paused. "But you will have seen her before, of course. Did you look at her, Mr. Turnbull, or did you keep an eye on the staircase?"

Did the answer come just a little too hastily? "No, I turned with everyone else. I am only a minor servant and don't see that much of Their Majesties."

"Then anything could have happened while attention was engaged elsewhere."

"Yes, I suppose it could."

"And you noticed nothing untoward, nothing at all?"

Digby shook his head. "No. I'm sorry."

"It must have been done at the speed of light." John paused, considering. "The pages and footmen - surely one of them might have seen something."

"They are all instructed to keep their eyes forward and nearly all of them do. The footmen are trained staff, of course, but the boys are not, being pages-of-honour."

"What is that exactly?"

"They are not servants but all members of the nobility. They help on state and important occasions. Ordinary pages are of lower rank than footmen."

John drained his wine. "The boys all seemed very helpful, doing their best. Indeed, I thought how well behaved they were." He watched as Digby refilled John's glass. "Is there some sort of tradition about there being thirteen of them?"

The other man stared. "What is that you say?"

"Why do you have thirteen pages? I always thought it was considered an unlucky omen."

Digby Turnbull shook his head. "There are only twelve, Mr. Rawlings. We would never have thirteen. As you say, it is not a happy number."

"But there were thirteen present at the levee. I counted them myself."

"I think you must have been mistaken, my friend."

"But how? I noted it particularly."

"Impossible," answered Digby Turnbull, and looked slightly annoyed.

John relapsed into silence, sipping his wine and thinking hard. If he pressed his new acquaintance on the point it was obvious that he was going to get angry, yet the Apothecary knew quite certainly that he was right. There had been thirteen pages in attendance that day, there was no doubt about it, he had counted them and for sure had noted the strange number correctly. This meant that an extra boy had been present at the very time that George Goward fell to his death. An odd coincidence to say the least of it. Yet to antagonise Digby Turnbull over the issue would be fatal. The Apothecary assumed his 'foolish me' expression.

"I must have been mistaken. I do beg your pardon. However, I am sure Sir John would be interested to speak to the pages who were present. Would it be a great bother for you to give me a list of them?"

"Not at all," Digby answered, cheerful again. "I'll get one drawn up tomorrow. What about the footmen?"

"I'm sure the Magistrate would like to have a record of them as well."

"You're going to have your work cut out, you Public Office people, talking to all those involved."

"Indeed we are," John answered, affecting a sigh. He

changed the subject. "Did you know George Goward at all?"

"A little. His first wife came from Devon, from whence hail both Miss Chudleigh and myself."

"His first wife!" John exclaimed. "I had no idea that he had been married before he wed Lady Mary."

"Not many people have. It all took place in the West Country. I lived near Ashton, a remote village some fair distance out of Exeter. Miss Chudleigh spent her youth in Ashton - her family were local and have places bearing their name - and as I came from just outside so we were acquainted. Hannah Wilson lived in Exeter itself. She was a local beauty and several of us fell in love with her but George Goward, who was visiting relatives in the city, married her by eloping on the day of her twenty-first birthday."

"How fascinating. What happened to her?"

"I think he rather regretted what he had done, despite her great physical charms. He kept Hannah in the country, in very meagre circumstances, while he pursued his career in polite society in London. Then she became pregnant and died in childbirth. He arranged the funeral and promptly forgot all about her. A few years after that he married the widowed Lady Mary."

"What happened to his child?"

Digby Turnbull stared into the fire. "It was taken in by relatives. I don't know anything further than that. I lost all contact with Devon after I made my home in London."

"What an extraordinary story. Do you think Lady Mary knew that her husband had been married before?"

Digby shrugged. "I have no idea. I certainly didn't mention it."

"But Miss Chudleigh could have said something."

"She might. Who knows?"

There was a silence during which the clock in the great Tudor Clock Tower chimed nine. John finished his glass of claret.

"Mr. Turnbull, you have been of great help to me. I thank you for your time and patience."

"It is nothing. If Sir John is right and an act of murder has been committed within the palace walls, then it is my duty to give you every assistance. I shall send the list of pages-of-honour to the Public Office tomorrow, together with the names of the footmen who attended."

"You are most public spirited," said the Apothecary, getting to his feet.

"Anything I can do to help. I shall be removing to Kew Palace shortly but you can contact me at any of the royal residences."

"I thank you for your courtesy, Sir."

"Allow me to escort you across the courtyard, Mr. Rawlings. Do you know, legend has it that Henry VIII tethered his horse to that tree there."

"How incredible," said John as they strode out together into the darkness.


With a great feeling of guilt that Nicholas was being left alone too often in charge of the shop, and with a secondary notion that he might quiz his apprentice about Lucinda and her erratic behaviour, John set out really early for Shug Lane. So early indeed that he caught his apprentice up as he limped his way through the back alleys, heading in the direction of Piccadilly.

"Master," said the Muscovite, turning round and staring in surprise. "I had not thought to see you about at this hour."

"Then more shame me. I have been neglecting my duties."

"Not at all, Sir. How goes it with you and Sir John Fielding?"

"We have a complicated affair on our hands."

"I thought as ..."

But Nicholas got no further. For at that moment a door in the alleyway flung open and a negro boy about nine years of age, his hair cropped almost to nothing about his pathetic head, his clothing a worn and terrible grey serge suit, far too large for him, came careering into the road pursued by a red-faced man bearing a formidable whip.

"Help!" the child shrieked as he ran like a hound down Great Windmill Street towards Piccadilly.

"Come here varmint, come here nigger," yelled his pursuer, cracking the whip on the ground in the most terrifying manner.

"Dear God," said John and gave chase, followed by Nicholas, running as fast as he could.

But there seemed little hope of catching them up and the poor child started to scream as the red-faced man began to gain on him. Then came a moment of pure theatrical magic, or so it seemed to John. With a leap that would not have shamed a gazelle, the most beautifully dressed black man that the Apothecary had ever set eyes on jumped directly into the path of the chase, scooped the boy up and pushed him behind his back, in the same movement drawing a sword and putting the point straight to the pursuer's genitals as he panted to a halt.

"Out of my way, damn you," shouted the chaser.

"Out of mine," drawled the negro.

He spoke superbly, with the accent of a true English aristocrat, and every move betrayed a first-class education. John laughed audibly, aware that he could be looking at none other than that exquisite, that buck, that fop of fashion, Jack Morocco himself.

Morocco whirled the sword in his hand, as only a master of fencing could, and thrust the point right at the man's penis. "Well?" he said.

"Don't you dare attack me, you black dog."

"Don't insult me, Sir, or you'll sing soprano. Now be off with you."

"Give me back my slave."

"No, Sir, I'll not return the wretch to a life of beating and degredation. Here ..." Morocco reached into the pocket of his beautiful white breeches and negligently produced a coin which he flipped in the direction of the red-faced man. "... there's a guinea for you. I'll buy him"

"I want him, not your damned money."

"Really?" said Morocco, affecting a yawn and throwing another coin after the first. "Good day to you."

And he sheathed his sword and walked off, taking the weeping child by the hand. What happened next was very, very fast. The red-faced man lunged at Morocco's retreating back and in that split second the negro turned and floored him with a fist to the jaw that would have crashed down a man twice the size.

"Oh Masser, Masser, he'll kill us," shrieked the boy hysterically.

"On the contrary," Morocco answered. "And it's Master, by the way. If you are to stay with me you must learn to speak properly." He flicked his fingers and a coach which had been trundling at some distance behind him, came smartly up alongside. "Take this child back home and give orders that it is to be scrubbed and deloused," Morocco instructed the coachman. "Then return for me at White's. I've a mind to attend a morning concert at Ranelagh today. I shall breakfast there, I believe." He bowed in the direction of John and Nicholas, who were standing goggle-eyed, and sauntered down the road, buying some flowers from an early-morning seller and sniffing them as he went.

Nicholas turned to his Master. "Who was that?"

"Jack Morocco, it has to be. There simply couldn't be two answering that description. Strangely, he was at the levee the other day but I can't say that I really noticed him with everything else that was going on. And now I have to question him about the death of George Goward."

"Go to Ranelagh," said the apprentice with determination. "You can contrive to bump into him socially. It would be worth it just to meet him, let alone anything else."

"But Nick, I have to work."

"No, Sir, go home and fetch Mrs. Rawlings. Stir Irish Tom into a frenzy and he'll get you there in a trice."

"Nick, my friend, you are beyond price," answered John with enthusiasm.

"Oh, I'm sure you'll find a way of rewarding me," answered the Muscovite, and with that gave his Master a look in which thoughts of Lucinda were clear to see.

The wonderful pleasure gardens at Vaux Hall had a great and formidable rival in the Ranelagh Gardens, which bordered onto the Hospital of Maymed Soldiers at Chelsea. Yet even though Vaux Hall excited, Ranelagh was by far the most fashionable of all the London gardens. With an exorbitant entrance fee of two shillings and sixpence, the hoi-polloi were kept firmly at bay, even though this colossal charge did include tea, coffee, punch and other beverages. Added to this cost was the general expense of refreshments, the high prices ensuring that one mixed with only the very best people. It had been said of Ranelagh that in the genteel walks one could meet the first persons of the kingdom and it was for this reason, and this alone, that those who wished to be considered *bon ton* willingly paid the money to attend.

The Gardens, though smaller than those at Vaux Hall, were prettily laid out but John and Emilia, having arrived somewhat breathlessly after a rather hair-raising drive, hurried through them and into the great Rotunda or Musick Theatre. Here all was splendour. Booths, many dozens of them, filled the circumference, while dominating the centre of the building was the great fireplace, an enormous edifice which had once housed the orchestra but now had a vast fire burning within, supplying boiling water for all the many tea tables dotted around it.

Above the gallery, which housed more booths, were stately windows, cupolas rising from each one, all arching centrally and terminating mid-ceiling in a point. From this the chimney of the great fireplace descended, giving a grandiose and stunning effect. Lights were everywhere, thirty-six branches of globe lamps lighting the Rotunda, besides many others nearer to the cubicles.

John stared around. "Can you see any sign of him?"

Emilia shook her head. "Not so far, perhaps he's walking in the Chinese Garden."

"Not he. He announced his intention of attending a morning concert and the orchestra is already tuning up."

"Let's hope that nothing occurred to make him change his plans."

John was about to say what a total waste of time the visit to Ranelagh would prove to be if that were true, then realised how discourteous to Emilia such words would sound. For she was clearly enjoying herself, looking at all the sights with that angelic expression which he loved so well. He put his arm round her shoulders.

"Let's find a booth and have some refreshment."

"Then afterwards can we promenade? I love that way of listening to music."

John, who thought the fashion of walking round and round the Rotunda, dresses swishing, faces serious, while the orchestra gave its all, was no more thrilling than the plodding of a donkey turning a treadmill, smiled.

"It shall be exactly as you wish."

But at that moment the man he sought chose to make an entrance and it was no exaggeration to say that almost every head in the place turned, including John's and Emilia's. Framed in the doorway, clad in scarlet and silver, his wig very white against his dark skin, his arms full of flowers, which he threw to the ladies in the booths, a retinue of sharp young blades behind him, at his side a truly beautiful white girl with pale red hair that hung *au naturel* to her hips and seemed without artifice except for the fresh blooms woven into it ... Jack Morocco had come into the Rotunda. Whether by coincidence or design, the orchestra struck up a rousing air and the Duchess of Arundel's adopted son made his way to a decorated booth where he sprawled at his leisure like a Prince of Araby.

"Good gracious," said Emilia.

"Gracious indeed."

"Strangely, I saw him go into the levee t'other day. He must have borrowed the Duchess's coach because the Arundel coat of arms was on the door."

"It would never surprise me to hear that he has them painted on his own conveyance, he's such a showman," John said wryly.

"But that would be going too far surely. After all, did you not say that he started off as the Duchess's black boy?"

"I did, and he has climbed his way upwards ever since. Now quick, sweetheart, the booth next to his has just become vacant. I must get into conversation with the fellow by some means or other, and sitting next to him is as good a way as any."

They hurried across the floor of the Rotunda, attempting to look nonchalant as they did so; no easy feat. Beating another, older couple with the same intent, John and Emilia took their places and motioned for a waiter to come for their order. Meanwhile from the neighbouring cubicle came the sound of much jollity as champagne corks popped. Emilia pulled a face.

"Is that their idea of breakfast?"

"A very good one," the Apothecary said severely. "Impending motherhood is not making you prudish, I trust."

Emilia looked slightly put out. "I was only joking."

"Never joke about champagne," John answered, "it's far too serious a subject." There was an explosion of mirth from next door, followed by Morocco's voice rising loud and clear. "Gentlemen, I give you a toast."

"Hear, hear," said somebody.

"To ladies of beauty everywhere. God bless them all, especially those who have loved me."

A female voice spoke out. "I'll most certainly not drink to that."

"No more should you, Madam," a man answered.

Morocco came in again. "And let me add in front of witnesses that of those whom I dared to hope have cared for me, there is none more beautiful, nor one that has pleased me so well as my fair Aminta."

The girl laughed. "Smooth as silk, Mr. Morocco."

"If you so care to describe me."

"He has all the answers," John whispered.

"No wonder he got on in the world with repartee like that."

Morocco was speaking again. "So, gentlemen, we'll drink to the ladies, and for our second toast of the morning, Aminta the fair herself."

A golden opportunity was presenting itself and as John heard the scrape of chairs, he got to his feet, a cup of tea in his hand.

"The ladies," said Morocco, and as glasses were raised John put his head round the corner of the booth.

"Gentlemen, I could not help but hear what you said. Though it is only in tea, may I join in your sentiments?"

Morocco looked up and John saw the momentary gleam of suspicion in his brilliant dark eye. Then he said. "Of course, Sir. But give the man a proper drink, Carter. We can't have anyone going short."

And with that a glass was poured and handed to John who raised it on high and echoed, "The ladies," with the others.

"On your own?" asked Morocco when the toast was done.

"No, Sir, my wife is with me."

Emilia popped her head round the booth and waved a pretty hand.

"Charming," said the black man. "Now why don't you

come and join us? Some feminine company will please Aminta who is feeling somewhat outnumbered today."

Aminta, who was queening it, looked far from thrilled at the prospect but both John and Emilia ignored this and hurried into the two extra chairs provided by a waiter.

Jack Morocco flashed his strong white teeth in a welcoming smile, then frowned. "Now I've seen you before somewhere. Both of you. Where could it have been?"

"You presented me with a rose when I was out shopping the other day," Emilia answered.

Aminta gave a light-hearted laugh. "Oh, he does that to everyone. He's known for it."

"What a charming reputation to have," Emilia answered pleasantly.

Oh dear, thought John, those two don't like each other.

He studied Aminta surreptitiously. Very vaguely she reminded him of someone but he could not place who it was and gave up trying, instead appreciating her wood nymph beauty and autumn colouring. She really was quite breathtaking and the Apothecary wondered if she was the white mistress to whom Elizabeth Chudleigh had referred or if Jack Morocco had yet another lovely girl hidden away.

The black man was speaking. "But you, Sir. You are very familiar. I've seen you somewhere recently. I know I have."

"The investiture the other day. I was present and so were you."

"I was indeed. Well, well. Who were you accompanying? Or did you receive an honour?"

John gave a crooked smile. "Alas, no. I was with Mr. Fielding of the Public Office, Bow Street. Now Sir John of course."

"Ah, the Blind Beak, eh? Quite a character, I believe."

"You've never met him?"

"No, though I've seen him in court, of course. A great spectacle."

John cleared his throat, ready to brooch the subject. "Did you by any chance witness ..."

Jack Morocco held up an admonitory hand. "No sad talk this morning, I pray you. Let us drink and promenade and listen to music. Aminta, may I escort you?"

"With pleasure," she answered, laying her pale fingers amongst his.

The black man looked at John over his shoulder and his eyes quite clearly conveyed a message, though quite what that message was the Apothecary was uncertain.

"My dear sir, in case we become separated in the throng, be kind enough to give me your card. You look an interesting fellow and I would converse with you."

John reached into an inner pocket. "This is my business address. I shall write my private on the back."

"Excellent," said Morocco. He gave a jackanapes grin, downed the rest of his glass in a swallow, refilled it, downed that, then jumped to his feet, his legs already jigging to the music.

"Shall we walk, John?" asked Emilia.

"Yes," he answered abstractedly, well aware that Morocco had something to tell him that he was not prepared to divulge before the rest of the company.

They charged into the melee, Emilia enjoying the experience of strolling with the finest company while listening to the sweet sounds of the orchestra. Ahead of them sauntered Morocco, stared at by all and sundry, smiling and waving at complete strangers, totally unabashed that he was the centre of attention.

With a positive push to his pictorial memory, John conjured up the scene on the staircase as George Goward fell to his death. Shock and horrified surprise had been the expression on most faces; nobody had moved as the figure in salmon pink had plunged downwards. But as the Apothecary fought to recall it, another image came into his mind. A dark figure, standing alone, a figure that he had entirely forgotten was there but the image of which had been stored in the deep recesses of his mind, had broken the stillness. Thinking that nobody was looking at him, that he was totally unobserved, there had been a sudden flash of white teeth in an ebony face. As George Goward lay dying, Jack Morocco had smiled.

# *Chapter 10*

It had been a wonderful day, full of music and wine and flowers - for Jack Morocco had insisted on buying more and more nosegays to shower on his two female guests - but the homecoming had put a damper on the entire proceedings. No sooner were John and Emilia through the front door than the sound of raised voices coming from below stairs broke the joyful mood they had been enjoying but a moment before.

She turned to look at him. "What now, I wonder?"

John shook his head. "I've no idea, but whatever it is I'll sort it out. Go and sit down. You can leave this to me."

It was not just that Emilia suddenly had a tired look about her, it was also because he had the strangest feeling that Lucinda Drummond was somehow involved in the argument and that it really was time for him to act. Without further ado John strode down the stairs to the basement and into the kitchen, the servants' principal domain.

They were very surprised to see him, clearly not being aware that he had returned, for the footman who had let him in had not yet reported below stairs.

"Well?" said the Apothecary into the shocked silence.

"I must go to the mistress," said Dorcas, bobbing a curtsey. "I didn't realise you were back, Sir."

"I'd rather you remained where you are," John stated severely. He looked straight at Axford, the head footman. "Your arguing voices could practically be heard in the street. Would you be so good as to inform me what all this is about."

"It's Lucinda, Sir. She's run away."

"Run away? When?"

"This morning, Mr. Rawlings. A letter came for her and she asked me for time off so that she could visit somebody sick. In short, Sir, I did not give permission for her to leave so she took the law into her own hands, packed her things, and left the house."

"Do you know where she's gone?"

"No, Sir."

"Do any of you?" John looked from one face to the other.

Bridget, Emilia's second maid, sniffed. "She said nothing to us. She was always very secretive and aloof."

"Perhaps she found you equally unfriendly," the Apothecary replied curtly, and marched out.

"It's Lucinda, isn't it?" asked Emilia, lying on a chaise in the salon but opening her eyes as her husband came into the room.

"Yes, but don't judge her too harshly. Somebody close to her is ill - or so she says."

"Is it her mysterious mother?"

"I have no idea. But I have a very shrewd notion who will know."

"Nicholas?"

"The very same. I'd better go to the shop."

Emilia frowned. "Must you? We've had such a wonderful day together."

The Apothecary, who had no particular wish to turn out, full of champagne and food as he was, felt himself weaken. "Well, I'm sure an hour or two more will make little difference. There's nothing I can do till the morning in any event."

His wife sat upright. "Don't tell me you intend to go after her?"

"It's my duty to do so. After all, she's scarcely more than a child and she is under my protection."

Emilia made a derogatory sound.

"What is that supposed to mean?"

"I believe that young woman to have her head well and truly on her shoulders. Don't think I haven't noticed how Nick moons after her ..."

"He is particularly susceptible. Remember Mary Ann and his passion for her?"

"You told me of it, yes. But that is beside the point."

"Which is?"

"That I believe Lucinda to be a scheming minx who took you in utterly with her story of rape and molestation."

"I thought you liked her."

"Well, I've changed my mind."

"Emilia, have you no pity? I suspect that the poor girl's brother may be ill. And if so, I truly can't blame her for running to his side."

"What makes you think it is him?"

"Because she told me when we first met that he was a sickly child. That was why her mother sent her to join him at school, disguised as a boy."

"A likely tale. But if it's true, oh dear," Emilia answered.

John burst out laughing, sat down beside his wife and took her in his arms. "Are you tipsy, Mrs. Rawlings? First she's a minx, now you're sorry for her. Oh the mercurial mind of a pregnant woman."

Emilia frowned again. "Don't tease me. I don't know what I think about her, except that, whether she be good or bad, I don't really trust her."

But this convoluted argument could not be followed further for there was a sudden peal at the front door and the sound of a footman going to answer. A minute or so later, the servant appeared with a tray bearing a card. John picked it up.

"Digby Turnbull," he read. "Show him into the library, would you. I think he may have some information for me."

Kissing a somewhat tearful Emilia, John went to join their guest who was standing with his hands outstretched to the flames of the fire. He looked up as the Apothecary came into the room.

"Ah, Mr. Rawlings, I have brought you the list of footmen and pages-of-honour. I thought perhaps you would like to read it before it goes to Sir John."

"Why? Is there anything of interest on it?"

"Nothing that I can see. Of course, I am not in charge of the pages-of-honour, they are in the hands of a high-ranking courtier, but the footmen are my responsibility."

John scanned the list, noticing that all the pageboys did indeed have titles, the lowest rank being an Honourable. There was even a young Duke amongst their number.

"I suppose we shall have to speak to them all," he said to Digby with a sigh.

"Surely not. What could they tell you?"

"Only if they noticed anything unusual."

"I feel fairly certain that they would have been staring at the Queen along with everybody else. The poor woman is still an object of curiosity, even amongst the aristocracy."

John read the list once more, wondering why he had the feeling that it should be telling him more than it did. Noticing that only twelve names were written there, he considered the fact that he could have been mistaken about seeing thirteen boys. Yet the Apothecary felt absolutely positive that he had counted their number correctly.

"One of these young people acted very fast," he said, almost to himself.

Digby Turnbull stared. "What do you mean?"

"I saw a pageboy run for help. As I was kneeling beside George Goward I noticed one of them haring down the reception corridor."

"I don't know who that would have been. It would not have been considered correct for any of them to have left his post."

"He must have acted on the spur of the moment."

Turnbull seemed decidedly doubtful. "How very odd. You're certain of this?"

"Yes." The Apothecary looked thoughtful. "Perhaps he was running away in fright."

"But why? He would have seen no more than any of the other boys."

"Unless he stood the closest," John answered.

But his mind was racing on. If an extra page had been

there for some reason, however innocent that reason might have been, the fact that there had been a fatal accident would most certainly have drawn attention to his presence. The boy was quite clearly making an escape before somebody discovered him. Or possibly because he had seen something but had no wish to say what, so was getting out before he could be questioned. The Apothecary tapped the list again.

"This Duke of Guernsey, how old is he?"

"Seventeen or eighteen. The eldest of them all. A descendant of Charles II of course. Nice lad."

"Where can he be found?"

"I'm not sure. Would you like me to discover?

"Yes please."

"Why do you pick him out in particular?"

"I don't know. Perhaps through some deep-rooted idea that one should be able to trust the word of those born to high station."

"A misconception if ever there was one."

"You're right, of course. Still, as he is the most senior I should like to talk to him."

"I'll send you word of his whereabouts from Kew. I leave for the palace in the morning, rather early I'm afraid. So, if you've nothing further to ask of me I'll take my leave."

"May I offer you some refreshment before you go?"

"Thank you but no. Duty calls." Digby Turnbull smiled. "Will that be all?"

"One last question. How old would George Goward's daughter be now?"

Digby was silent a moment, considering. Then he said, "About sixteen, seventeen at the most."

John nodded. "Thank you. An interesting age indeed. Exactly the same as our missing Lucinda."


By this time it was far too late for the Apothecary to go to Shug Lane, a fact for which he was extremely grateful, so instead he decided to wait for Nicholas Dawkins to come home, then to hold a conversation with him before Emilia became involved. In the event, it couldn't have worked better. His wife, tired by the excitement of the day, retired to bed early and John was left to snooze before the library fire, waking as Nicholas, who as a trusted apprentice had a key to the house, let himself in through the front door.

"Nick," called his Master, "come here and have a sherry. There is much to talk about."

The Muscovite appeared a second later looking somewhat apprehensive. "Sir?"

John came straight to the point. "Lucinda's gone, run away from the house. Apparently a member of her family is ill. Tell me what you know about it." He poured a substantial glass and motioned his apprentice to a chair.

"It's her brother, Master."

"I thought as much. He's very sickly I believe."

"Very. He attends the school that she fled from. But now she has risked all and gone there to be with him."

"Oh my God. I'm sure that headmaster will force her back if he can."

"She says she will invoke her mother if she has to."

John refilled the Muscovite's glass. "Nick, who *is* Lucinda's mother? Do you know? If so I enjoin you to tell me. It would make things so much easier for the girl."

The apprentice shook his head. "Master, she has never confided in me, being determined to keep the secret. But I have taken a guess."

"Who? Who do you think it is?"

"Miss Chudleigh," Nicholas answered.

The Apothecary almost dropped his sherry. "Miss Chudleigh?" he repeated, astonished.

"Lucinda said that her mother was close to the court and had aristocratic connections. It is also widely rumoured - I have heard great ladies in the shop discuss it - that Miss Chudleigh, in the past, gave birth to a child, or two, which she kept utterly concealed from the world in general."

"Good gracious! But I must admit it would make an awful kind of sense. Even the close proximity of the school takes on another meaning."

"That is how I reasoned it," said Nicholas enthusiastically.

"Did you put this to Lucinda?"

"No, she is so vehement about protecting her mother's identity that I thought it would only provoke an argument."

"Um."

The Apothecary was silent, remembering something. How Emilia, whilst in Miss Chudleigh's house, had spoken of women who abandoned their babies and how George Goward had waved his fingers at the hostess and made a remark that some mothers put their newborn infants out to cruel guardians. Then another memory came. Of two people speaking in The Hercules Pillars, of the woman accusing the man of betraying her secret and saying that, if pushed, she would not hesitate to betray his. The Apothecary had seen the back of them as they left. Surely he would not be fanciful in thinking, in hindsight, that they might well have been Elizabeth Chudleigh and George Goward.

"Do you know, Nick, I think you might well be right," John said now.

"About what?"

"About Miss Chudleigh being Lucinda's mother. I think I shall have to call when I go to Kensington tomorrow."

"You are going to fetch Lucinda back?"

"I am going to see how I can help her, yes."

The Muscovite looked terribly eager. "Sir, may I come with you?"

"No, my friend, you may not. You would only complicate the issue further. Besides, the shop must open and only you are there to do it."

Nicholas shifted in his chair, "But I am so worried about her."

"I understand that. But I really think that this problem would be best left to me. Now, go and get some supper. You must keep your strength up if we are to succeed."

"But, Master ..."

"No further argument, Nick. My mind is made up."

With every sign of reluctance, his apprentice left the room, while John settled himself to read for a while before he went to bed. But yet again he was to be thwarted. The doorbell pealed once more and a hearty laugh in the hallway as the visitor was let in announced that his old friend Samuel Swann had called. John put the book aside and rang a bell for port to be brought up from the cellar, mentally preparing himself for a possible late night.

"My dear chap," said the Goldsmith, coming into the room like a boisterous dog, "how good to find you in. I have just come directly from the Public Office." He looked important.

"Really? Do tell me," John answered, masking a smile, for it was obvious that Samuel was simply bursting to reveal all.

"I called on Mr. Fielding - I mean Sir John. As you know, I've offered my services to help with the current case, and he has finally found something for me to do. Apparently there are two witnesses - a brother and sister called Witherspoon - who live in Islington. As you know, my dear papa lives there and Sir John thought that visiting him would provide a splendid excuse for you and I to bump into them, accidentally but on purpose if you see what I mean."

"He wants me to be with you?"

"Yes, indeed. I don't think he completely trusts me to handle them on my own, more's the pity." Samuel laughed robustly.

"And when does he want us to go?"

"As soon as possible. They were standing on the stair quite close to George Goward, or so it seems."

John felt very fractionally irritated. "Yes, I know. Miss Chudleigh told me of them. She says that their relationship is quite possibly incestuous."

Samuel's honest countenance looked deeply shocked. "Oh surely that can't be true."

"Well, we have yet to meet them. Perhaps they are riddled with corruption and vice and capable of doing anything."

"Oh dear."

"Anyway, my old friend, they must wait a day or two. I have another crisis on my hands. Lucinda has run away." And the Apothecary explained, while the port was poured and Samuel settled himself comfortably, all that had been going on, even down to the extraordinary fact that there had been thirteen pages-of-honour present on an occasion where normally there should have been only twelve.

The Goldsmith listened, very nearly open-mouthed when it came to the description of the incredible Jack Morocco. "Damme, what a character. Is he then a Moor?"

"No, African I imagine. The name is probably a jest on the Duchess's part."

"D'ye know, I've heard of him. I believe he teaches riding and fencing at a school for young bloods."

"He does at that. Not that he spends a lot of time there. He had a very beautiful girl with him this morning and appeared more devoted to her than to giving his lessons."

"From what I hear, she is just one of a string. And I believe his extravagant parties are the talk of town. He seems to lead an enchanted life."

"What a lucky man he is," said John. "For it occurs to me that the ultimate cruelty meted out to the majority of black boys is that after a life of pampering and cosseting, as much loved as a pet dog, they are sent back to slavery and degradation as soon as hairs begin to sprout upon their body."

"It doesn't seem very fair."

"Fair! It's downright evil. Better to go straight into servitude than be shown kindness only to have it snatched away for the sin of growing up."

Samuel sighed. "There's little we can do about it. Anyway,

about Morocco. You say he was standing on the staircase, close to where George Goward fell?"

"Yes, and there's something he wants to tell me. That much was obvious when we met at Ranelagh."

"Will you seek him out?"

"If he doesn't come to me first."

Samuel shifted his large frame. "I take it you're intent on finding this girl before you see the Witherspoons."

"I think she could be in danger."

"Then allow me to accompany you, my friend. I promised Sir John that I would help and I have no wish to delay longer."

There was no way in which Samuel could be dissuaded without hurting his deepest feelings and loving his old friend as he did, the Apothecary had no intention of doing that. However, there was a possible way out.

"I intend to leave for Kensington very early tomorrow morning. What about your shop?"

"My apprentice can manage for a day or so. May I beg a bed for the night?"

"Of course," John said with resignation.

"Then it will be just like the old days," Samuel answered cheerfully, leaving the Apothecary to smile to himself and wonder when, if ever, his old companion would finally grow up.

Despite Nicholas Dawkins's pleading looks, John did not waiver but sent his apprentice off to Shug Lane even earlier than usual. Then, deciding that they would breakfast at The Hercules Pillars, he and Samuel set off.

It seemed that the world and his wife were out that day, for the coaching inn was packed with a wonderment of characters. Two stages had arrived simultaneously, pouring their contents within, and at the same moment a private coach had disgorged its elegant passengers, very finely dressed in shades of crimson and puce, all these varied people rubbing shoulders together in the confined space inside. Lawyers and countrymen, aristocrats and actresses, excited children, a crying baby, tripped over one another in the fight to get fed and watered. In the midst of all, the same dog lay on its back, farting as it slept. A thin-boned woman with a myriad of red veins in her cheeks, dressed in the most unfortunate shade of pea green, decided to have an hysteric because of the crush and crashed down upon the unfortunate animal, forcing it to howl loudly in shock. John looked at Samuel.

"Shall we move on? This place is a bear garden."

"Worse. We'll eat somewhere else."

But at that moment, into the view of both of them, running her fine eyes over the assembled masses, tall and elegant, giving not an inch as she progressed, even though the osier hoops of her gown struck all those she passed, came Elizabeth Chudleigh.

"We stay," said John and Samuel in one voice.

"Attract her attention," instructed the Apothecary, and Samuel's vast height and windmill arms swept into action. Snatching his hat from his head, he waved it aloft like a flag.

"Miss Chudleigh," he boomed. "Over here, Ma'am."

She turned her head, her high hair crowned with a brimmed creation making an arc of colour as she did so. "Gentlemen, good morning," she called.

"Allow us to escort you to the dining parlour," shouted John.

"Gladly. But how to get through this melee?"

"Allow me," said Samuel and charged through the crowd to where she stood, sweeping her into his arms, osier hoops rising to preposterous heights above both their heads, then carried Miss Chudleigh as best he could towards the hall from which the dining parlours led.

"Oh Mr. Swann," she said, and fluttered girlishly, leaving John to think that his friend was not, after all, without his uses.

Once seated at the breakfast table, a difficult feat which had involved bribing a waiter, some semblance of order was restored.

"I'm on my way to Kensington, of course," Miss Chudleigh announced. "I take it that that is where you are heading, Mr. Rawlings."

"Quite correctly, Ma'am. I have a small errand to perform." He omitted to say what it was and a slight pressure to Samuel's elbow indicated that he should do likewise.

"Well, I am returning home for a few days, partly to oversee the building work, partly to get away from all this horror. It is now commonly spoken of that George Goward was pushed to his death but no one seems certain who could have done it. I believe it was his wife, of course."

"Why?" asked Samuel, genuinely interested.

"Because he had had several mistresses, including one particularly immature one, I believe, and Mary knew it."

"Really?" said John, eyebrows flying. "Who was the young lady?" Miss Chudleigh frowned, her beautiful face suddenly severe. "That's the problem. I don't know. Nobody did. The *beau monde* discussed it for a while but as no-one could come up with the answer they lost interest and went on to the next scandal."

"But surely Lady Mary must have realised who it was"

"Very probably. Perhaps she intends to kill her next." Miss Chudleigh's eyes sparkled and she warmed to her theme. "That may well be it, you know. She lost patience with the entire situation and is hell-bent on revenge."

"Did you know that George Goring had a daughter by his first wife?" John slipped his key question in quietly.

Elizabeth fell into the trap. "Oh yes, though he tried to keep the matter well concealed."

"So not many people were aware of it?"

"Not many."

John's pictorial memory switched back to that other occasion in The Hercules Pillars. Digby Turnbull, the dog voiding wind, the unseen couple and the words they had uttered: "Guilty conscience and guilty conscience alone," the man had said. To which the woman had retorted, "You bastard! Never forget that you are not without guilt." As they had gone out they had looked familiar. Had it been Miss Chudleigh and George Goward? Had it been they who had discussed terrible secrets. Had one of those secrets been that he had a hidden daughter? Or was it possible that both of them had daughters they wished to conceal?

"Does the name Lucinda Drummond mean anything to you?" John asked suddenly.

The wide eyes grew wider. "No, I don't think so. Lucinda Drummond..." Miss Chudleigh repeated. "No, I do not know her."

She was either a consummate actress or telling the truth.

"So she's not Goward's daughter?" John persisted.

"No."

"What is his child's name then?"

The great eyelids drooped, disguising the pupils beneath. "I believe she was named Georgiana after her father."

"Is she in London these days?"

Miss Chudleigh rallied. "Now how would I know that, Sir? George once told me that he had a child which was being brought up by relatives who lived not far from Chudleigh, a village named after my family, don't you know? As far as I am aware the girl is still breathing the fresh Devon air, a county famous for the beauties it produces."

She made a coy moue which John felt belittled her.

"So how old would the girl be now?"

"Again you ask me things I do not know. I imagine about sixteen or so - but that is only a guess," she said, confirming exactly what Digby Turnbull had said.

"So it is possible the beauty has left the county and come to London to make her way."

"One would hope not. Town is no place for a child. I was

twenty before I first came to London, chaperoned by my mama, of course."

"Of course."

Miss Chudleigh shot the Apothecary a very direct glance to see whether he was mocking her but was met with an expression of straight-faced sincerity.

"Perhaps," said John thoughtfully, "Lady Mary Goward will know something of the girl's whereabouts. After all she is the child's stepmother."

Miss Chudleigh burst into a peal of tinkling laughter. "Oh my dear young friend, how little you understand of the ways of the *beau monde*. Lady Mary, I'll have you know, has absolutely no idea that her husband's offspring even exists."


"Mr. Sebastian will not see you," said the servant, "and that, Sir, is final."

"Then you can tell him from me that I shall report the matter to Sir John Fielding himself."

"I doubt that will be of much concern to him, Sir." And the door of the Brompton Park Boarding School was banged shut in the faces of John Rawlings and his companion Samuel Swann.

"God's mercy," said John, angrily banging his great stick on the ground. "Now what do we do?"

"Find a pupil," answered Samuel solemnly.

The Apothecary stared at him. "What do you mean?"

"What I say. Wait until evening when they all climb out over the walls, as you tell me they do, then nobble one and bribe it."

"You make them sound like chimpanzees."

"Well, they act little better, do they not?"

John nodded. "Not a great deal, it's true." He frowned. "But I wanted to get home. Emilia does not care for nights alone in her present condition."

"Well, as soon as we've caught one we can go."

"But that may not be until late. No, I'll send Irish Tom home and tell him to call for us in the morning. I think a night with my revered father is indicated."

"Oh good," said Samuel, rubbing his hands together. "It is always a pleasure to be in Sir Gabriel's company."

And the Apothecary had to admit that the thought of spending time with his father, to dine with him and perhaps play cards, was enormously pleasurable. He wondered, very far from the first time, whether he was a suitable sort to be a husband and could only console himself with the fact that he was doing his best.

"So where to now?" said Samuel.

"Straight to Church Lane. It is just possible that Sir Gabriel might have picked up some information. He gets around the great houses playing whist and is bound to have heard gossip of one kind or another."

"Excellent," Samuel answered.

But this plan was to be thwarted. No sooner had Irish Tom turned the equipage in the direction of Kensington than they cast a wheel and the two passengers plus the coachman were forced to disembark.

"Now where?" the Goldsmith asked uncertainly.

"The Swan," John answered. "It's a coaching inn so they'll be able to tell us where the nearest wheelwright is placed and meanwhile we can sit down and take our ease."

"And listen to other people's conversations in case we learn something?"

"Certainly."

But as it turned out, in contrast to The Hercules Pillars, The Swan was almost empty, the stage and flying coaches having just left. So empty indeed that Irish Tom, having discovered the whereabouts of the wheelwright, asked in a jocular way whether there was a plague upon the place.

The landlord fortunately took this remark in good humour. "We have several visitors in the snugs, Sir. The

Duke of Guernsey himself is in The Ram, entertaining his brother to breakfast."

John turned to Samuel. "Now where have I heard that name before? And recently at that."

"I've no idea."

"Guernsey, Guernsey?" John repeated, but got no further. For from within The Ram came the sound of a chair crashing to the ground, followed by the thump of a falling body.

"You little bastard," shouted a voice, its tones aristocratic. "You dirty little gammer-cock. Why, I'll take my crop to you. Just see if I don't."

"No, Michael, no," shrieked a younger voice. "Please, no."

But there was the unmistakable sound of a thwack followed by a yell of pain.

John looked at the landlord questioningly. "Should we go in?"

"I'm not sure. It's the Duke and his brother."

"But we can't let one beat the other to death. I'll take full responsibility. Come on, Sam."

"Right," said John's friend, looking cheerful. "I'm in the mood for a good mill".

"Well now you've got one."

With that the Apothecary threw open the snug door and used the element of surprise to full advantage. Looking down at the two young men wrestling on the floor, he put his quizzer to his eye and drawled, "Your Grace, be so good as to stop, if you please. You're frightening the ladies, to say absolutely nothing of the horses."

"Quite right," boomed Samuel. "Stow your whids, Sir. Stow 'em, I say."

# Chapter 11

In the event, the Duke was too angry to stow anything and went on beating his brother round the arse with his riding crop despite the fact that by now he had a small audience. It was all too tempting to the onlookers just to leave them to get on with it, but the younger boy had contrived to get an injury to his neck and had started to lose blood. The Apothecary, looking with a professional eye, decided that it really must stop and, striding out to the stable yard, picked up a bucket of water which he pitched with deadly aim over the two combatants. There was a mutual gasp at the shock and the youths drew apart. Samuel and the landlord stepped in, pulling the lads to their feet and holding them fast.

"Well," said John laconically, thinking that he could hardly make matters worse for himself, "that is the first time I have ever thrown water over a peer of the realm."

"And you had better make it the last," said the younger boy, apparently not in the least grateful that he had been saved from a beating.

The Duke, who was mopping his face and hair with a handkerchief, glowered at him. "You should be overjoyed, you stinking cully. I'd have killed you else."

John held up his hand. "Gentlemen, please. This is not the place to air your private grievances. Now, your Grace, with your permission I will tend your brother's wound. I am an apothecary by trade and know how to staunch the blood flow."

Guernsey pulled a face, but nodded. "Very well. But I want nothing further to do with him. I'll order my coachman to take him back to his school when you've finished with him, Sir. I'm off to another snug."

John felt that his ears were growing outwards on stalks. "School, Sir?"

The young Duke turned in the doorway. "Yes. The little bastard attends the Brompton Park Boarding School."

"God's mercy!" muttered the Apothecary. "If I hear that name once more!"

"What's that? What did you say?"

"I said there's some blood on the floor. Samuel, would you be so good as to escort his Grace and get him a brandy for shock. I'll attend to the injured."

His friend rose to the occasion, bowing the youthful nobleman out, then giving an over-hearty wink before he, too, left the room. Alone with the Duke's brother, John removed his travelling coat and hung it over the back of a chair, then looked at his patient.

It was a grumpy creature he was examining, truly an obnoxious youth. Spotty, some of his pustules with yellow heads, his hair the same jaundiced colour, his eyes a watery shade of grey ... the Apothecary wondered at the contrast with his sibling. For not only was this boy plain but he had an ugly nature to go with it. As John gently cleaned the wound with warm water and a cloth provided by the landlord, the youth cursed to himself and once accused his helper of being a clumsy oaf.

"Ouch. Mind what you're doing, fellow."

John straightened up and began to put his coat back on.

"What are you doing? Where are you going?"

"To find your brother and have a drink with him. I'm not tending anyone who treats me with such contempt. Wash your own wounds. Good day to you."

"But you can't leave me."

"Oh yes I can," said John, pulling his coat into position. "Go back to your school. Let them clean you up."

The creature looked mutinous. "Very well. But I'll tell the headmaster of you."

The Apothecary snapped his fingers. "I give that for his opinion." He paused as a moment of divine inspiration came. "What do you know of Lucas Drummond?" he asked.

The boy literally rocked on his feet. "He's run away," he said hoarsely.

"And not returned?"

"No. Though some say he stole back a few nights ago. Claim they saw him."

"Oh? Then did he not stay?"

"No. And now Fred Drummond has gone as well. Lucas must have come for him."

"And you would know nothing about any of that?"

The boy rallied unpleasantly. "Who do you think you are to ask questions of me. I'll have you know I'm Lord Arnold Courtney."

"Bad luck," said John, and left the room without bowing.


He found Samuel and his young companion comfortably ensconced in The Ewe, a decanter of brandy and two glasses set on a table which stood before a large log fire, beside which they had settled themselves. Drawing up another chair, the Apothecary joined them.

"Well, Sir," he said forthrightly. "I have left your brother to his own devices. He was so intolerably rude that I refused to treat him further."

"Quite right. He's a wastrel and a mistake," said the Duke gruffly.

"What do you mean by that, Sir?"

"He should never have been born. My mother died when I was a babe in cradle and my father - not a man to go without his connubial comforts for any length of time - promptly impregnated a distant cousin of his. A stupid, brainless creature if ever there was one. Arnold and the rest of my siblings are all half brothers and sisters. Anyway, after my father had produced four more children, he died. I succeeded when I was twelve."

"And may I ask how old you are now?"

"Three months off seventeen. I have left school and am

studying the finer things with a tutor. I have too much to do with the estate to attend university."

He had a very direct way of speaking, something that went well with his open countenance, topped with his mass of red hair, which he wore tied, clearly not bothering with a wig on informal occasions. His eyes a clear untroubled blue, very light, almost Arctic in shade, stared at the world without guile. He was as pleasant as his half brother had been disagreeable.

It was while he was studying the young man, wondering why he seemed vaguely familiar and also where he had heard his name before, that the answer came to John in the morning's second moment of inspiration.

"The investiture," he said loudly. "You were at the recent investiture. You were one of the pages-of-honour."

The Duke of Guernsey looked startled. "Indeed I was. How did you know?"

"I was also present. Accompanying John Fielding who received a knighthood." The Apothecary assumed his solemn expression. "What a terrible outcome, was it not?"

The young man's light eyes did not falter. "It certainly was. I was standing on the right, quite close to the balcony, and looked down on the scene like a bird. All I could think was that he seemed to fall so slowly."

"Yes, he did, you're right," John answered reflectively. His voice changed. "Tell me, Sir, how many of you pages were on duty that day?"

The Duke stared and the candid eyes started to cloud. "What an odd question. Why do you ask?"

"Because I must be losing my faculties, I think. For I could have sworn that I counted thirteen present. Yet good sense tells me there could have been only twelve."

Guernsey lowered his eyes, the lids drooping slowly, rather as if he were shutting out the light. "There were twelve, Sir. You were mistaken in what you thought."

He was lying, that was crystal clear. It was as plain as day that there had been thirteen boys present and the Duke knew it. But why was he hiding the fact?

The Apothecary exchanged a look with Samuel and cleared his throat. "Forgive me pressing the point, Sir, for you might well say that it is none of my business. But the fact is that not only did I accompany Sir John Fielding t'other day, I am also one of his associates. And in that capacity he has asked me to find out all I can about the death of Sir George Goward. Indeed, Sir, you were one of the people on my list of people to speak to."

The eyelids shot up and the Arctic eyes gazed into John's in bewilderment. "Was I? Why? I had nothing to do with it."

"Only because you were there," the Apothecary answered soothingly. "I merely wanted to know how much you saw."

"Nothing really. I confess I craned my neck when the Queen passed along the balcony."

"But you must have seen her before, at the coronation for example."

"She was a dot in the distance then. On this occasion she was quite close."

Samuel joined the conversation, doing his version of putting a witness at their ease. "Ugly ain't she, damme. Or so runs the consensus. Would you agree, Sir?"

The dignified peer of the realm fought with the boy's natural exuberance, and the boy won. The young nobleman burst out laughing. "Dreadful, and slow-witted with it, so they say. The King should have married Sarah Lennox and hanged convention by the neck."

"Are you unconventional, Sir?" asked Samuel, guffawing.

"I would hope so," the Duke answered seriously. "I would not like hide-bound regulations to govern my every action."

John seized his opportunity. "That's a rather unconventional school your brother attends. I have heard the strangest reports about it."

Guernsey's eyes were averted once more. "What sort of reports?" he asked, his voice slightly muffled.

"That there was a girl there, dressed as a boy. Put in the place by a harpy mother to care for a sickly brother. That this same girl was forced to have intercourse against her will by one of the older boys. That she ran away and became a maid-servant to a professional man in London, a man who is fearful for her safety, a man who even now is seeking her. But it seems this girl has returned to the school in secret, and decamped again, taking the ailing brother with her. That is, according to Lord Arnold, who told me of it this very morning."

There was a long pause, then the Duke said, "What did he say to you?"

"Just that. The bare outlines of the tale. Why, do you know more?"

The red hair tossed and the Duke showed his metal. "No, Sir, I don't - and I rather resent your attitude. As you represent Sir John Fielding I am quite prepared to answer questions about the fatal investiture but I fail to see what the Brompton Park Boarding School has to do with the matter."

The Apothecary looked duly chastened. "You're right, of course, your Grace. There may be no connection whatsoever except that you have a brother at the establishment - and there are some who will swear there were thirteen pageboys present at the investiture."

Guernsey coloured angrily but said nothing. Instead he stood up as there was a clattering of wheels in the courtyard. "Ah, my coach has returned I see. Gentlemen, I must take my leave of you."

John and Samuel rose and bowed.

"Thank you so much for your help," said the Apothecary. "Here is my card just in case anything else should occur to you."

Guernsey took it with a certain reluctance and placed it in an inner pocket. Then said, "Good day," and sauntered out with as much nonchalance as he could muster.

The two friends looked at one another. "Talk about concealing things," said Samuel, pouring himself a severe glass.

"He knows so much and is saying so little."

"But how to break him down."

"Well, I couldn't. That would have to be a task for Sir John. Unless he has an attack of conscience and contacts me, of course."

"I suppose it's possible. He seems quite an honourable young man. Do you think he guessed you were Lucinda's employer?"

"Indeed he did. But even the most upright and truthful can lie in their teeth in order to protect someone."

"But who could he be protecting? He clearly doesn't like his half brother."

"Think, Sam. Who is the victim in all this?"

The Goldsmith frowned, then his brow cleared. "Good gracious!" he said. "Do you really believe so?"

"It's possible."

"Well, I'll be blessed," said Samuel, and downed his brandy.

It was dark by the time their coach was roadworthy once more and John, anxious though he was to see Sir Gabriel, decided that he would rather return home.

"But have you found out all you wanted about the School?" the Goldsmith asked.

"Indeed I have. Lucinda went back and stole her brother Fred away. Now, presumably, they have gone into hiding."

"But where?"

"That I don't know. But I truly feel that the time has come to pool information with Sir John. Much as I love my father, he will have to wait. I shall bring Emilia to the country at the end of this week and we can see him then."

"So your fears for Lucinda are calmed?"

"Not completely, but somewhat. I'm sure she wouldn't have taken Fred away unless she had somewhere to go."

"The uncaring mother?"

"Possibly but not probably."

"I shall be interested to hear what the Blind Beak has to say about all this."

"So," answered John with feeling, "shall I."


"The thirteenth pageboy," said Sir John Fielding. "You are really sure he is connected with this case?"

"Positive, Sir. I am far from convinced that he had anything to do with the murder, but he was most certainly seen by me running away while Sir George lay dead or dying on the floor. Therefore he is a vital witness. What made him bolt like that? My belief is that he saw something and either had no wish to tell what it was to those in authority, or was so shocked by it that the poor boy was overcome with fright and took to his heels. And it's because I am certain he knows something vital, he really must be found and questioned."

Joe Jago cleared his throat. "But Mr. Rawlings, only Mr. Turnbull and the Duke of Guernsey know who the boy is - and they have refused to talk. In fact both have refuted what you have to say."

"I could order them into court and put them on oath," rumbled Sir John.

"Let's leave that as a last resort," said the Apothecary. "Maybe one of them will crack and come forward."

The Blind Beak, sitting in his snug, Joe Jago, John and Samuel all crammed into the crowded space, sighed deeply. "This case is not progressing at all. There is so much still to be done. The Witherspoons are yet to be seen and questioned; Lady Mary Goward, who could well be guilty, must make a statement; Jack Morocco has given Mr. Rawlings a look indicating that he has something further to say. And now we learn that Goward has a daughter, presumably alive and well and living in Devon. So somehow she has to be traced. Mr. Rawlings, you have connections in the West Country, do you not?"

John went cold with guilt, remembering the woman he had met while on honeymoon with Emilia, conjuring her up in his mind till he felt he could almost smell her heady and exotic perfume.

"Er, yes," he said, and Joe Jago coughed.

"Perhaps you could write and ask one of them to search the Parish Register. We have a rough idea of where and when the birth happened, do we not?"

The Apothecary could not answer, lost in a dream world, in which he and Lady Elizabeth, Marchesa di Lorenzi, made love before a log fire in a ruined house in which only one wing was inhabited while the rest lay empty and abandoned to the elements.

"Mr. Rawlings?"

"Sorry. Yes. I'll see if Sir Clovelly Lovell can investigate."

"A wise choice," said Joe Jago, and winked a most disconcerting blue eye.

The Apothecary took a grip on himself. "When is Sir George's funeral?"

"Next week," answered Sir John, "and what a pother it has caused. Lady Mary had so many vapours that at first nobody could get near her to make the arrangements. However, it seems that all is finally settled. The poor man is to be laid to rest next Tuesday."

"I shall go," volunteered Samuel stoutly. "I might spot something of interest."

"Very good of you," said Sir John, smiling a little. "Jago will represent the Public Office. What about you, Mr. Rawlings?"

"I will if I can, Sir. But as you said, there is much still left to do."

"Then may I suggest that the Witherspoons come next."

"Tomorrow," said John. "Samuel, would you like to stay the night so that we can leave early? I know that Emilia will be delighted to see you.

"A pleasure," answered his friend, beaming at the world in general.

"Gentlemen," said the Blind Beak, rising, "if you will come downstairs into the salon I shall offer you some refreshment before you leave."

The Goldsmith turned to his friend, raising his eyebrows in question. John grinned. "Well, we've missed dinner and are so late now that we may as well be hanged for a sheep as a lamb."

"Are you sure?"

"Certain."



But turning into Nassau Street from Gerrard Street, John wished that he had gone straight home. It was Emilia's sadness, rather than her anger, that always cut him to the heart. And tonight he felt doubly guilty because he had been thinking of Elizabeth di Lorenzi and had suffered all the old wild stirring that memories of her always brought.

"You're very quiet," said Samuel.

"I'm worried about Emilia."

"Will she be in militant mood?"

"No, sad and sniffing more likely. Oh God, Sam, I am a terrible husband."

"You most certainly are not," said his friend stoutly, throwing a jovial arm round John's shoulders. "Why Emilia looks one of the happiest women in the kingdom. I envy you having a loving wife, I truly do."

"Well, don't rush into anything," the Apothecary answered thoughtfully. "Be quite sure that you have made the right choice."

Then he thought of the power of Elizabeth's personality and wondered if he could ever have married her, had his situation been different. Perhaps the two of them beneath one roof would have been too dramatic, too confligrational. Maybe they would have been better as permanent lovers, though even that had never happened between them.

"You're in a funny frame of mind," stated the Goldsmith. "Now pray become more jolly before we go within."

"I'm sorry," said John. "I've probably imbibed too deeply and have reached the melancholic stage."

They stepped out of the coach, which Irish Tom promptly drove round to Dolphins Yard, which lay behind Nassau Street and was the place in which the carriages and horses were kept.

"Please be very apologetic and gentle," whispered John as he inserted his key in the lock.

Then he stopped short. The house rang with gaiety and was full of light. From the music room came the sound of Phyllida Kent's harpsichord being played more than deftly, indeed extremely well, by someone other than John's wife. Then the tune changed and Emilia's voice was raised in song.

"Bravo, bravo," said a man enthusiastically. "Why, you're so damned pretty I've just got to kiss you."

"You shouldn't," answered John's wife, giggling.

"Why not? A beautiful woman is born to be loved."

"But I am *en ceinte*."

"You are? But I adore pregnant women. They bloom so nicely. May I kiss your baby too?"

"Most certainly not."

"Who is this blackguard?" said John furiously. "I'll cut his culls off."

"I heard that," called the voice from the other room, a very cultured voice full of laughter and fun. "Well, just you stop right there, Mr. Rawlings. Otherwise you will never know what it is I want to say to you."

John turned to Samuel, his eyes bolting in his head. "God almighty," he said, then let out shout of laughter. "It's the black buck himself. It's Jack Morocco."

# Chapter 12

The harpsichord rang out again, this time playing a bravura piece by the late Mr. Handel. Without meaning to, John and Samuel found themselves marching into the music room in step to it, a fact which sent Jack Morocco and Emilia into hysterics, particularly in view of the glum expression on the Apothecary's face. And the more they giggled, the glummer he got. So much so that Samuel began to grin at the sight.

"What's so funny?" said John truculently, glaring at them.

That was the final stroke. The other three laughed till they wept, Jack Morocco throwing his arms round his companions as he doubled up with mirth. In the midst of all this frivolity, John sat down on a small chair, one leg crossed over the other, his expression furious, waiting for the storm to pass. But it didn't, in fact it got even worse, Samuel whirling like a mill as he clutched his aching sides.

To his horror the Apothecary realised as he tried to sit back nonchalantly, that one of the chair's supporting legs was decidedly loose. The thought of collapsing to the floor in full view of the howling mob that his wife and friends had disintegrated into was too much even to contemplate. With what dignity he could muster, he stood up.

"I am going to the library for some peace and quiet," he announced and strode out, only to hear the laughter redouble behind his departing back.

He was hungry and had drunk too much but that did not deter John from ringing for a decanter of port and a glass. Then he sat, attempting to read the paper, while from the music room came more renditions on the harpsichord, punctuated by cries of "Good health, Sir. To your eyes, Madam," indicating that spirituous liquor was being consumed.

The Apothecary seethed, then in the midst of feeling put-upon and down-trodden came the horrible thought that he was getting set in his ways, that he was middle-aged and acting it.

"I'm thirty," he said aloud.

"And behaving as if you're fifty," answered a voice from the doorway. It was Emilia, coming towards him with her hand outstretched. "Oh John," she went on, "don't sit there all alone. Jack Morocco is going in a minute and he really does want to speak to you first. Shall I send him in?"

"Is he still screaming like an ape?"

"No, he's quietened down. We all have. It was just that you looked so solemn ..." Her lips quivered but she forced them to stillness. "Sweetheart, we've missed you. No gathering is complete unless you are there."

He pulled her onto his lap. "I resented him flirting with you, that was the trouble."

Emilia smiled and kissed him lightly. "Jack Morocco was born to flirt. No doubt he flirted with the Duchess when he was a little boy, no doubt it was his lovely flirtatious character that made her decide to adopt him. How could a joyful soul like that be sent to the plantations? I could never have done that to him if I had been his mistress."

John smiled a little wryly. "There are mistresses and then there are mistresses, you know."

She tweaked his nose. "Don't be difficult. You know exactly what I mean. Now, are you going to see him or aren't you? It's nearly ten o'clock and I have ordered a cold collation to be served when Jack has gone."

"Jack now, is it?"

Emilia stood up. "I shall get annoyed in a minute. Now what do I tell him?"

"To step into the library and join me for some port."

It really wasn't surprising that he had the *beau monde* at his feet, John thought, as the black man stepped into the doorway a moment later. For Morocco was one of those people who brought the sunshine of his native Africa with him. Even his dark eyes, so knowing and yet alive with good humour, sent out brilliant sparks of warmth. As John rose to meet him, Jack bowed low, as beautifully presented and well mannered as if he had been the Duchess's true flesh-and-blood son.

"Thank you for coming to see me," said the Apothecary. "and let me apologise for my ill-humour of earlier on. I have had rather an odd day and, to tell the truth, was feeling somewhat out of sorts."

"My dear fellow," the black man drawled in aristocratic tones, "the fault was entirely mine. To have been seized with laughter in that way was quite intolerably rude. I do trust that you will forgive such a childish display."

"I not only forgive but wish that I had been in high enough spirits to have taken part. Tonight, Mr. Morocco, I looked at my thirty-year-old self and felt frightened."

"Of age? Surely not. Youth is in the spirit, in the heart and in the mind. The outer casing may look older but as long as the eternal stream bubbles, then there is nothing to fear."

"My father says that."

"And so say I to my mother, the Duchess. Within she is but a girl; as young and as fresh as the day she bought me."

"You remember it?"

"I," said Jack Morocco solemnly, "remember everything."

And suddenly, just for a second, he was all-wise and all-knowing, looking at the Apothecary from eyes that had known generations of suffering. For no reason that he could account for, John felt tears sting at his lids. Then it was over. An easy smile crossed the handsome black features, Jack Morocco leant negligently back in his chair and sipped from his glass of port.

"You wanted to speak to me?"

"I rather thought," said John, "that you wanted to speak to me."

"Yes, so I did, I'd quite forgotten. It was on my mind to do so that day at Ranelagh but that was hardly the place to say what I had to."

"Which is?"

"That George Goward was pushed to his death," Jack stated, then smiled and emptied his glass.

The Apothecary's stomach lurched to his boots for here was the first confirmation that Sir John Fielding had been right, that none of them was engaged on the wild goose chase that every one of them had silently considered.

John decided to be frank. "The Principal Magistrate is also of that opinion. But what makes *you* think so?""

"I half saw something out of the corner of my eye."

"What?"

"I saw a pair of feet creep past."

"Whose?"

Jack Morocco sighed and held out his glass for refill. "They must have been the murderer's. But even before you ask, I did not see the rest of the killer. It was all so quick. By the time I registered the move, the person had gone."

"How do you know it was the one who pushed Sir George?"

The black man shrugged exquisitely. "I don't really, except for the fact that they were out of breath, as if they had just made some physical effort."

"I see. Tell me about the feet. Were they small or large?"

"Very small." Jack shook his head. "They must have belonged to a woman. Or perhaps an extremely short man."

"Did anyone else see anything? What about the pages and footmen lining the staircase?"

"They all seemed to be staring at the Queen. But you would have to ask them."

"That is already being done by the Runners, Sir John's court officials. I just wondered if any of them cried out or made some sign that they had shared your observation."

"None that I noticed."

John stared into space, considering, then came to himself. "But the shoes must have given their owner's sex away. Were they a female's?"

"They were black and heeled, with a silver buckle. The sort that could be worn by a fashionable man or a woman who didn't trust herself balancing up too high."

"Why do you say that? Were they low?"

"Not enormously so, but on the low side, yes."

A picture of Lady Mary Goward, fat and puffing, her large white stockinged legs thrust into tight shoes, came vividly into the Apothecary's mind.

"Mr. Morocco ..."

"Jack, please."

"Jack, who do you think wore those shoes? Have you any idea at all?"

"The grieving widow," said the black man, and flashed his jackanapes grin.

"Why her?"

"Because she always hobbles about in footwear that's too small. Also the gasping sounds. Whoever gave that push was not in the best of health."

"I believe she was standing quite close to you."

"Precisely. All she had to do was heave into his back, then shuffle to her original position. Small wonder nobody saw anything. She would hardly have to have moved at all."

"Would that series of events fit in with what you saw?"

Jack Morocco looked serious. "You must remember, my friend, that it was all over in a trice. I had hardly time to register anything before I heard Goward scream."

Into the Apothecary's mind came that vivid picture of a flash of white teeth in a dark face as the victim lay dead. "Jack, did you like George Goward?" he said.

Again, that elegant shrug. "I hardly knew him. He was not my sort. But he once hurt a friend of mine, very badly indeed. Perhaps it is my old tribal blood that stirs within me, but I neither forgive nor forget an injury done to someone close to me. Their enemy is my enemy; loyalty is an attribute that I do not lack, Mr. Rawlings."

And what a dangerous enemy he would make, the

Apothecary considered, with his entree into high society, his easy manner, his deadly ability with a sword, and the protection of his powerful adopted mother. Somewhat to John's disappointment, he began to consider whether the story of the creeping feet was, after all, a fabrication.

He sighed reflectively. "I suppose you won't tell me how Goward upset your friend."

"You suppose correctly." Jack laughed and stood up. "Will that be all?"

"You have been more than helpful. I shall report all this back to Sir John. By the way, who else was standing near you?"

"The Witherspoons - an odd couple. La Chudleigh, of course. And, as you know, the grieving widow."

"You don't care for her, do you?" said John curiously.

"I adore the Chudleigh. She is so full of hidden secrets."

"I meant Lady Mary."

"Oh her. No, not particularly."

"Another insult to a friend?"

"In a way," answered Jack Morocco, suddenly serious again. "In a strange sort of way, you're right."


The ride to Islington the next morning was not a happy one, for the heavens opened and water deluged from the sky, soaking Irish Tom, swathed in oilskins though he was. Despite the fact that it was broad daylight, even though somewhat gloomy, the coachman came to a halt at The Angel coaching inn to join up with other conveyances, including a farmer with a cart, so that they might cross the fields leading to the village in a bunch and thus avoid the attention of highwaymen. To compound the soaking driver's ills, there were several coaches already waiting and thus he was denied the chance of some ale and a chat with his peers. As he slammed back onto the coachman's box, Tom cracked his whip into the air. John turned to Samuel.

"We'll have to leave him at an hostelry while we track down the Witherspoons. Otherwise I fear a terrible ride back."

"Is he always this moody?"

"No more than any other Irishman deprived of his drink."

"What do you think of my idea that we should call on the Witherspoons on the pretence that we are looking for my father?"

"I believe the direct approach might work better. They're bound to respond to the name Sir John Fielding. After all, they must have seen him at the investiture."

"I wonder why they were present."

"No doubt we shall find out."

"If we ever get there," said Samuel gloomily, peering through the curtains of rain to where the village of Islington lay nestling amongst its delightful fields, not very far away from them but seeming a great distance because of the terrible conditions.

Though not nearly as fashionable as Kensington, Islington had its share of persons of *bon ton*, for it positively teemed with places of amusement. Mr. Sadler's theatre and pleasure garden, once famous for its wells but now much better known as a place of entertainment, led the field. For there one could see Miss Wilkinson, the graceful wire-dancer and player of the musical glasses, and other artistes of similar calibre. However, if water drinking, public breakfasting and dancing were more to one's taste, then the delightful New Tunbridge Wells, prettily situated close to the New River Head, lay close by. From there it was but a step to the London Spa tavern, with the New Wells theatre and gardens, a serious rival to Sadler's Wells, a mere hundred yards distant. And for those who enjoyed skittles, the Merlin's Cave tavern, situated in fields near the river head, was the place to visit. These being but a few of the many haunts of delight near the village.

And it was to a house not far from the tavern, standing

in its own grounds, also close to the river head and obviously owned by people of certain social standing, that John and Samuel made their way. As they dismounted from their coach and plunged through the rain to the front door, the Apothecary thought that they must present a sorry spectacle indeed as representatives of the Public Office.

A girl answered the bell, not a servant but obviously a member of the family. John removed his tricorne, sheltering in the pillared porch against the deluge.

"Is Miss Witherspoon in?" he asked.

"Yes," the girl answered cheerfully. "Who wants her?"

"My name is Rawlings and I am here as a representative of Sir John Fielding, the Principal Magistrate."

"My!" said the girl. "That's impressive."

She was an elf, a thin, small-breasted, mischievous, enchanting elf, with a face lively as quicksilver and a smiling humourous mouth.

"Will she see me, do you think?" John persisted.

"You're looking at her," said the elf, and moved back from the front door, motioning the visitors into the house.

John was amazed to the point of shock, while Samuel's mouth hung open. In the Apothecary's mind, the Witherspoons, ever since Miss Chudleigh had mentioned them, had been a middle-aged couple of rather unpleasant mien. The sort who had lived together always, surrounded by jugs of lemonade and sweet cakes, and who might well have indulged in unwholesome practices, driven to it by the fact that nobody else would look at them. But this sprite was so far a cry from such horrors that John found himself disbelieving what he was seeing.

"Is there an elder Miss Witherspoon?" he asked.

The girl chuckled. "Sorry to disappoint the Magistrate but I am the only one. Not respectable enough for you?"

"On the contrary. It was just that I had imagined someone rather older."

She grinned. "I am fairly young but on the other hand I'm very rich. Will that make me more suitable?"

"By Heavens, yes," said Samuel with brimming enthusiasm.

She shot him an amused glance. "And you are?"

The poor fellow blushed to beet. "Samuel Swann, goldsmith of London. I'm - er - assisting Mr. Rawlings."

"To do what?"

"Miss Witherspoon, don't tease," said John. "We are here about the fatal fall of Sir George Goward at the investiture the other day. Witnesses have said that you and your brother stood quite close to him on the staircase. We wondered if you had seen anything that might throw some light on the matter."

The elf attempted to look serious, a difficult task. "You'd better come in, Mr ...?"

"Rawlings, John Rawlings."

She held out her hand. "Christabel Witherspoon." The elf dropped a small curtsey. "A terrible mouthful, is it not?"

"On the contrary; a charming name. Is your brother at home?"

"He is in his studio. He's a portrait painter, you know. Quite famous."

"Not Julius Witherspoon?"

"Certainly."

"Good gracious," said John, and wondered at his own lack of initiative that he had not enquired further about the brother and sister.

"Do you want to see him?" Christabel asked.

"Not yet. Leave him in peace a little longer. Perhaps we could speak to you first."

The elf nodded. "Follow me to the salon, gentlemen. There you may sift me for information."

As she moved in front of them to lead the way, John and Samuel stared at one another, still both reeling from the shock of her.

"Beautiful," whispered the Goldsmith, much to his friend's amusement.

"Gentlemen, come in," she called over her shoulder, and opened the door to a small but prettily appointed and very feminine room. This, John guessed, was Christabel's private sanctum.

She motioned them to sit down. "I wondered if somebody might call."

"Did you? Why?" asked the Apothecary.

"Because Goward was so detestable that I am sure he was murdered. Why, I'd have done it myself if I'd thought quickly enough."

It was too much. First her elfin looks and her youth, now this frankness of speech. All John could think of saying was, "Good gracious."

"Don't look so startled. You came here for the truth, didn't you?"

"Well, yes."

"Then don't be shocked by it, I pray you. We've known the Gowards for years, in fact they bought a country place here shortly after he married that fat frump Mary."

John and Samuel exchanged another glance, not knowing how to deal with this at all.

"He was always mooning round here, his eyes falling from their sockets over my sister. Look, there she is. My brother painted her when she was fifteen."

She motioned to a portrait on the wall and the two men turned to stare at it. A consummate beauty gazed back at them, clad in crimson, her skin the colour of a white rose, hair so black that it seemed to gleam on the canvas, a pair of wonderful dark blue eyes, glittering with vitality. Truly one of the loveliest girls he had ever seen, John thought. The image of such a creature being pursued by the loathsome Goward was repellent to say the least of it.

"What happened?" he asked.

"Simply put, he seduced her. And all at such a vulnerable

time. Our father had died and Mother was one of those silly, feeble females who simply cannot manage on their own. So she went into a final flutter and died as well."

It was so comically said that the Apothecary found himself wanting to laugh, and yet it was such a tragic story.

"Anyway, in the guise of strong friend of the family, he bedded her then got bored with her when she became *en ceinte*."

"She had a child?" exclaimed Samuel.

The elf looked serious, a difficult task for her. "Fortunately not. She miscarried after a fall, a fall which broke her back by the way."

"Oh my God!" said Samuel, who was so involved with the tale that he was leaning forward on the edge of the chair, turning his hat in his hands.

"What happened next?"

"Julius and I cared for her as best we could. But she was such a creature of the wild; she loved riding and dancing and being in the countryside. She simply couldn't bear to be confined to one room. Very simply, gentlemen, she saved up the syrup that had been given her to relieve the pain and took it all at once, thus causing her death. She was eighteen years old."

"It seems George Goward had much to answer for."

"He did indeed." Christabel stood up and pulled a bell rope. "May I offer you some coffee?"

"How very kind of you,"

"Very," echoed Samuel, who had a look on his face that John knew only too well.

"So why were you at the investiture?" the Apothecary continued.

"My brother, my funny little brother, was receiving some kind of medal. He had painted a portrait of the King's sister, Princess Augusta, which actually made her look quite human. God's sweet life but don't these Hanoverians surround themselves with hideous women - faces like dogs, the whole damned bunch of 'em ..."

167

This was too much for John, who guffawed loudly, Samuel joining in somewhat over-enthusiastically.

Christabel grinned at them. "I see you agree. Anyway, Julius was being rewarded for his services. Did you not notice him?"

"What does he look like?"

"Sadly, somewhat dwarfish. He was born with a curvature of the spine which makes him appear rather hunched. In fact he's an odd little carcass. But I love him dearly and that is why I stay with him and keep house. Though now he has been rewarded by the King perhaps some female will disregard his lack of looks and marry him."

"So that's how you came to be there. Now tell me, did you notice anything while you stood on the stairs?"

"If I had," Christabel answered roundly, "I most certainly wouldn't tell you. Whoever did it deserves to be elevated to the peerage."

"Hear, hear," said Samuel, letting the side down completely.

Fortunately, at this juncture coffee was served, and the general disturbance covered any gaffes that might have been made. John made the taking of his cup an excuse to marshal his thoughts. If anyone had a motive for murder it would be the Witherspoons, both brother and sister. He wondered, almost absently, what size shoes they wore. If Julius was described as dwarfish, then his feet would be small. But by the same token, Jack Morocco could have made up the entire story of the creeping feet to attract attention away from himself.

"Would you like to see Julius now?" asked the elf. "For there is nothing more that I have to tell you."

Have or won't, the Apothecary thought. Out loud he said, "That would be most kind. Shall we go to his studio rather than call him from his work?"

"In either event it means disturbing him. But, yes. Perhaps you would like to see some of his canvasses."

"I'd be honoured," said Samuel, brimming with the enthusiasm of the newly smitten.

It was indeed a small man who turned to look at them as Christabel opened the studio door, having knocked and been told to enter. In fact the curving of his spine gave the momentary impression that Julius Witherspoon was a hunchback. But probably through years of habit, he straightened as soon as he saw that he had visitors and made a small, polite bow. He was not really handsome at all, other than for a pair of fine eyes, similar to those of the girl in the portrait. But those apart he was pale and had that sense of strain common to people who have struggled with pain and deformity. Yet if beauty had been denied him, a compensatory great gift had been bestowed. The canvas he was working on was quite stunning.

It was of a woman in riding dress, her hair like flame beneath a small hat with a feather, her skin the colour of ivory, her eyes brandy wine. Yet it was the sitter's expression that Julius had caught so brilliantly. John gazed, totally absorbed, feeling that he knew her, that he could sense her mischief and her pride, her kindness and her rebelliousness. Then his eyes were drawn to the background of the painting. He looked at a wild lake, hyacinth blue, at mountains rearing above, at the colours of autumn tingeing the trees. Then he realised that the girl herself was the embodiment of autumn and that the artist had contrived, most cleverly, to bring another depth of meaning into what could have been simply a portrait of a young woman.

"This is a masterpiece," said John. "You are a genius, Sir."

The little crooked man smiled and his whole face lit from within. "How very kind of you."

"It is the truth," said the Apothecary. "If I can afford your fee I would like you to paint my wife."

"I would be delighted. But tell me, to whom do I speak?"

Christabel answered. "He is John Rawlings, Julius, and he is here on behalf of Sir John Fielding, the Magistrate. They believe that someone pushed George Goward down the stairs."

"Really?" said the painter, and dabbed gently at his canvas.

"I've told them everything, including the fact that I would have done it myself if I'd thought about it."

"And I would have helped you," Julius replied.

It was futile to ask further questions. The Witherspoons, even if they had seen anything, which the Apothecary doubted, would remain totally silent. He changed the subject.

"I'll take up no more of your hospitality. It has been kind of you to see us."

"Sorry we couldn't be of greater assistance."

"You were very honest." John turned to his companion. "Samuel, I think it's time we were on our way."

The Goldsmith cleared his throat, then looked at Christabel earnestly. "Miss Witherspoon, my father has retired to Islington and I often come to visit him. Would it be in order for us to call one day?"

She looked at her brother and a silent current of amusement passed between them. They were clearly very close, to the point where they could communicate without speaking. It was small wonder that unperceptive souls might accuse them of an unnatural love, though the Apothecary felt certain there was another explanation.

"You aren't twins by any chance?" he said.

"Of course we are. How did you guess?"

"You have a certain rapport, an empathy that only exists between those who've shared the womb."

Samuel cleared his throat once more. "Miss Witherspoon?"

She turned to him, her elfin face contrite. "I'm so sorry. Of course you may call. Might I know the name of your father? It is possible that we are acquainted."

"Samuel Swann, which is also my name."

"Ah, Mr. Swann. Of course. I often see him at the theatre. A nice old fellow."

"Yes, he is rather," said Samuel, and Christabel, approving of this answer, looked at him and smiled.

John turned to Julius. "It has been a privilege to meet you. You have a great gift. I will discuss fees with you another time, if I may."

"Of course. Would you care to see some more canvases before you leave?" And without waiting for a reply he began to pull some out from a pile stacked against the wall. He was certainly not weak, despite his deformity, and the Apothecary noticed as well that his feet were small and neat, encased in a pair of low heeled shoes. The fact that Julius was a genius did not exempt him from the possibility of being a murderer, John thought.

His work was breathtaking, though. He seemed to have the knack of seeing into the sitter's soul and conveying their idiosyncrasies with strokes of his brush. Dignitaries revealed themselves as corpulent, sagging old men; spindle-legged, double-chinned, purple-veined. Their wives looked on the world from the bored, dead eyes of women who have never done a hand's turn, or the shrewish gaze of those whose small tight lips only parted to criticise and argue. Yet it was the last canvas of all that left John breathless.

As Julius lifted it on to the easel, the Apothecary saw that it was a portrait of Lady Mary Goward, enormous within a chair, her pink and white complexion and vacuous expression brilliantly captured. Beside the chair stood an equally enormous boy, his body distorted by roll upon roll of flesh, his legs thick and unwieldy, his face scarcely visible for wobbly chins, even his eyes peering out from puffs of fat.

"Good God!" John exclaimed. "What a terrible child. Who is he?"

"It's her son, Frederick, poor thing. Goward gave him a life of hell because he was so big. Said he couldn't bear to see him round the place."

"I believe he mentioned that to me when we first met."

"I didn't realise you knew Goward."

"I only came across him briefly. We were not friends."

Julius gave a bitter laugh. "He had none. Anyway, he refused to pay for this portrait.

Said I hadn't caught the essence of his wife or his stepson. Said I had made them look too bad-tempered!"

The Apothecary shook his head. "I can't speak for the child but you have portrayed Lady Mary exactly, even down to her fat restless fingers."

"I admit that I was pleased with it," Julius said.

John stared at the portrait, feeling that there was much it could tell him, but the more he looked the less he seemed to see. Yet his pictorial memory, the gift that allowed him to conjure up a scene exactly as it had been when it had taken place, absorbed every detail of the picture so that he might carry it with him and look at it again when he was alone.

# Chapter 13

Samuel, dragging Miss Witherspoon's name into the conversation as frequently as he possibly could, talked all the way back to London, then begged pardon of John that he must leave him, saying that he would walk the rest of the way to his shop in Puddle Dock Hill. The sudden quiet was an immense relief, giving the Apothecary the chance to sort out all the information he had received and to plan what he was going to do next.

High on the list, of course, was to continue the search for Lucinda and her brother, for the thought of the two youngsters wandering around unprotected was alarming to say the least. Yet were they wandering, John wondered. Or had they gone to someone's house, perhaps their unfeeling mother's and had she finally done her duty and taken them in? And was Nicholas right? Was Miss Elizabeth Chudleigh, rumoured to have given birth to at least one child, harbouring them right next door to that unpleasant school from which they had both decamped?

"Kensington," said John. "But before that a visit to Bow Street." He called up to Irish Tom, who was in a far better mood having spent an hour in The Angel while his master visited the Witherspoons. "Tom, we'll go straight to the Public Office, if you please."

"Certainly, Sir," answered the coachman, and whistled to himself, thinking that there was a pleasant little hostelry situated quite close to their destination.

Sir John Fielding, as good fortune would have it, had not sat down to dine but was enjoying a sherry with his wife Elizabeth. Even more fortunate, thought John, was the fact that their adopted daughter, Mary Ann Whittingham, was out visiting and was not present to disrupt sensible conversation with idle chatter.

"My dear friend," said Sir John as the Apothecary came into the room. "How are you proceeding?"

"I am a little further forward. I have seen the Witherspoons who both have a motive for murdering George Goward and admit quite freely that they would have done so if they had been quick witted enough. But, and this is most significant, Jack Morocco has been to visit me."

And he told the Magistrate the story of the creeping shoes and the black man's assertion that George Goward had been done away with.

"You think it is possible that he made it up?" the Blind Beak asked.

"He might have done, he's full of mischief. But on the other hand I feel inclined to believe him because it bears out what you said, Sir."

"Yes." There was a long silence, then Sir John said, "Have you written to your friend in Devon yet?"

"Emilia was doing so this morning. She is asking him to check the parish registers for the birth of Goward's daughter."

Once again the Beak was very still, an old trick of his, leading those who did not know him better to believe he had dropped off to sleep. "There's a thread to all this but I'm damned if I can grasp it," he said eventually.

"I feel the same. By the way, is the questioning of the footmen and pages-of-honour complete yet?"

"Yes, they've all been interviewed, and I can tell you this much. There is a conspiracy of silence regarding the thirteenth page boy. All of them categorically deny that he was there."

"How very bizarre. Tell me, Sir, did anyone see anything untoward?"

"They say not. Whoever moved on that staircase must have been so quick and clever that it was over before it was even noticed."

"Jack Morocco firmly believes that it was Lady Mary herself. He thinks the shoes could well have been hers."

John Fielding sighed. "Tiresome woman. I am due to see her two days after the funeral. Elizabeth will accompany me there, won't you, my dear." He took his wife's hand.

"I shall be intrigued. Having missed the investiture, to say nothing of the murder, at least I will be able to get a look at the principal suspect."

"Could I accompany you?" John asked.

The Blind Beak looked a little dubious. "Well, Jago will be there of course. But if I were to say that you had come in your professional capacity, lest she feel faint, then I am sure it can be arranged."

"I would much appreciate it." John rose. "Sir, will that be all? I would like to get back to join Emilia at dinner."

"Indeed you must. But just one last thing. Has young Guernsey contacted you?"

"No."

"Then seek him out again, my friend. He has a country estate, very fine apparently, out at Marybone, not far from the Gardens. If anyone will tell you the identity of the thirteenth pageboy, it will be he. Runner Ham interviewed him and found him to be an honest lad. Try your best with him, Mr. Rawlings."

"I certainly will, Sir."

"And let me know as soon as you hear from Sir Clovelly Lovell."

"Of course."


By the time the Apothecary rejoined his coach, all Irish Tom's troubles were behind him, and he was singing merrily up on the coachman's box. Delighted to find him in a better frame of mind, John gave the driver his orders.

"Tom, I want you to take me home then change the horses and go straight to Kensington. Spend the night at Sir Gabriel's, then return for us at eight o'clock. Tell him that we are coming for the weekend and there is much afoot."

"It will be dark any minute, Sir."

"Never mind. You have done the journey so many times that it will make little diference."

There was the sound of muttering, to which John said, "Think of the pleasures of The Dun Cow, Tom," and peace was restored.

As arranged, they left town early and had reached Kensington by the time those members of the *beau monde* who had residences nearby were first stirring in their beds. John turned to Emilia.

"Do you think I dare call on Miss Chudleigh?"

"At this hour?"

"That's partly the reason. If she is concealing Lucinda and her brother in the house, then I might catch them unawares."

"But you can't ask to search the place. You haven't the right to do that."

"No. But I might find the children at breakfast, or hear them moving about. I think it's worth incurring her wrath. The only thing is, what excuse can I make?"

Emilia's angelic features hardened and she suddenly looked extremely cynical. "My darling, an attractive male would not need an excuse to call on Miss Chudleigh, particularly, I imagine, when she is *deshabille*."

John looked shocked. "You have a wicked mind. Such a thought would never have occurred to me."

"Much! Now make your call. I'll go on and take breakfast with your father."

In the event, Emilia was uncannily correct. Having been informed by a footman that Miss Chudleigh was not yet up, the Apothecary sent in his card. A few moments later the man reappeared and said that the mistress would receive the visitor after all - in her bedchamber. This was a custom often adopted by the London belles of fashion, where it was considered chic to entertain from one's bed, but the very thought of it made John feel decidedly nervous as he followed the servant up the curving staircase and along a fine and spacious landing.

Miss Chudleigh, scantily clad about the shoulders and breast but wearing a great deal of cleverly applied make-up, reclined against lace pillows, her hair covered by a pretty cap trimmed with blue satin bows. In her hand she held a bone china cup, from which she sipped delicately. She looked at John over the rim, the enormous eyes artless.

"Mr. Rawlings, to what do I owe this honour?"

"I was passing and came in on the spur of the moment," he answered truthfully.

"Really? Just to see me? I feel flattered indeed."

Oh God, he thought, I just hope she doesn't try to drag me into bed with her. He forced a smile. "Of course to see you, dear lady."

"May I ask why?"

John attempted to look roguish. "Perhaps I wanted to discover if you are as beautiful in the morning as you are the rest of the time."

Elizabeth Chudleigh gave a silvery laugh and patted the bed beside her. "Come and sit down."

"I'll take a chair if you don't mind."

She pouted. "Why?"

"Perhaps I don't trust myself," John answered and raised a brow, wondering whether he looked as anxious as he felt.

Miss Chudleigh's hands began to play idly with the bow at the top of her nightgown. "I should have you thrown out, Sir."

"I'll try to behave myself, I promise." Before she could answer, the Apothecary lifted his head as if he were listening to something.

"What is it?" asked his companion.

"I thought I heard children's voices."

"There are no children here, Mr. Rawlings."

"A pity," said John musingly, and leaned back in the chair,

folding his hands behind his head, and giving her what he hoped was a smouldering glance. "You would have made such a beautiful mother. I have a theory that all lovely people should have a child and leave their perfection behind them on the earth."

"How poetic."

"Possibly so, but would you not agree with the sentiment?"

She changed the subject, rather significantly he thought. "Would you like some champagne? I believe that a glass or two in the morning is extremely beneficial for the health."

"You may well be right. Yes, I would love some."

Miss Chudleigh pulled a bell rope hanging conveniently over the bed. "Now, you are to stay where you are until the servants are dismissed. I would not wish you and I to be the subject of gossip."

"Perish the thought." John moved his head again. "Are you sure there are no children in the house?"

"No, definitely not. The wind must be bearing the sound from the school close by."

"The Brompton Park Boarding School. Lucinda Drummond, the girl I mentioned to you, attended that place dressed as a boy."

"How shocking."

"Indeed. What is even worse is that she was raped there."

"I can't believe it."

"It's true enough. Do you know, for a while I believed her to be George Goward's daughter, then I thought perhaps she was yours."

Miss Chudleigh went very white but her predicament was saved by the arrival of a footman. For one terrible moment John thought that she was going to give orders for his physical removal but she merely ordered champagne, a bucket of ice and two glasses. He could not help but notice that she pulled the bed coverings high, hiding her provocative neckline while the servant was in the room, but that as soon as the man had gone Miss Chudleigh slipped the coverlet down again.

"Is this not a truly glorious autumn?" she said, her colour restored, her eyes wide with innocence.

The ruthless side of the Apothecary's nature gained control. This was the moment, he thought, to regain the advantage and risk being manhandled out. "So Georgiana Goward and Lucinda are not one and the same person?"

Miss Chudleigh looked decidedly impatient. "Why are we talking about this girl? I've told you for once and for all that I do not know her." She stared at John angrily, the lovely eyes hard as steel.

"Forgive me. London society thrives on gossip as well you know. Cruel though it is, rumour reached my ears that you had secretly given birth to a child, and as the wretched Lucinda told me that her mother was one of the most beautiful members of the *beau monde*, the exquisite to end them all, I cannot be blamed for supposing it to be yourself."

This was a total falsehood but well worth the telling as Miss Chudleigh's lips parted and her eyes widened.

"I think you flatter me, Mr. Rawlings. But no, the girl is not mine. I wonder who this paragon mother can be."

"I have been trying to find out for days with absolutely no success. So the rumours about you are not true? I find it hard to credit that you obtained that sparkling loveliness without knowing the bloom of motherhood."

He was flattering her so hard he thought his tongue was going to fall out, yet she was vain to a degree that was incalculable.

"Do you truly find me beautiful?"

"Exquisite."

"You have seen very little of me."

Help, here comes the seduction, the Apothecary thought. He stood up and crossed to the window. "One can imagine."

There was a knock on the door and servants with trays

appeared, setting everything down with a flourish. "Would you like me to pour, Madam?"

"No, Mr. Rawlings can do that. And Merrill..."

"Yes, Madam?"

"Pray see to it that I am not disturbed for a while."

"Very good, Madam. But what if the Duke should call?"

"That is a different matter."

John, who had remained staring out over the grounds, now turned to look at her and audibly gasped. Nudity was clearly something from which Miss Chudleigh did not shy. She was out of bed, standing stark naked and smiling at him impudently.

"Was it true that you once went to a masked ball wearing nothing but your mask?" he asked, gulping.

"I believe I had on three fig leaves."

"I won't ask where they were placed."

"There, there and there." She pointed.

"You're perfect," he said. "But then you know that."

"Well, Apothecary, have I ever had a child?"

"If you have, there is not a mark on you to show it."

She smiled at him, her face cat-like. "When I went to that ball I had given birth only two years previously."

Her vanity had trapped her. Here was the truth at last.

"So you are a mother?" Her smile broadened and she nodded slowly. "Where is the child now?"

"He died in infancy. It was not ... convenient ... for me to raise him so I put him into the care of foster parents, and there he perished."

"Is that the truth?"

"Of course. Why should I lie to you? I can assure you that my little boy has nothing to do with this girl you are looking for. He has been gone these fourteen years past. But let us speak of more pleasant things. Talk of death makes me sad. Mr. Rawlings, do you find me attractive?"

She had crossed the space between them and had woven her arms round his neck.

"Very," John gasped, not at all sure where to put his hands.

"Well then,"

"Well then what?"

"Why don't you show me how much?"

"I am a married man."

Miss Chudleigh gave a careless laugh. "I've never known that stop anyone before."

"Not even an apothecary?" asked John wildly.

She looked surprised. "Why should they be any different?"

"Because we regard all people as our patients and therefore treat them with respect."

"Rubbish," she answered roundly, and giving him a hearty push backwards onto the bed, leapt on top of him, nuzzling his face between her breasts.

Momentarily, John knew what it must be like to drown, then he was saved by an urgent knocking on the door. With a hiss of rage, Elizabeth got to her feet, pulling a wrap around her.

"What is it?" she called angrily.

"Madam, the Duke is here. I told him you were still sleeping and he is taking coffee below."

"Oh, merciful Heavens." Elizabeth rolled her eyes. "Mr. Rawlings, you must leave at once. Turn right out of my door and you will come to a back staircase. Then you must go through the kitchens and out that way."

"But ..."

"No buts. I cannot have the Duke upset."

"Very well." John decided to make a good exit. Bowing low, he kissed her hand. "What can I say, Madam, but thank you for the pleasure that wasn't quite mine. Good day to you."

With that he snatched up his cloak and hat and hurried from the room, wondering in a wicked little part of his mind whether he was sad or glad that the Duke of Kingston had arrived just in the nick of time.

"So the lady has had a child, has she?" asked Sir Gabriel, dressed for strolling into the village with his daughter-in-law and son.

"Yes, but as I said to you, I do not believe it to have any bearing on Lucinda's disappearance. Nicholas was wrong, I'm sure of it. Somebody else is the girl's mother."

"But who?"

"George Goward's first wife?" asked Emilia.

"Um," said her husband and fingered his chin. "Why is that man omnipresent?" he asked after a while.

"What do you mean?"

"I pick up a runaway and out of the kindness of my heart offer her a position in my home. That should have nothing to do with the case in hand, namely Goward's murder. Yet somehow, time and again, I come up with the idea that the two things are connected."

"If Lucinda is his daughter, then they most certainly are."

"But she said her mother was highly placed in society, and according to Digby Turnbull Goward's wife died when the girl was born."

"Supposing he was wrong, or lying," said Emilia, in a voice that she used especially when she was talking of mysterious things. "Supposing she left Devon and became a member of the *beau monde*. What then?"

"I think another chat with Turnbull is indicated at this stage," put in Sir Gabriel. "He's in Kensington. I saw him last night. I shall invite him to dine with us."

"Father," said John, "how do you always manage to come up with the right answer?

Sir Gabriel smiled. "My dear child, it is just a matter of age and experience. And don't you grin at me like that, young man. Just because you are preparing for fatherhood doesn't grant you immunity from your own parent."

Emilia intervened. "Let us stroll forth. I need to breathe some fresh air again. London's streets become more noxious by the second."

"Allow me to offer you my arm," said Sir Gabriel gallantly. "It is very good for my reputation to be seen walking out with a beautiful woman."

"Even one who is growing rounder by the day?"

"It is at that time that they are the most beautiful of all."

They set forth for The Cold Bath, a short, pleasant walk from their house, and there sat down in the small tea garden attached. Though nothing like the Peerless Pool in London, the Bath offered an invigorating swim for those hardy enough to brave itswaters. John had been in on several occasions, though never lingering long, but today, feeling the need to plunge into icy water after his extraordinary encounter with Miss Chudleigh, he left Sir Gabriel and Emilia drinking coffee and eating buns oozing with butter, and went to the bath house.

The attendant taking money and handing out towels, looked dubious. "Bit crowded in there today, Sir. Might be worth waiting a while. Got the boys from the Brompton Park School in."

The Apothecary hesitated, not particularly enjoying packed swimming pools but knowing that his father and wife would not want to linger too long, particularly as they had a dinner guest.

"I'll just have a quick plunge."

"It's your choice, Sir."

Within the bath house, which was small indeed in comparison with the cold bath at the Peerless Pool, was a heaving mass of juvenile humanity, yelling with one voice as it took to the water. John, clad in drawers and shivering slightly, hesitated on the brink, wondering if he had been foolish even to contemplate such a venture. Then a hand made contact with the small of his back and the next second he was gasping as he plunged beneath the surface into water so bitter that it would not have disgraced a polar sea. Fighting his way upwards, John's head broke free and he panted in air, only to feel something wrap itself round his feet and pull

183

him downwards again. Dragged into the icy depths, the Apothecary kicked wildly.

It seemed that no one was taking any notice of the struggle going on in their midst, and it occurred to John that this was no more than a schoolboy prank, that his life was not actually in danger. But for all that he fought wildly to free himself from the hands that had now reached up and were grabbing at his waist, Then the full import of what was happening dawned on him. It was a jape for sure, for the assailant was undoing his drawers and pulling them off. In front of all

those horrible children, John was faced with the prospect of climbing out of the bath, cods naked.

His head came above water again and with a mighty effort he reached down and grabbed the hair of the little beast who had attacked him. Tugging viciously as he felt his drawers finally depart, John hauled with all his strength and up came the spluttering face, pustules and all, of Lord Arnold Courtney.

"I might have guessed," said John and pushed the boy down again, holding him under till it was no longer safe to do so, then pulling him up once more.

"Right," the Apothecary continued, "answer a question or I'll drown you."

"Damn you," said the boy, and kicked in the direction of John's privy parts. Then he called, "Help" to his peers, who ignored him and continued to scream at one another about the temperature.

John's fingers closed on the boy's neck. "So you want to be rough, do you?"

Arnold shook his head, unable to speak. The Apothecary released his grip very slightly.

"The other day I asked you about Lucas Drummond and when I did so you went white as a sail. You knew damned well that he was a girl, didn't you? And shall I tell you why? Because you were the one who took advantage of her and caused her to run away in the first place. That's why your brother was beating you, wasn't it?"

Arnold drew in breath, then sneered. "So what if I did? She was more than willing."

The Apothecary's grip tightened once more. "She predicted you'd say that. Well, my fine friend, I intend to call on your brother and confirm his suspicions about you. Then I shall leave you to his tender mercies."

"I care nothing for him."

"Next time there might not be anyone there to intervene. Think about it. Now, do you want to go under water again or are you going to tell me where she's gone?"

Arnold shook his head. "I don't know and that's the truth. She stole Fred out by dead of night, then vanished. I swear it."

He wasn't lying, John felt sure of it, but he pushed him under again for good measure, then with as much gravity as he could muster, hauled himself out and made a stately progress to the changing booths, attempting to close his ears to the cheers and catcalls of the pupils of the Brompton Park Boarding School as he made a dignified exit.


Digby Turnbull shook his head. "But surely," he said, "Hannah Goward must have died to enable George to marry Lady Mary. I mean, he couldn't have committed bigamy, could he?"

"I suppose anything is possible. After all, the West Country is a long way away. News might never have spread to London," John answered.

"I don't agree with you. It only needs one letter, one visitor, for the story to come out."

"Mr. Turnbull has a good point. We live in a small world. It is difficult to conceal anything these days, John," added Sir Gabriel.

The Apothecary smiled feebly, thinking of Elizabeth di

Lorenzi still hidden away in Devon and no one aware of her existence. "You're probably right," he said.

The three men were sitting at port, Emilia having retired to another room to read for a while before she went to bed, and it had been John's father who had steered the conversation round to the death at St. James's Palace. Not that there had been any reluctance on the part of their guest, who seemed more than anxious to catch up with the state of affairs.

"I am amazed that the case remains unsolved," he said now.

"I doubt it ever will be. Nobody seems to have seen the moment when he was pushed, or won't admit to it," the Apothecary answered gloomily. "Besides there are so many people with a hearty dislike of George Goward - Mr. and Miss Witherspoon to name but two. As well as those who had no respect for him - Jack Morocco and Miss Chudleigh amongst the foremost. Anyway, with all those suspects, who to choose without more evidence?"

His guest frowned. "But I thought Elizabeth Chudleigh was a friend of his."

John wondered briefly how discreet he should be, then decided to tell the truth. "I believe he could have been blackmailing her about an incident in her past."

"Her child, I suppose," Digby Turnbull replied. "Oh, don't look surprised. A great many people knew about it. However, there is one thing about her even more intriguing."

"And what is that?"

"It is believed in certain quarters that she is married. That her son was legitimate but that she and her husband parted company soon after he was born and that now they have nothing further to do with one another."

"But what about the Duke of Kingston?"

Digby smiled cynically. "Indeed. What about the Duke?"

A great diamond flashed on Sir Gabriel's finger as he

toyed with his glass. "Court life, great God. What next one wonders."

"Perhaps young George will breathe some new life into it."

"He is already exhibiting signs of being a bore," stated Digby frankly. "Anyway, enough of that. Was it Lady Mary who pushed her husband?"

"Sir John thinks so. Jack Morocco agrees - that is if one can believe his tale of small feet and heavy breathing. I, personally, have absolutely no idea. Unless his unknown daughter were present and killed her father for deserting her."

"But how could that be? We know exactly who was there."

"But do we?" John said reflectively. "Do we?"

And with that an idea was born that absolutely refused to go away.

# Chapter 14

He had fully intended not to attend the funeral of Sir George Goward, but the more John thought about it the more he felt he would be missing a unique opportunity of studying the principal suspects. Yet his conscience bothered him. He was turning into an absentee shop owner. Indeed if it were not for the stalwart Nicholas Dawkins, pale and sad these days in the absence of Lucinda, he would not have any business left at all. However, visits to patients had not been neglected. By working at some rather unorthodox times, John Rawlings had managed to keep his clients happy and had only sent Nick out to dispense simple remedies to those with minor ailments.

For reasons best known to herself, Lady Mary Goward had decided to dispose of her husband's mortal remains in Islington, rather than in the London parish where she had her town house. So yet again the difficult journey through Holbourn, Hatton Garden, Clerkenwell Green and St. John's Street was undertaken by the Apothecary, rook-dark in mourning clothes, while Irish Tom wore a black ribbon on the arm of his many-caped driving coat.

The waiting convoy at The Angel consisted almost entirely of mourners. John saw Sir John Fielding's coach, the great man inside, together with his wife and Joe Jago. Emblazoned with the Duchess of Arundel's escutcheon, a grand carriage was drawing up at the same time as the Apothecary's own. Out of it, looking like something from an Araby fable, leapt Jack Morocco, gallantly reaching upwards to assist his passenger to dismount. It was the beautiful girl who had been with him at Ranelagh, John saw. Today, drained of colour, the red hair scarcely visible, swept up into a great black hat, she was like an injured animal, a vixen run beneath a carriage wheel and left at the roadside to suffer. Full of curiosity, the

Apothecary found himself following them into the coaching inn to down a brandy before the ordeal ahead.

Elizabeth Chudleigh was already inside, seated alone at a table, a glass of strong liquor in front of her. Oddly enough, Digby Turnbull was also present, though neither had seen the other, he, too, fortifying himself for the occasion. It occurred to John that, other than for the Witherspoons, the group who had stood close to George Goward on the Grand Staircase was once again gathered together. And then, as if he had conjured them up, Julius and Christabel walked in, the little artist leaning on a stick, his sister straight as an arrow beside him. She looked around her.

"Good gracious. But don't I know you all?"

"Morocco, Madam," said Jack, and as he bowed before her a bevy of diamonds twinkled about his person.

"I saw you at St. James's Palace, Sir."

"And I you. Mr. Witherspoon, may I say how much I admire your work. I would like to commission without hesitation a portrait of my beloved mother, the Duchess, one of myself, and also one of Aminta, my dear friend."

The girl curtsied to the new arrivals, and John thought that if he had been a painter he would have liked to capture her today, her beauty intensified by her extreme pallor, the curls that had escaped her hat glowing against the whiteness of her skin.

Miss Chudleigh raised a languid hand. "Mr. Witherspoon, I don't think I have had the pleasure, though of course I have seen you round and about. Pray, will you and your sister join me?"

It was uncanny, John thought. All the people who had watched George Goward die, forming into little groups before they trooped off to see him laid in the earth. Present amongst them there might well be a murderer, hiding their black heart beneath a show of mourning. Very carefully, the Apothecary studied each one.

Elizabeth Chudleigh, her powdered hair swept high, a

dark hat with bobbing feathers atop, was as self-seeking and ruthless as they come, he decided. If she wanted something, nothing would stop her getting it, be it man, riches or a title. More and more certain that the whispered conversation he had heard in The Hercules Pillars had been between herself and the dead man, John considered that they might have been discussing the fact she had contracted a marriage long ago and was still bound to it. Apparently news of this shocking state of affairs had not yet reached the ears of the unworldly Duke of Kingston. Would Miss Chudleigh have been prepared to kill to stop George Goward betraying her?

John's gaze fell on Digby Turnbull, that most honest-looking of citizens, for here lay motive indeed. Originally from Devon, an associate of Hannah, the Beauty of Exeter and Goward's first wife, could there be another story beneath the surface? Digby had admitted that he amongst many other admirers had also loved Hannah. Had it been more than a youthful passion and had he sworn revenge when she had been left behind in the West Country while her husband promoted his career in town? Had he, the servant of the Crown, seized his chance at the palace and heaved his old enemy to his death?

Then there were the Witherspoons, at present sitting quietly with Miss Chudleigh. The funny little carcass, as Christabel had described Julius, was a genius; no one could deny that. Had the death and defilement of his elder sister unhinged him slightly? Were not intellect and insanity meant to run hand-in-hand? Had he gone mad with grief and seized the chance to kill when it presented itself?

And what of Christabel? She had admitted to loathing Goward for the same reasons as her twin. Had it been she who had hurled him down the staircase, her small shoes moving into Jack Morocco's line of vision as she did so?

This brought John's thoughts to the Negro himself. Today, dressed all in black, even his wig consisting of long dark curls, he looked a truly fascinating prince of the night. Yet if he had been the one to end Goward's life, then the motive itself was not readily apparent. Though there remained the inescapable fact that he had grinned as the victim had died. He had admitted to not liking the man but was there more to it than that? Could his great friend, as he had described Aminta, been one of George's many conquests at some time in the past?

So, with the exception of Lady Mary Goward, all the suspects were there, gathered in The Angel to get a little liquid courage before the rigours of a funeral. Yet were they, thought John. For who had been the enigmatic thirteenth pageboy? And why had all the other boys denied seeing him? Surely they, of all people, must have noticed a stranger in their midst? With a determination that somehow he must get young Guernsey to reveal the truth about that day, John went to join Digby Turnbull.

Even though the clouds overhead were black as crows, the rain held off. Yet though the mourners might be spared that, a howling gale which shook the rafters of the church to the extent that the funeral bell tolled a few times on its own - a highly sinister occurrence - seemed to come up from nowhere. Accordingly the service was conducted to the sound of moaning and wuthering, a dismal accompaniment that unnerved everyone present.

John had been, even as he left the house, convinced that today Lady Mary would give a spectacular display of major hysterics, and he was not to be disappointed. She had walked up behind the coffin quietly enough but then, billowing like a black barge, she had suddenly risen from her pew and flung herself over the casket, causing it to rock slightly on its trestle. John and Joe Jago, who were sitting at the back with the Fieldings, exchanged a glance, then simultaneously rolled their eyes heavenwards.

"We're for it," whispered the clerk out of the side of his mouth.

"What's happening?" demanded Sir John, not quietly.

"Lady Mary's about to go orff," Joe replied, and grinned in an unseemly manner.

"Apparently she's in regular high bridle because her son is ill and cannot attend her," Elizabeth Fielding murmured.

"How do you know that?" asked her husband, still in the same loudish tone.

"Another mourner told me outside the church."

"Ha," said Sir John but made no further comment.

The Apothecary looked round. Elizabeth Chudleigh sat just behind the family pew as befitted her status, real or imaginary. Jack Morocco, too, not one to conceal himself, had taken a place well near the front, where he fixed the coffin with a dark unreadable gaze, looking neither to right nor left. Beside him, his lady friend, even paler than before if such a thing were possible, gazed at her prayer book and did not look up. John stared to see her expression, but Aminta's face was concealed by the veiling of her hat which fell forward as she bent her head.

The Witherspoons sat near the back, their look grim and unrelenting. Julius's lips moved silently and it occurred to the Apothecary that even here, in church, he was sending Goward to his eternal rest with a curse. Behind the brother and sister was Digby Turnbull, his expression bland, revealing in no regard that he and the deceased shared a history that went back a very long way and had known a great deal of drama. But it was to Lady Mary that John's eyes were drawn once again as she let out a cry that would not have disgraced a she-wolf and bodily embraced the coffin.

A female attendant, very slight and small, rose from her place in the front pew and grappled with the wailing widow, attempting to get her back to her seat. But Lady Mary was in full swing and would not be gainsayed.

"I feel vomitous," she announced to the congregation at large.

"Oh God," said John, and with the utmost reluctance rose from his place at the back and marched down the centre aisle, his feet ringing out noisily on the flagstones, to where the green-faced woman stood.

"Madam, if you will step outside," he ordered firmly, "I will administer to you."

She rolled her eyes piteously. "But it's very windy beyond."

The Apothecary looked harsh. "Madam, you cannot vomit over the coffin. Out with you." And gripping her elbow he stalked to the door, dragging her with him, she clutching a handkerchief to her mouth and making quite the most hideous noises.

Once outside he pushed her behind a gravestone, standing well clear himself. Then, having half suspected that this kind of thing might occur, John fished from his cloak pocket a syrup made from the juice of balm with added sugar, already bottled, and uncorked it.

"Drink this," he said shortly when she returned, looking much the worse for wear.

"What is it?" she asked suspiciously.

"A cure for vomiting. Lady Mary, you must take it. You cannot go on like this. The entire funeral is being held up because of your lack of control."

"But I have lost my husband." She pronounced it lawst.

Thoroughly tempted to ask where, John controlled himself. "Tragedy strikes us all at some time in our lives. It is up to one's personal pride to conduct oneself as well as possible in the face of it."

"If only my boy had been here, My little Frederick."

"But I thought he was ill."

"Yes, according to the school. He has never enjoyed good health."

A mental picture of Julius Witherspoon's portrait of an obese mother and son came into focus in John's brain, and he considered that a child afflicted with so much excess poundage would be far from fit indeed.

"But surely you told me that the boy was not Sir George's child?" he said.

"Yes, I did. He is the son of my first husband."

"Then in fact this funeral is no place for him. Such sombre occasions can affect children very adversely. Probably his indisposition is a blessing in disguise."

Lady Mary snorted with annoyance. "What rubbish, Sir. My son would have wanted to pay his respects to his stepfather. Besides, what about me?"

"What about you is that you should get back into the church and conduct yourself with dignity, Madam."

"But Sir George was brutally done to death."

"All the more reason for you to comport yourself with enormous gravity and grandeur."

"But I cannot help my failing health."

"That, Lady Mary, should be discussed with your physician at some future date. Now, are you going to keep the congregation waiting even longer?"

She blew out her cheeks at him, like a furious pug, but clearly bit back the words she would like to have said and marched ahead into the church. With a sigh of relief, John slipped quietly back into his place beside Joe Jago.

He had always found that the procession to the graveside revealed a great deal and this occasion proved to be no exception. Lady Mary, obviously having taken his words to heart, waddled majestically into the churchyard supported by the parson and the small female attendant. Elizabeth Chudleigh wept bitterly, or appeared to do so, her face obscured by a dainty handkerchief as she threw earth upon the lowered coffin. On the other hand Digby Turnbull seemed to fling with relish, almost as if he were saying good riddance. But the most surprising gesture came from Jack

Morocco. Walking slowly with Aminta clinging tightly to his arm, her face now obscured, the veils on her hat totally pulled down, the black man threw a single red rose onto the casket.

John turned to Joe, who was eyeing Miss Chudleigh for all he was worth. "What was that for I wonder."

"A red rose for love, Sir," the clerk answered, wresting his attention back to his surroundings.

"But Jack Morocco had no love for the deceased. He grinned when the man died, I told you that."

"Apparently, Mr. Rawlings, all is not as it seems."

"Obviously not," John answered thoughtfully, and having no wish to scatter earth, a custom he did not care for, made his way back up the path.

Very late and very much out of breath, Samuel stood there, apologising to anyone who would listen, particularly Miss Witherspoon.

"My carriage cast a wheel so I walked."

"Not from London surely?" asked Christabel.

"No, from my father's house. I spent last night with him." He turned to John. "Did all go smoothly?"

"Eventually, yes. Lady Mary threatened to vomit in church ..."

"Uh!"

"But I managed to get her outside in time. Other than for that there were no high tantrums. However, all may change in a moment. Sir John is waiting in the porch for the widow to return and he will then request an interview with her."

"That will not please her."

"But it will do her the world of good." John turned as the Witherspoons began to move away. "Are you going?"

"Yes," answered Christabel, "we only came to make sure he was really six feet under. I know it sounds strange but we had to see for ourselves."

There was an awkward silence during which Samuel shuffled about, obviously longing to make a further assignation with her but somehow lacking the courage. Loving everything about his old friend, John helped him out.

"Why don't we all repair to The Angel? My coach can take you home later, as the weather is so inclement. I am sure one or two others will be joining us there."

"Are you not going to the wake?" Julius asked.

"Certainly not. Nor, I imagine, will many of those of our acquaintance."

"In fact," said Samuel, "it will be interesting to see who does attend."

Joe Jago came up the path, a weeping Miss Chudleigh on his arm. John, looking at him with all the affection of old acquaintance, saw that the clerk's neck had gone extremely red and that his light blue eyes had a glazed expression in them.

"... you must call on me," she was saying between sobs. "It is at times like these that I feel so alone, Mr. Jago. So very alone."

She peeped round her handkerchief and caught John's eye. He winked and grinned and she glared at him robustly.

Joe cleared his throat. "I shall make a point of it, Madam. When would be convenient?"

She whispered a reply, but the Apothecary caught the words, "As early as you please."

So he was next, thought John, and decided that, all things considered, Miss Chudleigh might possibly do the clerk a world of good.


The red rose thrown into the grave puzzled him for the next half hour, particularly as it was not long before Jack Morocco and Aminta walked into The Angel as well. From the open door of The Unicorn, the room that he and Samuel were occupying with the Witherspoons, he saw them go past, the vixen-girl as pale and drawn as before, making their way into another snug. So even after that token of love they had not gone back to the house to eat cakes and drink sherry. It was all very strange to say the least.

John turned to Julius. "Lady Mary seemed much put out that her son was ill and could not attend her at the funeral. Tell me, was the child sickly when you painted him?"

"Well, he had all the woes of the very fat. He was constantly out of breath, could not run, even had difficulty in walking. I felt desperately sorry for him."

"What happened to him? Did he lose flesh?"

"I don't know. George really took a dislike to him so the mother sent him away to school instead of standing up for her son."

"Rather typical I would have thought."

"Very."

"Strange that she never had a child that her new husband could dote upon," John said thoughtfully.

"There were rumours," answered Julius.

"Really? What were they?"

"That despite her size she was voracious as far as men were concerned. Apparently, she'd given birth before she was married and so already had a babe out of wedlock. Then, and this is really bizarre, she told George she was expecting his child but when it was born, the baby was black."

"What?" said John, shooting to the edge of his chair and startling Samuel and Christabel who were engaged in what appeared to be delightful conversation.

Julius laughed aloud. "It is only gossip because the whole matter was extremely hushed up. It seems she had made free with one of her slaves but took a chance that the pregnancy was caused by her husband and only discovered her mistake at the actual birth."

"What happened?"

"George, who knew exactly which side his bread was buttered, decided to forgive her her trespasses, and the child was taken away."

"By whom?"

"I have no idea. But presumably by someone who could sell it into slavery later and make a handsome profit for a pretty little black boy."

"God almighty," said John, hitting his forehead with his clenched fist, and saw once again the red rose go hurtling down into the grave's gluttonous maw, thrown by the black hand of Jack Morocco.

# Chapter 15

It appeared that Miss Chudleigh and Digby Turnbull had gone back to attend the wake, which was logical as both had known the dead man for several years. The question remained, however, whether Sir John Fielding would go to Lady Mary's house, representing the Public Office. But in the end it seemed that the Blind Beak had shied away from visiting a place he did not know and had decided to brave The Angel instead. Thus, the occupants of The Unicorn heard the familiar tap of a cane amongst all the other noises of the inn and John, recognising the sound, rose to meet him and lead him into the place where they were all sitting.

Sir John was accompanied by his wife and clerk, one walking beside him, Joe steadily behind so that he could hurry to assist should the Magistrate fall. The Apothecary, who by this time had drunk far more than he should have done and was feeling enormously sentimental as a result, watched the three of them silently for a moment, thinking how inextricably his life was now linked with theirs and of all the many strange and sad things they had come across in their time together.

"Mr. Rawlings," said Joe, seeing him.

"Come in here, please do join us," the Apothecary answered, hoping that his speech was not blurring. To the Magistrate he said quietly, "Mr. and Miss Witherspoon are with us. He is the noted portrait painter Julius Witherspoon, she is his twin sister. As I told you at Bow Street, they both hated George Goward because their beautiful elder sister was his mistress, abandoned by him when she became pregnant."

"He was indeed a true blackguard," said Elizabeth with feeling.

"Be that as it may, they are interesting company, particularly as they were standing close to Goward on the Grand Staircase."

"Fascinating," said Sir John, "pray introduce me, Mr. Rawlings."

"Sir," said Julius, having bowed politely, "I would deem it a privilege if you would sit for your portrait. I should not want a fee, merely the honour of leaving your likeness for future generations."

"I should be duly flattered," the Blind Beak answered. "However, as I do not find travelling as easy as I used, I wonder whether you could come to Bow Street and paint me there."

"It would be an honour," Julius answered.

John smiled benignly, suddenly seeing himself in the role of one who brought great people together.

The delightful Christabel spoke up. "Julius, I think a portrait of Lady Fielding would be another splendid notion."

"I shall paint the two of you together," her brother announced.

"And I," said Sir John, sipping from the glass that John had just handed him, "shall commission a painting of my clerk and right hand man. Joe Jago's image shall adorn the walls of Bow Street also."

The clerk, who was obviously in a highly charged emotional state after Miss Chudleigh's invitation to call, flushed deeply. "But Sir John, surely I am not worthy?"

"You are more than worthy, my friend. For do you not realise that without your eyes it would be almost impossible for me to carry out my duties?"

The eyes that the Blind Beak was referring to, filled with sudden tears. "Oh Sir John," Joe said in muffled tones.

"Come, come, my friend. Do not distress yourself."

But John, observing silently, felt certain that Joe Jago was suffering the pangs of falling in love and was far more likely to be weeping because of his passionate condition than through anything else. Decidedly tipsy as he was, the Apothecary raised his glass.

"A toast to beautiful ladies," he said, apropos of absolutely nothing.

"Yes indeed," Joe responded fervently, as did Samuel, gazing adoringly at Miss Witherspoon.

"My beautiful wife," Sir John added gallantly, raising his glass to Elizabeth.

"History repeats itself, does it not?" said a voice from the doorway. "Surely this was how we met at Ranelagh, Mr. Rawlings?"

It was Jack Morocco and his lovely pale companion.

Sir John Fielding moved his head in the direction of the sound. "Do I have the honour of meeting Mr. Morocco at last?"

"You do, Sir."

The Blind Beak stood up. "Sir, if you would not consider it an imposition, there are one or two questions I would like to ask you about the day of the fatal investiture. And now would seem as good a time as any. May I suggest that we withdraw to a private room and that Mr. Rawlings and Joe Jago accompany us."

The Negro hesitated, his dark eyes clouded. Then he said, "Why not? But surely Mr. and Miss Witherspoon should be questioned too. They were standing right by me."

Sir John took his seat once more and turned in their direction. "My friends, would you object?"

"Of course not," said little Julius, heaving his crazy carcass out of the chair. "Better to be interrogated in the comfort of an inn than at Bow Street."

Lady Fielding spoke up, looking at the pale Aminta. "Miss ...er..."

"Wilson, Ma'am."

"Miss Wilson, would it upset you to be left with myself and Mr. Swann for a short while? I assure you that we are very civilised and will try to give you good company."

It was so charmingly said that the ground was cut from beneath Aminta's feet. She had no option but to say, "No, of course not."

John saw the flamboyant Jack Morocco look truly caring

just for a second before he flashed his usual dazzling glance. "Aminta, you have only to say and I'll refuse to go."

"To deny the Principal Magistrate would not be clever, Jack. I'll be perfectly all right with Lady Fielding," Aminta answered in a quiet, well-modulated voice.

"I'll take care of her," said Samuel loudly, and laughed a boisterous laugh that filled the room.

John saw Christabel wink at her twin and hoped fervently that Samuel wasn't going to be disappointed in love yet again.

Aminta spoke, this time quite firmly. "As there are only three of us and far more of you, I suggest, if Lady Fielding agrees, that we are the ones to find somewhere else to sit. Mr. Swann, please lead the way."

And she stood up, revealing that she had more strength of character than was at first apparent.

"Certainly," said Sam, who had seen the wink, was accordingly thoroughly flustered, and led the ladies out with much over-compensatory noise.

There was a moment's silence after their departure and then the Blind Beak got straight to the matter in hand.

"Lady and gentlemen, I don't doubt that you have already told Mr. Rawlings all that you saw and heard on the day that Sir George fell to his death but for my benefit, would you be so kind as to say it once more." He turned towards Christabel. "Miss Witherspoon, pray begin."

She cleared her throat. "Sir John, I am sure that Mr. Rawlings has already informed you that I hated George Goward."

The Magistrate nodded silently.

"But as it happens I did not give him the deadly push."

"Do you know who did?"

"No, but even if I knew I wouldn't say. All I can tell you is that there was a movement close by me and some whispered words, but I did not see who uttered them."

"What were the words you heard?"

"What price slackness now."

"Slackness!" Sir John exclaimed. "Are you sure?"

"Not totally. But it was something like that. Why? Did you hear it too?"

"Yes," the Magistrate answered. "But I thought he or she said, 'What price greatness.'" He paused then said, still facing Christabel. "Miss Witherspoon, give me your opinion if you please. Was it a man or a woman who spoke?"

She frowned. "It is hard to say, and I refuse to hazard a guess for fear of betraying someone. All I can tell you is that the words were whispered and the voice had a strange quality to it, almost unearthly."

Sir John signed deeply. "I, too, cannot decide." He turned towards Julius. "Sir, did you hear anything?"

"I was a little further away and only heard the whisper, the words themselves were not clear."

"Did you see anything?"

"Only Goward falling to his death. Which sight, though shocking, held a certain fascination for me. For like my sister I disliked the man, but it was not I who pushed him, of that I can assure you."

The twins exchanged a glance, noticed by nobody except John, who happened to be staring at them while they were speaking. Were they telling the truth, he wondered, or were they both accomplished actors who, as twins, had spent years weaving fantasies about themselves and half believing them?

Jack Morocco spoke up. "Sir John, I saw and heard something. Has Mr. Rawlings told you what it was?"

"Yes. But tell me again in your own words."

"It was the sound of physical exertion and then a pair of small feet came into my sight line. They were encased in low heeled buckled shoes, neither masculine nor feminine. The most striking thing about those shoes was their lack of size. So whoever wore them had particularly small feet."

"Like me," said Julius Witherspoon, and stuck his shoes out before him to show how tiny they were.

"You heard no whispered words, Mr. Morocco?"

"There was something but I could not make out what it was. No, the thing I remember most clearly was the sound of exertion."

"Did that lead you to any conclusion?"

The black man looked thoughtful, moving a little in his chair, the sprinkle of diamonds he wore catching the light as he did so. "Not really, except perhaps that the person who did the pushing wasn't immensely strong. That it was hard for them to do so."

Sir John Fielding gave a grunt of satisfaction. "Excellent. That was what I had thought myself."

The Apothecary, through a wine-haze, looked at Jack Morocco as intently as he could. He had just told his story well, and most believably at that. But it was his hand that had thrown a red rose onto George Goward's coffin. For what purpose if it was not as a token of love? Before he could stop himself, John found that he was asking a question.

"Jack, why did you throw a flower onto the casket when you told me quite clearly that you had no time for Goward? That he was not your sort?"

The Negro stared at him, thoroughly startled, and John knew for certain that he thought he had been unobserved. Eventually he said, "I considered it polite to do so."

"Polite!" echoed Joe Jago, clearly astonished.

Morocco looked aloof. "It is a custom of my people," he said coldly. "Now, can we drop the subject if you please?"


It was as well, thought John, that Emilia had decided to stay in Kensington with Sir Gabriel. For by the time he had taken the Witherspoons back to their home and had driven Samuel, who sighed gustily every so often but said very little, back to the City, it was midnight before he put his key in

204

the lock. Worse for wear though he might be, the Apothecary still noticed that two letters awaited him on a tray in the hall. Picking them up, John decided to read them in bed.

The first was from Sir Clovelly Lovell of Exeter.

My Friends,
I much Regret the Tardiness of this my Reply, but the Ways have been Foul with Flooding, and there are Branches over the Ways caused by High Winds and Torrents of Rain.

I found the Information You Seek in the Parish Register of St. Mary Magdalen, Chudleigh Knighton. It Read: Baptised, 28th April, 1744, Georgiana Aminta, Daughter of Hannah Goward and George Goward, of This Parish. The Mother's Death and Burial are Recorded a Few Days Later.

Trusting that This is of Help, I Remain, Your Friend
C. Lovell.

So that was it! Georgiana Aminta. George Goward's missing daughter was not only in London but her lover had stood within feet of her father just before he had plunged to his death.

Good God, thought the Apothecary, and wondering at the strangeness of life fell fast asleep, the second letter, still unopened, in his hand.

# *Chapter 16*

The Apothecary woke the next morning feeling absolutely terrible and swearing to reform. Indeed he was so far gone in suffering that he was forced to mix himself a potion before he could even face going downstairs to breakfast. Once there, however, and after several cups of strong tea, he felt somewhat better and able to tackle the correspondence which had arrived for him while he had been at the funeral.

Having re-read Sir Clovelly Lovell's letter, John wondered if he had jumped to a conclusion too rapidly. Aminta, though not common, was far from an unknown name, and there was simply no reason, other than for an odd coincidence, why Jack Morocco's friend should be George Goward's daughter. Yet the Apothecary had a feeling that would not go away, a feeling so strong that he knew he could never totally reject the idea until he had found out for sure.

The second letter addressed to him was in an unknown hand, yet there was a clarity and youthfulness in the writing that immediately made him think of Lucinda Drummond. With fingers that shook a little, though this probably caused by his excesses of the previous day he thought wryly, John opened the paper.

It was indeed from her and he read the message eagerly.

My Dear Mr. Rawlings,
How Ill you must Think of Me that I left You as I did. Having Heard from My Brother that he was Grievous Sick I could abandon Him at the School No Longer. I Stole Him away and for Two Days we Lived very Poorly. Yet a Lucky Meeting brought us Face to Face with our Saviour Who has now put Us under His Protection. Thank You for Your Many Kindnesses to Me. My Greatest Regards to Mrs.
Rawlings. I remain, Sir, Your Friend, L. Drummond.

"Oh dear," the Apothecary sighed. And a mental picture of Lucinda's protector as a loathsome, leering old man with lecherous intentions flashed into his mind. Still, there was nothing he could do about it. There was no address and no indication of where the letter had been posted. The trail, as far as his erstwhile servant was concerned, had gone dead. Wondering whether his apprentice had also received a communication from her, John left the house and headed for Shug Lane.

Nicholas, as usual, was ahead of him, dusting and tidying and looking very long-faced. The Apothecary, certain that he could guess the reason for it, put on his sympathetic expression and lead the conversation in the direction in which he felt the Muscovite would like it to go.

"I had a letter from Lucinda yesterday."

"So did I," Nicholas answered miserably.

"Ah ha. What did it say?"

"That our friendship, hers and mine, must remain only that and could not progress to anything further."

The Apothecary was frankly astonished. "What a strange thing to write. You haven't seen her recently, have you?"

"Of course not, Master. How could I? I've no more idea where she is than you have."

"Then why put such a thing?"

Nicholas grew slightly less pale than usual. "Because I became fond of her while she was in your household - and she knew it."

"But why, out of sky blue, write that?"

Then he saw it, even as he said it, but Nicholas had already worked out the answer for himself.

"She has met someone else, Master, and is warning me off. Which is utterly foolish as I shall probably never see her again."

John nodded. "You're right, of course. But women don't think like that, Nick. In her eyes she will have done the honourable thing by telling you, regardless of the fact that she is no longer in touch."

The Muscovite sighed. "The older I get, the less I know. I don't think I shall ever meet a female that I understand."

"Will any of us?" asked John, and burst out laughing.

Nicholas did not join in. "But who is this man? And how has she grown so attached to him in such a short space of time?"

"Because he's rescued her and her brother from living on the streets. In her letter to me she said that she had been saved and put under someone's protection ..."

"Filthy old fart catcher," Nicholas interrupted.

John raised an eyebrow. "... and she has no doubt switched allegiance in gratitude. Nick, you must put the past behind you."

"Again?"

"Yes, again. Wherever she is, at least she is safe."

"But not from his disgusting advances."

"He might not be disgusting. Poor devil, he could be a kindly soul with purely honourable intentions."

"Then why did she write that to me?"

Shaking his head, the Apothecary found himself unable to reply.


They had a good morning, working hard in the compounding room, John enjoying the freedom of being away from the puzzle of George Goward's death. Yet however hard he tried, he wasn't really away from it at all. Over and over again, he found himself running through the various points and coming up with nothing but a series of loose ends. Everyone seemed to have a motive for doing away with the dead man, yet there was no one at whom one could actually point the finger. The more he mulled it over, the more convinced John became that Sir John was right and that the widow was responsible, tired, no doubt, of Goward's mistresses and general bad behaviour.

"She's got to be interviewed - and interviewed soon," he muttered.

Then another idea came. Just supposing Lady Mary *were* Jack Morocco's mother, having allowed one of her black servants to make free with her. Supposing that the victim, short of money perhaps, had decided to blackmail his own wife. What a motive that would give her.

"By God!" said John.

He had spoken aloud and Nicholas looked up questioningly from the table at which he was pounding herbs. But at that moment a voice called, "Shop," and before he could say a word, the Muscovite was forced to remove his apron and go through.

"Is Mr. Rawlings in?" John heard a youthful voice say.

"Who wants him?" Nicholas asked.

"I am Miss Aminta's black boy and I come with an invitation from my masser ... I mean master."

Nicholas laughed. "Are you the jackanapes that Jack Morocco rescued in the street?"

"I am he," the child answered with dignity.

John stepped into the shop and gasped at the transformation. The dirty little rascal in the suit of clothes too large, had been turned into a miniature black prince. A scarlet turban with a twinkling jewel supporting a cheeky white feather, matching red trousers shaped like those of a Turk, an embroidered waistcoat, a miniature dagger tucked into a stiffened taffeta waistband, adorned the former ragamuffin.

"Well, well," said the Apothecary, "and what does he call you?"

"Ebony, Sir."

"No other name?"

"Ebony James Morocco."

The Apothecary smiled at the sweet pretension of it all. "Well, Ebony James, what does your master want with me?"

"For me to give you this, Sir." And he produced from his belt a gilt-edged card.

John studied it in surprise. "A supper party? Tonight?"

"Yes, Sir. I have been told to await your reply, yes or no."

209

"Well, yes then."

"I have also been instructed to ask whether Mrs. Rawlings will be joining you."

"No, she won't. She is in the country at the moment."

"That is a pity, Sir," Ebony James said seriously. "Because my masser say that she is one of the prettiest girls in town."

"How very saucy of him and how very observant."

The boy, still not sure of himself, though growing more confident by the minute, gave a nervous smile. "Thank you, Sir."

The Apothecary glanced at the card again. "I see that the supper is to be held in Grosvenor Square. I didn't realise the Duchess lived there."

"She doesn't, Sir. Those are Mr. Morocco's private apartments."

"A very good address," the Apothecary answered, and wondered who paid the bills to support the black man's extravagant lifestyle.

Ebony James shifted his feet. "Would it be in order for me to go now, Masser? I have other cards to deliver."

"Of course, of course." The Apothecary searched along the shelves and found a bottle of perfume. "Here, give this to Miss Aminta with my compliments. Tell her I look forward to seeing her."

The boy bowed. "Thank you, Sir. Good day." And he was gone, trotting along the lane in his beautiful gear, attempting to avoid the spray of mud sent up by the carriage wheels of those driving round town.

"Isn't it strange," said Nicholas, "how one moment of good fortune can change a life. When that child bolted into the street to avoid a whipping, fate led him to Jack Morocco and an assured future. Just as Mr. Fielding, as he then was, saw the goodness in me and asked you to take me as an apprentice. Everything hinges on the flip of destiny's coin."

"The art of life," John answered seriously, "is to know that the coin is flipping and to act on it."

"What do you mean?"

"That many people do not recognise their golden opportunity for what it is and ignore it, continuing with their mundane lives until the moment has passed - for ever." He became brisk again. "I must call at Bow Street to tell Sir John what I have learned about George Goward's daughter."

"Is she Jack Morocco's mistress, do you think?"

"I did at first but now I'm not so sure, so the Beak's opinion will be very helpful."

"Will you ask her when you see her tonight?"

The Apothecary fingered his chin. "If the moment presents itself, then I certainly will. On the other hand I would hate to embarrass the girl on a social occasion."

"You're very considerate, Sir."

"Not always," John answered, as, unbidden, a picture of Elizabeth di Lorenzi came into his mind.

He had never seen anything quite like it. The house in Grosvenor Square, an address that was considered the height of *bon ton* by the *beau monde*, had either been most cleverly converted or custom built as apartments, John was not certain which. And of these apartments, Jack Morocco had the finest. Situated on the first floor, it had a large salon with three big windows from which one could step out onto a long ironwork balcony. Leading from this salon were bedrooms and a parlour, together with a silk wallpapered dining room. Indeed, the whole place was decorated and furnished to a fabulous degree.

There were hothouse flowers everywhere, in fact the apartment was totally full of them, giving out a strong heady scent which filled John's nostrils. There were also flowers of the human variety. Every good-looking young person in London, both male and female, seemed to be present, vying with each other for shrill small talk and expensive dress. The main topics of conversation, as far as the Apothecary could

211

make out as he pushed his way through the groups, were the opera, the theatre, horses, grooms and fashionable clubs, together with the latest balls, assemblies and ridottos. It was all very boring and very trivial and John, having secured himself a glass of champagne, looked around for someone with whom to converse on a sensible level. As good luck would have it, Aminta sat alone on a small couch and he headed in her direction.

She was very much a young woman with her own style, clearly refusing to bow to fashion's latest decree. Where all the other females present were following the trend for enormous hairstyles, *en poudre* and with swaying plumes atop, Aminta wore hers down, hanging straight, almost to her waist, its colour the bold rich red of autumn trees, its texture fine as silken threads. Into these very beautiful tresses flowers had been woven, so that in her apple green open robe and blossom white underskirt, she looked like a wood nymph, or rather the spirit of an orchard, John thought.

He bowed before her. "Madam, we meet again."

The tremendous pallor which had enveloped her at the funeral had gone, so had the look of an injured vixen, but still Aminta had a haunted manner, as if she were concealing something from the world.

She looked at him blankly, then said, "Mr. Rawlings, is it not?"

The Apothecary bowed again, "Your servant, Madam."

"I did not realise Jack had invited you,"

"He did, but only this morning. Where is he by the way?"

She smiled faintly. "Showing some beauteous female round the place, I expect."

So she wasn't the only one, John thought. Morocco clearly believed that there was safety in numbers.

"You don't mind?" The words were out before he had time to curb his tongue.

Aminta shrugged delicately. "No, of course not. Jack was

born to flirt and charm. Without being able to do so, he would die."

"You do not fear that one day he might leave you?"

She looked thoughtful. "If he does, he does. There is nothing I can do about it."

"You are a very philosophical young woman."

"I have had to learn to be. I was brought up by foster parents, you know. An aunt and uncle. They were not unkind to me but they were very strict. In order to make life tolerable I had to plan that I would leave for London as soon as I had saved enough money for the coach and lodging at the other end."

"And did you?"

"Yes. But life in town was not as I imagined it. It seemed there was little work open to me other than prostitution or maid servant."

"Which did you pursue?"

"Neither. I had always wanted to act and so I took myself off to the Theatre Royal and asked them to help me."

"What happened?"

"I got a job selling fruit in the intervals." The girl laughed. "I think if I had stayed long enough I might have been allowed to set foot upon the stage. But then I met Jack and he did not approve of my being a lowly fruit seller. So he put me under his protection."

The Apothecary thought of asking the key question about her antecedents but decided to wait a while longer, not wanting to frighten her away. "Tell me more about Mr. Morocco," he said. "I find the man quite fascinating."

"Well, he was the Duchess's black boy." At that she turned to lay her hand on Ebony James's shoulder, for he was sitting close by, a necessary adjunct if her pale beauty were to be shown off to its fullest advantage. "She loved him so much that she did not send him away at puberty. Now he acts as if he were her son." Aminta indicated the apartment with a sweep of her arm. "These hothouse flowers are always here, they are not just for this evening's entertainment. As to the rest: a box at the opera, a horse and groom in Hyde Park, a coach, the best clubs, and fashionable dinners and suppers for his coterie of hangers on."

"And a beautiful white friend," John added.

Aminta smiled. "Why not say mistress? It's true enough."

"I wasn't sure about that."

The girl shook her head. "It is not something that society wishes to know."

"But what about these people?" John indicated the guests.

"They are young and are too afraid of losing Jack's generous friendship to voice anything openly. But behind his back the knives are out."

"So you do not believe you have a future together?"

"Fine company, or those that consider themselves to belong to that set, would turn their back if we were to marry. Isolation would become the order of the day and Jack is too gregarious to tolerate such a situation."

"You have been very honest with me. Do you mind if I ask you something else?" She shook her head.

The moment had come to find out the truth, John thought. "This great journey of yours to London. Was it from Devon by any chance?"

Aminta looked astonished. "Yes, it was. How did you know?"

"Mostly guesswork. Tell me, Madam, is your full name Georgiana Aminta Goward?"

She went pale as she had been at the funeral and appeared so frightened that the Apothecary instantly regretted his forwardness. "Be calm," he said. "I mean you no harm by asking that. It is simply that I am assisting Sir John Fielding in the hunt for your father's murderer and everything about Sir George's past must come out if we are to shed any light on the present."

Aminta turned away, shaking. She was such a delicate being, such an elfin creature, that John began to think himself ruthless to the point of cruelty that he had been so blunt with her.

"Please," he said, "don't be alarmed. I am truly acting as a friend."

She turned to look at him once more and he saw that the agonised vixen had returned, white as snow, her hair flaming round her colourless face.

"I can tell you now," Aminta said, her voice low and somehow menacing, "that I didn't kill him despite the fact that he treated me like filth. I literally have never met the man in my entire life, and that's the truth. I was handed to my foster parents as soon as my mother died. And then, if rumour be correct, when he remarried his new wife wanted nothing whatever to do with me. Thus I was abandoned, totally and utterly."

"So she knew of your existence? Miss Chudleigh believed that Sir George would not have informed her."

"Oh she knew all right. But she and my father were not the sort to love children. Lady Mary, fat and foolish; he the most selfish being to strut. Her son was sent away, I was kept in darkest Devon. That is how they wanted it. Mr. Rawlings ...." She looked at John in a blaze of sincerity. "... the closest I ever got to my natural father was at his funeral yesterday."

"Was it you who threw the rose?"

"Jack threw it on my instigation. Despite all George Goward had done - or rather not done - it was he who breathed life into me. The rose was the one and only respect I ever paid him."

I wonder, John thought, if it was your lover who exacted the final revenge for your neglect? And yet again the memory of the black man's grinning face as Goward lay with skull smashed at the bottom of the Grand Staircase, came back to haunt him.

The supper party was superb; everything that money could buy lavished on the guests and Jack Morocco himself proving to be the perfect host. Despite feeling somewhat older than the rest of the visitors, John enjoyed himself thoroughly, while Aminta seemed to have recovered her old spirits and laughed and danced along with everybody else.

Looking at her, considering her beauty to be almost unworldly, the Apothecary again asked himself the question as to whether a man would kill for her. Without doubt, the answer was yes. Yet would Jack Morocco risk losing all his material benefits, his wonderful lifestyle, just to be avenged for his mistress's neglected past? If he thought he could get away with it, he would, John concluded. In fact there was little he wouldn't put past the black man in the way of daring and contempt for authority. Yet, observing him, charming all who came in contact with him, it was impossible not to like him. A great desire that Jack should not be the one who must be brought to justice came over John and he did something totally foreign to his nature. He actually wished that the guilty party would be Lady Mary Goward, whom he was due to visit, in company with the Blind Beak, the very next day.

"More champagne," said a voice at his elbow, and John saw that his host had come to join him.

"Thank you."

Morocco snapped his fingers and a footman appeared instantly. "I saw you speaking to Aminta earlier. How did you get on?"

"Do you mean do I like her? If so, the answer is yes."

"Let's not mince words, John. Did she tell you her story?"

"I had guessed it anyway. The parish records showed the birth of a daughter to George Goward, a daughter who bore the name Georgiana Aminta. I worked the rest out for myself."

"You Public Office people are quite cunning, I'll give you that," said Jack, downing a glass and immediately taking another. "Checking the parish records, eh. So now you know why I didn't like Goward and have no time for that wife of his either."

"Yes." John looked his host straight in the eye. "Jack, there's something else. A rumour circulates that Lady Mary, despite her size, is a lascivious woman. It is said by the locals of Islington that she gave birth to a child out of wedlock and that that child was black. Was it you? Goward's widow your mother?"

The great dark eyes changed and the Apothecary saw in them a look that he had glimpsed once before. A look of immense sadness and knowing, as if all the terror and trials of those snatched from their native land to act as unpaid servants to white men had entered the soul of Jack Morocco.

"I ask you, John, could that woman have produced a creature like myself?"

"It does not follow that her children must be as vacuous and vacant as she."

"That's true enough, but the answer is no. If the rumour is reality, then the child is not me. I was born on board a slave ship. My mother gave birth to me in the horrors of that foetid crowded hold where people of my race were chained in order to be transported from their families and homes into servitude. The experience killed her but I lived; I lived because, by God, I was tough and determined. I was baptised in our first port of call because they all expected me to die, but I wouldn't give them the satisfaction. Some maiden sisters in Bristol brought me up but when I became too lively for them, forever involved in japes and jollys, they sold me off. You know the rest. I owe everything to the Duchess. She loves me and has given me a life of luxury and pleasure. So whoever Lady Mary's love child - a misnomer if ever there was one - might be, it is certainly not myself."

"This case is full of unexplained children," said John, musingly. "Miss Chudleigh's unwanted offspring, George Goward's daughter, Lady Mary's bastard, to say nothing of her fat son, my ex servant Lucinda, the thirteenth page boy. How do they all fit in, I wonder?"

"And how many of them are still alive?" Jack Morocco added.

"Most, it would seem."

He relapsed into silence, Sir John's words that there was a thread somewhere repeating themselves in his head. There had to be a connection but what it was remained a mystery. Yet at least the Apothecary felt he might now make some sort of progress. When he had asked the Duke of Guernsey about the thirteenth page boy there could be no doubt that the young man had lied. If he could somehow or other persuade him to tell the truth then perhaps the rest of the pieces would fall into place. But meanwhile there was something even more important to do. Tomorrow, in company with Sir John and Lady Fielding, he would see Lady Mary Goward and she would finally have to answer for herself.

# Chapter 17

Rather oddly, considering his dislike of the woman, Lady Mary Goward's London home was a mere stone's throw from Jack Morocco's private apartments. Whereas he lived in Grosvenor Square, she had a large and fashionable house in South Audley Street and no doubt they must have seen one another when strolling round town. But today, John thought, as the coach carrying himself and the Fieldings from Bow Street drew up at the graceful house in which the dead man and the fat lady had lived together, there was little chance of being seen by anyone. It was pouring hard, the sky dull and leaden, the streets awash with all the accumulated filth of days.

It seemed that the widow had left Islington the day after the funeral, preferring to do her mourning in her more accessible London residence, where she could receive sympathetic visitors, no doubt, and weep profusely over continual cups of tea. As the Apothecary stepped down from the carriage to assist Elizabeth Fielding and Sir John to disembark, he wondered just what sort of condition they were going to find Lady Mary in, and checked yet again that he had a small medical bag with him. He had also taken the precaution of putting on rather an old suit of clothes just in case he was unable to sidestep her habit of regular vomiting.

The Blind Beak himself was in a very bad mood and not prepared for any nonsense, as he had informed John during the journey.

"She'll not shilly and shally with me, by Jove she won't," he had said as they left the Public Office behind them.

"Do you still think she is the guilty party, Sir?"

The Magistrate had grunted. "I have thought so for so long that I am now beginning to doubt it. She's too obvious, if you know what I mean."

"And there were several people present who had a grudge against Goward."

"Yes. Including your friend Digby Turnbull. Wasn't he in love with Sir George's first wife?"

"At the least, very attached to her. I wonder if he knows that Aminta is Hannah Wilson's daughter."

"I should make a point of telling him then closely watch his reaction," Sir John had answered, and after that had relapsed into total silence, a sure sign that he was thinking things through.

The interior of the Goward establishment was as fine as its outside. Having climbed the stairs, beautifully curved and displaying wrought iron balustrades, most elegantly designed in the shape of a lyre, John entered a room almost self-consciously stylish. Deep red in colour, it had a marble fireplace, the mantelpiece supported by two scantily clad caryatids. Over the fire hung a very fine painting, a large chandelier throwing light onto it and also on to the figure in black, a handkerchief raised to its eyes, which reclined on a sofa, sobbing loudly.

"Great God," muttered Sir John, and tapped his way into the room and to a chair, in which he sat without invitation.

"Sir John and Lady Fielding and Mr. John Rawlings," boomed Lady Mary's footman, somewhat late in the day.

The Apothecary noticed with enormous interest that the man was in his forties and jet black, clearly a servant who had been kept on from boyhood. Was this, John wondered, the father of Lady Mary's bastard. And, if so, had Jack Morocco been lying in his teeth about his parentage?

"I can't receive you," wailed the widow pitifully. "As you can see, I am in disarray."

"I cannot see, Madam," said the Magistrate angrily. "And even if I could I should not take pity on you. The Public Office has left you entirely alone during the time of your troubles and this arrangement to speak with you has been made for some considerable time. You may plead indisposition for as long as you wish but here I sit and here I stay. Mr. Rawlings, be so good as to administer salts if you please."

The Beak was clearly furious and even his wife looked alarmed, laying a calming hand on his arm. He completely ignored this and made a gesture to John, who stood shuffling from foot to foot, to calm his patient down.

"Lady Mary," the Apothecary said placatingly.

She glared at him, her eyes piggy with weeping. "I don't want your horrible salts."

"Then do without," thundered Sir John. "But know that I shall order you into court if you refuse to cooperate."

She howled the louder but took the proffered bottle and sniffed gingerly.

"Would you like some soothing physick?" John asked.

"No, I shall do naught but bring it back."

The Apothecary groaned audibly and the Blind Beak hissed with rage. "Madam, you must take your emotions in hand. I refuse to allow this procrastination one second longer."

"But my husband has only just been laid to rest."

"Then it is time to let him lie in peace and discover who was responsible for pushing him to an untimely death."

"He wasn't pushed," said Lady Mary mulishly. "It was an accident - and that is all I have to say about it."

"If I may remind you, Madam, you stated to Mr. Rawlings at the funeral that you husband had been done to death, or words to that effect at least."

"Well, I've thought it over and changed my mind. He tripped and fell. There's an end to it."

"That is not the opinion of myself and a certain other witness. Now, tell me all that happened. Everything, from the moment you entered St. James's Palace to the time of Sir George's plunge."

Lady Mary glared at John. "You're the other witness aren't you, you wretch?" she whispered.

"No, I'm not," he whispered back. "Now get on and answer or you'll find yourself charged at Bow Street."

She looked furious but slowly started to speak. "George and I travelled to the investiture by coach. We waited in the long reception hall with everybody else. Then we climbed the stairs and went through the various apartments. Then I went to sit with the guests and George waited with the rest of the recipients."

"I believe you were taken ill on the way in," Sir John interrupted. "What happened?"

"A page-of-honour escorted me to a closet. I was vomitous."

"Again?" the Magistrate asked rudely.

She ignored him. "The page sent for water and cleaned the front of my dress."

"That was very good of him."

John spoke. "Did you by any chance notice that there were thirteen pages present that day instead of the customary twelve?"

The porcine eyes glinted in his direction then John distinctly saw Lady Mary turn away from him so that the expression in them would not be revealed. She knows, he thought.

But her lips said something different. "Of course not. How could I have done?"

"Very easily I imagine. By counting, as I did."

"Well I didn't count them." She turned to the Blind Beak. "Shall I continue?"

"Yes, of course."

"After the ceremony was over I went to go down the stairs with everybody else. Then Her Majesty..."  Lady Mary simpered. "... passed along the landing and I turned to make obeisance."

Only she could have put it like that, thought John.

"At that moment George missed his footing and fell. That is all I have to say," the widow finished.

"You saw nothing out of the ordinary? Nobody moved near you?"

"I can't even remember who was standing close."

"Then let me refresh your memory. Julius and Christabel Witherspoon, who are neighbours of yours in Islington; Jack Morocco, the Duchess of Arundel's adopted black son; and close behind, Miss Chudleigh and a servant of the King's household, Digby Turnbull."

"I didn't notice," Lady Mary repeated obstinately.

"Well, take it from me, they were there. Further, one of them saw a pair of shoes move quickly as the push was executed. A pair of shoes not unlike your own," Sir John said harshly.

Lady Mary emitted a scream loud as a trumpet. "How dare you? Are you accusing me? You shall not get away with this, Sir. I shall go to the highest in the land with my complaint against you. You shall be stripped of your office. Apologise I say."

Sir John remained amazingly calm. "Madam, I have accused you of nothing. I merely pointed out that the shoes that were seen were not unlike the ones you wear yourself. They were small and rather tight, that is all."

"Who saw this?" she asked truculently.

"That I am not at liberty to disclose."

"Because there's no such person," Lady Mary retorted. "You say these things to discomfit your victims. Anyway, I'm telling you for once and for all, George fell accidentally."

"You are entitled to believe that," Sir John answered, and suddenly looked benign, a complete change of tack. "Tell me your life story," he said, almost as if he were requesting a fairy tale.

"I beg your pardon?"

"I said tell me your life story. You were born Lady Mary Milland, were you not? Daughter of the Earl of Grimsby?"

"That is correct."

John could not help but notice that the widow's little girl voice had returned and presumed from this that she was starting to calm down.

"What happened next?"

"I married young, very young, indeed scarcely seventeen, the Earl of Lomond, an ancient Scottish peerage. I then had my son, little Frederick, but when he was only two years old, his father was killed in a hunting accident. Then I met George and we were married shortly afterwards."

"How fortunate that a widow and widower should come together like that," Sir John stated comfortably.

She shot him a look of pure surprise and the Apothecary could almost see the words of denial forming on her lips. Then Lady Mary realised that the Public Office knew far more than she had reckoned on and that to contradict would do her more harm than good. "Yes," she said shortly.

"I believe your husband had a daughter by his first wife but that you did not wish to take her into your household," the Magistrate continued.

"It was for the girl's own good," Lady Mary answered, her voice now very small. "She was being brought up by her mother's sister and was tremendously happy. She would not have enjoyed London life."

So Aminta had not lied. Lady Mary had known all along that the girl existed.

"Did you ask her?" John said caustically.

"There was no need to," the widow answered crossly. "The situation spoke for itself."

"I see. I have also heard that your son was sent to boarding school because your husband did not care for his appearance. Is that correct?"

"Of course not. He was sent to school to be educated. George was very fond of Frederick."

"Even though he teased him mercilessly about being obese?"

The little girl voice had vanished. "Who told you this?" hissed Lady Mary angrily.

"People who knew you at the time. The artist Julius Witherspoon and his sister to be precise. Mr. Rawlings has seen a portrait of you and your son that Sir George Goward refused to accept because he said you both looked too large."

Lady Mary's face worked. "How dare you, Sir? What is the point of these questions? What are you trying to prove by asking me about the past and throwing insults into the bargain?"

"By enquiring about the events leading up to a suspicious death, the reason for that death frequently becomes clear. Despite your contradiction, I believe that your husband was murdered and that somebody had a grudge against him. What I am trying to elucidate is, from the many who disliked him, which one actually gave him the fatal thrust."

"You're wasting your time. George was very popular."

Sir John ignored this, turning the black bandage which he always wore over his eyes in her direction and sitting motionless, an old and unnerving ploy.

"Thank you for telling me your story, Lady Mary. Now, is it complete in every detail? You have omitted nothing?"

"Why should I?" Her tones had altered completely and a definite note of defiance was clearly audible. The Apothecary automatically fished in his bag for something calming.

"No reason, no reason," said the Blind Beak cheerfully. He paused, then asked silkily, "You only had the one child?"

"I've already told you. Sir George and I did not have any children."

"I remember you saying that. But what I meant was, did you have another child, perhaps before Frederick was born? And maybe another, conceived while you were married but proving to be unsuitable?"

Lady Mary rose to her feet, looming like a great crow in her mourning clothes. "What are you insinuating, Sir?"

"Nothing. Again I am only repeating rumour and gossip, a necessary part of any investigation I fear. Apparently it is said in Islington that you bore a child out of wedlock when you were a very young girl. Further, that you had a child while married to Sir George Goward but that it was black."

Lady Mary lost all colour and mouthed frantically, no sound coming from her lips.

The Blind Beak continued ruthlessly. "Is this a fact, Madam? Answer me, I pray you."

The widow's face turned the shade of raw liver and she made a choking sound as she clawed the air frantically. "Frederick," she gasped, then fell in a dead faint at the Apothecary's feet.

It was more than a simple faint, of that he felt certain as he knelt at her side and felt her pulse. Lady Mary's face had contorted, her lip down on one side, her eyelid drooping as if she had palsy. Further, her arm had twisted in a peculiar way and was lying half underneath her.

"God's life!" John exclaimed forcibly. "I think she's had an apopletic fit."

"What?" called the Blind Beak, turning towards the sound. "What's happening?"

"It's Lady Mary. I believe she's had a seizure."

"You must ring for the servants," said Elizabeth, rising from her chair and hurrying to join John. She leaned forward to look into the widow's face. "She seems palsied indeed. I declare the strain has been too much for her."

"That and her own precarious state of health. With the amount of extra weight she carried it is small wonder that she has been struck down."

Elizabeth's anxious gaze met the Apothecary's. "John's questioning didn't bring this about, did it?"

"In a way. But this kind of seizure could have come upon her at any time, rest assured." He searched frantically in his bag. "I'm not carrying anything really suitable. I hadn't envisaged this sort of eventuality."

"Have you nothing that will bring her back to consciousness?" asked Lady Fielding, frantically tugging a bellrope.

"Only Black Horehound for hysterics. That and my salts. I

will do what I can but I think a physician should be sent for immediately."

"Is the woman seriously ill?" asked Sir John from his chair.

"She has certainly had a seizure, Sir."

"Did I cause it?"

"She was very unfit and the questions you asked her obviously hit home. Yet I can't believe that someone with nothing to hide would have been as upset as she."

"If I have brought her low then I have much to answer for," the Blind Beak said seriously.

"You alone could not have done it," John answered with equal gravity. "The apoplexy might have attacked at any moment. Please believe that."

The door to the salon opened and the black footman appeared. "Yes, Sir?"

"Your mistress has been taken ill. Kindly arrange for her to be carried to her room and for a doctor to be summoned at once. Meanwhile, I will treat her."

Without much hope, John administered a spoonful of the horribly bitter Black Horehound and after a moment, much to his surprise, Lady Mary choked violently, twitched and opened one eye. Then she tried to speak but with no effect. It was as he had feared; an apoplexy had left her palsied and dumb. There would be no further statements from her for some considerable while. The mystery of her children was, for the time being anyway, going to remain just that.

The journey back to Bow Street was conducted in sombre silence, Sir John Fielding obviously feeling more than guilty that Lady Mary had collapsed whilst being questioned about her past. However, his spirits were greatly restored by the sight of Julius Witherspoon who had called without an appointment on the chance of being able to make some preliminary sketches of the Blind Beak and his wife. Having decided that this would be in order, the older couple went to change into more suitable garments, leaving John alone with the painter.

"And where is your delightful sister?" the Apothecary asked, hoping that his friend Samuel was not totally out of the picture.

"She is shopping in town and is to go to the Theatre Royal later with Mr. Swann. Christabel and I are both planning to spend the night in London."

"So you will be on your own this evening?"

"Yes."

"Then do come and dine with me. My wife is in Kensington at the moment, staying with my father, so I would really appreciate your company."

"I've a better idea as you are temporarily a bachelor," Julius answered. "Let us dine at my club, the Pandemonium. They are due to meet tonight at the Blenheim Tavern in Bond Street and I had half promised to be present. I think you should come."

"I should very much enjoy that," the Apothecary answered, and leaving the little artist to start his sketches, hurried back to the shop to put in as much time as he could before the time to dine.


It seemed that the Pandemonium Club rejoiced in the most extraordinary initiation ceremony to which John, proposed as a new member by Julius Witherspoon, suddenly found himself subjected. Almost as soon as he had entered the Blenheim Tavern, Julius had suggested that he should join their ranks, a proposal met with much acclaim by several other rowdy members, one of whom, the Apothecary was astonished to learn, was Thomas Gainsborough, the celebrated painter, presently living in Bath but in London on this occasion to execute a commission.

"Well?" Julius had asked.

"Do you think I'm worthy?"

"As worthy as any of us. I'll send word through that a new member is proposed."

Julius slipped through a door leading to a room beyond, which he firmly closed behind him so that John could not see inside.

"You're for it," said Gainsborough in his Suffolk accent, and laughed heartily.

"They will admit you," Julius announced solemnly, returning and, before the Apothecary could utter another word, he had slipped a blindfold over John's eyes.

Unable to see a thing, John heard the door open and found himself being led through by the elbow, Julius on one side and the great Gainsborough on the other. There was a roar of greeting as the three appeared and judging by the sound, the Apothecary imagined himself to be in a large room occupied by an equally large number of people. Feeling his way cautiously, he discovered that he was standing at the bottom of an almost perpendicular ladder, that his guides had let go of him and that the order to mount was being shouted from every quarter. Glad that he had had nothing to drink in the way of alcohol, the Apothecary slowly climbed the steps, about dozen in all, and then was ordered to remove his blindfold.

He was standing on a platform, far too narrow for his liking, looking down at a table round which were seated the club's officials. John's eyes bulged in his head, for here were the great men of the arts, all staring up at him, completely straight-faced. Gainsborough's rival, Joshua Reynolds was there, David Garrick, whom John had met before during the fatal incident at *The Beggar's Opera*, and even the great Dr. Samuel Johnson, the most clubbable man in London according to his friends.

Reynolds, whom John recognised from a portrait he had seen of the artist, appeared to be the president, for he wore a rather extraordinary cap and gown, and had a gavel lying on the table before him. David Garrick, wearing a long black robe and a mask, which did not in the least disguise his recognisable features, had placed behind him on a perch a live owl, which he appeared to be consulting about John's suitability as a new member. As well as these two, there were twelve other dignitaries, all masked and gowned. The rather frightening effect of this solemn gathering was enhanced by the fact that a cauldron of spirits of wine stood on the table in front of them, throwing a most eerie light on all of their faces. John gulped, wondering what he had wandered into.

"Examine the candidate," boomed Joshua Reynolds.

Garrick spoke, disguising his voice but insufficiently to deceive the Apothecary. "Sir, were you present at your birth?"

So this was the way of it. Sheer absurdity, not meant to be taken seriously.

"I can't remember," John answered gravely.

"Do you hear that, Screech?" Garrick asked the owl, which winked an eye but did not reply.

"Sir," the actor asked again, "think carefully. You are out shooting and a covey of partridges takes flight. There are thirteen in it. You kill two birds with the first barrel, and one with the second. How many remain? Take care what you reply, Sir."

This was an easy one, John thought. "Why, ten remain, of course."

Garrick turned to the owl. "Hear that, Screech? Ten remain. Foolish fellow." He regarded the Apothecary once more. "Only three remained, Sir. The ten live birds flew away."

"Fine," chorused the other judges. "One bottle of claret."

So it went on. Ridiculous questions being met with equally ridiculous answers and fines of bottles of wine being imposed. Finally, though, they considered the Apothecary absurd enough and he was allowed to descend from his perilous platform and was offered membership, his subscription to be yet another bottle of claret.

This was the moment of unmasking and John watched in

amazement as various other actors, together with prominent young men about town, appeared from behind their disguises and greeted him.

"Well, well, Sir," said someone close to his ear.

The Apothecary turned to see who had spoken to him. Then his eyes widened in astonishment. Present with this raffish crowd of artist and theatricals and not appearing in the least uncomfortable in their presence was that most ordinary-looking of gentlemen, that sober and serious servant of the crown, Digby Turnbull himself.

# Chapter 18

"I never realised," said John, frankly astonished, "that you were a member of the Pandemonium, Sir."

Digby laughed. "It would sound pretentious if I told you that everyone who is anyone does belong. But the fact remains that if one is interested in the arts in their varied forms, this is the club to join."

The Apothecary looked round. "I see a good selection of rich young blades as well." A thought came. "Tell me, is the ubiquitous Jack Morocco a member?"

"Naturally. He belongs to every good club in town."

John was silent as it slowly dawned on him that the three men who had stood near George Goward on the staircase were all linked. Sir John Fielding believed that a thread connected the children in this case. Was there another thread, the thread of belonging to the same club, associating all the males?

"Was George Goward a member?" he asked.

Digby Turnbull shook his head. "Good God no. He would have considered the Pandemonium far too artistic for his tastes."

"I see. His widow was taken ill today, you know. She collapsed while being questioned by Sir John. It seemed to me that she had had an apopletic seizure."

Digby made a contemptuous noise. "I'm hardly surprised. The woman couldn't take a step out of doors without being ill. Do you remember that scene at the funeral? What was that all about?"

"She was in an hysteric because her son was ill and his school wouldn't release him to attend."

"Doesn't he board at Brompton Park?" Digby asked thoughtfully.

"Yes. Why?"

"Because I have an appointment there tomorrow. I simply demanded that Sebastian see me. His little rowdies are making trouble again."

Thinking of his shrivelling experience in the Cold Bath at the hands of the horrible Arnold, John nodded sympathetically.

"I wondered if you might like to come with me. You might get a chance to see the boy and learn his version of events."

"Sebastian will probably throw me out," the Apothecary answered.

"Let him just try," Digby stated with a fighting look in his eye.


It had been an amazing evening which John thoroughly enjoyed. However, he left relatively soon despite all the requests from his new acquaintances to stay on. For before he had parted company with Digby Turnbull they had arranged to meet early the next morning to drive to Kensington in John's coach. It seemed that, trusted employee of the crown though he might be, Turnbull had no conveyance of his own, using the carriages attached to the various palaces he visited.

They met at eight o'clock in Nassau Street and got aboard as soon as Irish Tom brought the coach round from the mews, then they clipped off at a good pace and had left the City of Westminster and were at The Swan in excellent time. There they stopped for breakfast, during which the Apothecary was unusually silent, remembering the two strange incidents that had occurred in the place: his first meeting with Lucinda Drummond, dressed as a boy, and the fight between the Duke of Guernsey and his half-brother. All part of the network of odd children, he thought.

Digby Turnbull broke in on his reflections. "D'ye know I'd like to meet that Goward boy myself. Just out of curiosity."

"He's hugely fat. I've seen a portrait of him. I believe his stepfather gave him no mercy over it, poor child." John paused, then said, "I wonder if he knows about his mother's apoplexy. I suppose somebody will have informed him."

"I doubt it. The welfare of children seems to be the last thing considered in that household. You'll probably end up doing it yourself."

"Heavens, I hope not," the Apothecary answered. "I don't even know the boy. I have no wish to be the bearer of ill tidings."

"Well, I think you should prepare yourself."

"Oh dear," said John, and cut another slice of ham to fortify himself for what might lie ahead.

It seemed that some word of Digby Turnbull's royal connections must have reached the ears of the nasty Mr. Sebastian for this time he received his visitor with cordiality and a certain amount of obsequiousness. However, at John he glared angrily, his face taking on its customary purplish tone. Digby, observing this, came in quickly.

"I insist that Mr. Rawlings be allowed to stay. He is my friend and confidant, and besides he has an urgent message for Frederick Goward, - that is, unless the child has been informed already of his mother's indisposition."

Mr. Sebastian looked genuinely puzzled. "Frederick Goward? I do not have a pupil of that name."

John came in. "He's probably called something else. He's Lady Mary Goward's son by her first husband."

"Oh," said Sebastian, ceasing to frown. "You must be referring to Lomond. Well, I'm afraid he's not here."

"Lomond?" repeated Digby, a slight edge in his voice. "Do you mean the Earl?"

"Of course I mean the Earl," the headmaster replied irritably. "His father was killed when he was just a child."

"Of course!" exclaimed the Apothecary. "I remember her telling me that she was first married to the Earl of Lomond."

Digby shook his head slowly. "I never knew that there was any connection. John, do you realise what this means?"

"No, what?"

"That the Earl was present at the investiture. He is one of the pages-of-honour that attends on state occasions."

"The thirteenth page boy!" exclaimed the Apothecary. "Great God, he was there when his stepfather died."

They turned to Sebastian with one accord. "Did you say that Lomond wasn't at school?" John asked.

The headmaster's heavily jowled face flushed to an alarming hue. "Actually, the boy's sick and can't be seen."

"Those are two contradictory answers," said Digby coldly. "I'm afraid, Sir, that as an employee of the royal household I have the right to know the whereabouts of one of its pages-of-honour. Is Lomond ill, in which case I insist on seeing him. Or is he absent?"

"The latter," said Sebastian furiously. "The little devil has left school and not informed me of his whereabouts."

"How long ago was this?"

"A few days."

"Is that why he didn't attend his stepfather's funeral?"

"Yes."

"But you told his mother he was unwell."

"He often is; a terrible sickly boy is Lomond. So it was only half a lie. It was just that I had hoped to retrieve the wretch before the burial and by the time it happened it was too late to change my story."

"This school seems to specialise in runaways," John remarked with sarcasm.

"What do you mean, Sir?" the headmaster asked nastily.

"Well, first Lucinda Drummond, whom you insist upon calling Lucas. Then her brother Fred. Now, the Earl of Lomond. What kind of a record is that?"

"Are you trying to be amusing, Sir?" snarled Sebastian.

"Of course not."

"Then you clearly do not know the facts."

"What facts?"

"Fred Drummond and the Earl of Lomond are one and the

same person. Drummond is the family name of the Earls of that title."

John leapt to his feet. "God's holy life, but I've been so blind. The thread between the children is beginning to make sense at last."

Digby looked at him in amazement. "What are you saying?"

"I am saying that I must get back to London and see Aminta Wilson."

"Why?"

"Because, my dear friend, she is the Beauty of Exeter's daughter, and she is also stepsister to both those unfortunates born to Lady Mary Goward."

The honest citizen looked positively shocked. "Aminta is Hannah's child?"

"She most certainly is. And it is quite likely that at this very moment she is sheltering both Lucinda and Frederick, protected, of course, by that man of fashion, Jack Morocco himself."

"But why him?"

"Because he could well be Frederick's half-brother."

"I think," said Digby Turnbull, rising to his feet and bowing to the headmaster, "that I need a very large brandy." And he made a hasty exit.


As is the way of the world, Jack Morocco could not be found anywhere. Having hurled himself back to London, still without seeing his wife or his father, John found that the trail had gone cold. The Negro was not at the Duchess's house, though the servants there parted with the information with the utmost reluctance. Nor was he at his own apartments, the Apothecary learned.

"The Master has gone to the country, Sir," the head footman announced.

"Whereabouts, do you know?"

"I have no idea, Sir. He didn't say. He could be anywhere. He has friends in all counties."

"Miss Wilson, has she gone too?"

"She is with him. They could even be visiting Devon. She comes from that part of the world."

It was hopeless. Tired and disgruntled, John climbed back into his coach and ordered a weary Irish Tom and an even wearier set of horses, to return to the village of Kensington where, he announced, he planned to spend the next day or two.

All the way there the Apothecary kept puzzling through everything he had learned. If Jack Morocco were Lady Mary Goward's son, then the picture was complete. She would have had Lucinda out of wedlock, Frederick by her first husband, and Jack by a black servant. Yet the Negro's story of having been born on a slave ship had been convincing indeed. With his head pounding in concentration, John Rawlings stared out into the darkness.


"Do you mean to say," asked Emilia, "that my servant Lucinda, who had poor Nick making sheep's eyes at her, is Lady Mary Goward's bastard daughter?"

"Not only that. She is half-sister to the Earl of Lomond, that fat little fellow whose portrait I told you about. Strangely, I don't remember seeing him at the investiture though Digby Turnbull assures me he must have been there."

"It was very crowded. One fat boy might well vanish amongst that throng."

"You're quite right. Oh, I have missed your good sense," said John, and cuddled his wife close. "You're getting rounder," he told her.

"I know; fatter and fatter. I'll end up like that poor Lomond soon."

"Never. His obesity was a disease. No wonder Lucinda was sent to look after him. He must have had difficulty in getting around."

"So how are you going to find them?" Emilia asked.

"I have no idea. My intuition that they might have gone to Aminta could be completely wrong."

"Would they have known about her? I mean, why should they?"

The Apothecary spread his hands. "Again, I don't know."

"You said that that young Duke of Guernsey lied about the thirteenth page boy. So he must be aware of something. Why don't you ask him where they are?"

"It's worth a try, I suppose."

"Indeed. But not," said Emilia firmly, "until you've had one day off to clear your head."


That day, being a Sunday, the entire family with servants set off to attend divine service in Kensington Church, walking the short distance in an orderly fashion. John, feeling staid, escorted Emilia, while Sir Gabriel, leaning upon his great stick, walked ahead, raising his hat and bowing to various acquaintances on the way.

One day I will be like this, thought the Apothecary, and rather shied away from the idea of having to settle down to total domesticity.

The church was packed with ordinary folk, while in the boxed pews near the front sat those of rank and fortune. Miss Chudleigh, somewhat flushed, John observed, made a grand entrance, depositing a small yapping dog into the arms of a servant, who took it outside where it continued to make a din. But it was not to the members of the nobility that John's eyes were drawn but to a figure at the back, lustily singing and taking part with vigour. Hardly able to control his face, John saw that Joe Jago, having presumably spent the night with Miss Chudleigh, had joined the commoners and was attending service at a respectful distance. The Apothecary could not resist it. Turning round quite deliberately he caught Joe's eye and gave a gracious bow of his head, then winked meaningfully.

Sir John Fielding's clerk, very red in the cheeks, made a brief bow back and returned his eyes to his hymn book.

Emilia looked up enquiringly. "What is it?" she whispered.

"Nothing at all," answered her husband. "Only the happy feeling that all's well in some people's world."

And with that he gave his full concentration to the service, though a smile still lingered about his lips.

# Chapter 19

There had once stood in the pretty village of Marybone a fine manor house with beautiful and spacious gardens. These gardens, however, had become detached from the dwelling in 1650, and had been converted into bowling greens and further rural walks attached to The Rose Tavern, sometimes called The Rose of Normandy because of its Huguenot associations.

Nearly one hundred years later, in 1738, the then proprietor of The Rose, Daniel Gough, advertised and opened Marybone Gardens as a place of evening entertainment. From then on he enlarged and improved the premises so that when the Gardens were taken over by John Trusler in 1751, they included a substantial garden-orchestra containing an organ, and a Great Room for balls and suppers.

John Trusler, being a cook by profession, decided to improve the food on offer, and rich seed and plum cakes and almond cheesecakes, all made by his daughter, became a speciality of Marybone. Further, the Gardens opened daily for public breakfasting in the Great Room, followed by a concert which began at noon. And it was to this breakfast, on the Monday following his visit to Kensington Church, that John Rawlings escorted Emilia and Sir Gabriel, both of whom had declared a longing to leave Kensington and mingle with the *beau monde*.

They had all returned to Nassau Street late on Sunday night, John's father walking round the house with a quiet reflective air, as if he were remembering the past when he had lived there with his wife and adopted son. The Apothecary, sensing something of this, insisted that a fire was lit in the library and that he and Sir Gabriel sat there and talked before they went to bed, as they had always done in the past.

"And so what steps will you take next?" his father asked when John had told him everything that had recently occurred.

"First of all I must find Lucinda and Lord Lomond. At the very least they have to be told that their mother is ill."

"So it was Lady Mary that Lucinda was protecting all the time."

"Yes, though I truly don't think she deserved any loyalty whatsoever."

"Tell me again about the black child that Milady is supposed to have had."

"The rumour is that she became pregnant while married to Sir George, tried to pass the child off as his, but that when it was born it was the wrong colour, so her plan was foiled."

"And she didn't keep it?"

"Certainly not. It was probably given away, or even sold. It occurred to me that it might just be Jack Morocco."

"But how could that be? Surely he is far too old."

The Apothecary had stared at his father, wondering how he could have been so obtuse as to not see this for himself. If Frederick was twelve, then the black child must be no more than ten. The dark dandy's connection with the Gowards had to be through his relationship with Aminta alone.

"Did everybody hate George Goward?" Sir Gabriel had asked, picking up John's train of thought.

"Yes. Elizabeth Chudleigh thought he might blackmail her because it is said that she is still married though she pretends to be single. Julius and Christabel Witherspoon detested him for impregnating then deserting their older sister. Aminta Wilson must have felt betrayed, knowing that he was her father but had never even bothered to see her. Jack Morocco, who loves her as far as he is capable of that emotion, disliked the man for that very reason. Digby Turnbull loved Aminta's mother and could well be seeking to avenge her."

"Which one pushed him?"

"If only I knew."

"Was it Lady Mary herself?"

"Very possibly." John had shaken his head ruefully. "But if her power of speech does not return then we will never find that out."

"It seems to me," Sir Gabriel had said thoughtfully, "that you most probably will not solve this mystery at all."

"I agree," John had answered, and with this sobering thought they had retired for the night.

But now it was morning and everyone was more cheerful, particularly as a good table in the Great Room had been secured and the delicious smell of Miss Trusler's baking was being carried on the air to awaken the appetite.

Having ascertained the whereabouts of the Duke of Guernsey's estate, the Apothecary had decided to breakfast with his family then leave them to enjoy the concert while he went to call.

"Supposing he is not there?" Emilia asked, sipping chocolate.

"Then I shall leave a card and return on another occasion. Anyway, you two are perfectly happy here for a few hours?"

"I could spend all day in the Gardens," Emilia answered.

"And I," added Sir Gabriel gallantly, waving to an acquaintance he had just noticed at another table. "It will be most pleasant to catch up with old friends."

"And make some new ones," his daughter-in-law added saucily, smiling at a handsome gentleman.

But the Apothecary was too busy eating a huge breakfast to rise to this and merely winked his eye at her.

An hour later he was back in the coach and heading away from the Gardens towards Love Lane, which cut across the fields in an easterly direction. Fronting on to this lane, separated from one another by the open spaces of Marybone Park, were three inns, The Queen's Head and Artichoke, The Jew's Harp House and The Yorkshire Stingo. The Queen's Head was very old, reputedly once being the house of a gardener to Queen Elizabeth. Though humble, it none the less had a garden for skittles and bumble-puppy, and served cream teas in shady bowers. The Jew's Harp was also very modest, though here the attractions were bowery tea gardens and skittle grounds. The third was a little more ambitious for already extensive tea gardens were being laid out and there was a bowling green attached. But it was to none of these idyllic rural retreats that John made his way, though he felt fairly certain that Irish Tom would be weighing up the possibilities of each as he passed. Instead he turned left at The Jew's Harp House and continued on to where an imposing pair of gates, a crest in ironwork atop, led onto an elm drive. Here he waited while the lodge keeper swung the gates open, then the coach passed through into the parkland beyond.

The first Duke of Guernsey had been a bastard of Charles II by one of his many mistresses and it was he, so John believed, who had started to build Fishergate Park. Other, later, dukes had added their own touches so that now a truly magnificent pile rose to greet the eye as Irish Tom eased the horses round a bend in the drive and the house came into view. Protected by a great archway, an equestrian statue dominating its highest point, two exquisite wrought iron gates shutting the house off from the world, Fishergate Park stood square, three massive blocks joined together by two smaller. On the roof of the central block stood an Italianate tower, a vast arched doorway at its centre.

"He's very young to own all this," remarked Tom from the box as the second pair of gates were swung open to give them admittance.

"I just hope he's at home."

"Wouldn't they know that at the lodge, Sir?"

"Not necessarily. Just look at the size of the place. There's another drive leading from the back, crossing over that marvellous bridge. He could have gone out that way and no one would be any the wiser."

"A secure and secret spot to hide in."

"It certainly would be," said John, and was seized by that customary frisson which told him something was afoot.

Gaining admittance to the house was more difficult than it had been to get into the grounds. After a great deal of tugging at bell chains and thunderous knocking, the vast door in the central block was opened by two footmen who took John's card, then closed the door again.

"I reckon the little bastard who owns this could do with a good hiding," said Irish Tom loudly. "Who does he think he is, giving himself all these airs and graces?"

"He's a descendant of Charles II and he's alright really. It's his half-brother who's a true tripehound."

"I've a mind to sort him out and all," Tom stated, clearly rattled by the fact that his master had been kept waiting.

"He's only a boy so it would be an unequal contest. Mind you, I did nearly drown him recently. A very satisfying experience."

With a great deal of squeaking the front door opened again and John was ushered into a Great Hall of immense proportions, so immense that it rose into the tower under which it had been built. A huge fireplace with not only a painting but also a full-sized statue above, dominated one end of the hall, the other was taken up by arched glass doors leading out into the grounds. Standing by the fireplace, warming himself and looking totally unconcerned that he should be meeting someone from the Public Office, was the youthful Duke himself.

"Oh, it's you," he said as John made a formal bow. "I was expecting one of those Beak Runners. Do you work for Sir John Fielding then?"

"Occasionally I do. I am helping with this case because I was present at the investiture when the fatality took place."

"Is it true George Goward was pushed?"

"Yes, we now have another witness who saw something."

"Really? I've already told you that I didn't. But I forget

myself. Come up to the Double Cube Room. It was built nearly a hundred years ago and is full of surprises."

"Such as?"

"Well it was planned as a Double Cube Room - sixty by thirty by thirty - but still it is somewhat out of kilter. The windows aren't symmetrical; the fireplace isn't completely opposite the centre of the painted ceiling. It's mysterious - and fascinating, because nobody can explain it."

The Duke mounted a staircase leading from the Great Hall and John, following him, thought how mature the young man suddenly seemed, how capable of handling any situation, how sure of himself.

"Did you know George Goward at all?" he asked.

Guernsey turned his head and frowned. "No, the investiture was the first occasion on which I'd set eyes on him."

"I see. Apparently his stepson was at school with your brother. I just wondered if you might have come across him there."

"I can't say that I did. No."

"Ah. Well, by the most extraordinary chance, it now seems that this same stepson is the boy who has run away. The one I told you about who had a sister at the school, disguised as a male."

The Duke did not reply, striding along the corridor at the top of the stairs, then throwing open a pair of double doors and ushering his visitor into the room that lay beyond. Overwhelmed by its magnificence, John looked around him.

A beautifully painted ceiling edged by glorious gilt surrounds drew the eye upwards at once, but as it lowered again intricately carved doorways, huge windows, family portraits in gilt frames, two full sized gold figures over the fireplace, framing a picture of the Duke and his half-siblings, all came into view.

"Glorious," said John.

"It's my favourite place," Guernsey answered casually. "Now take a seat, do. Tea will be brought." He waited for his guest to find a chair, then sat down opposite, crossing one fine young leg over the other. "So, Sir, tell me how I can help you further."

"It's about the pages-of-honour," said John.

As they had on the previous occasion, the light blue eyes clouded. "What about them? I have told you everything I know."

"Your Grace, with respect, I do not think that you have."

"Are you calling me a liar, Sir?"

The Apothecary remained calm. "How could I be so churlish? It is simply that, beyond a shadow of doubt, there were thirteen boys present that day. I personally saw one of them run down the long reception room after George Goward fell. At the time I thought he was hurrying to get help. Now I believe that he was getting away as quickly as he could before he was noticed. Your Grace, I am not accusing this boy of being a murderer; the fact that he was there is probably a mere coincidence. But I do need to know why he was present and who he was. Please help me."

There was a long silence during which the Duke got to his feet, walked to the window and stared out over the park. Eventually he spoke with his back turned.

"It would be dishonourable of me to dissemble. There was another boy present. I saw him too. But he had nothing to do with the murder."

"How do you know that?"

Guernsey continued to stare out. "I just do. You will have to take my word for it."

John raised his mobile brows. "So you know who it was?"

"Yes."

"And why he was there?"

"That too."

"Are you going to tell me?"

The Duke turned on his heel and gave John the most powerful stare. "No, Sir, I am not. I have given my word as a gentleman to keep silent, so silent I will keep."

"You could well be impeding the course of justice."

"Then justice be damned. The boy had nothing to do with the death of George Goward. It is another matter entirely that caused him to be present at the investiture. Now let us drop the subject and take tea like civilised folk. You'll get nothing further out of me so I advise you not to try."

For one so young he commanded a great deal of authority and John knew quite certainly that to persist would do more harm than good. With as good a grace as he could muster he made polite conversation over the tea cups, though all the time his mind was racing as to how he could discover the identity of the thirteenth boy. For with him lay the key, he felt it instinctively. The page had seen something, John was certain, for why else should he run away like that? An idea came.

"Was your brother at the investiture, Lord Guernsey?"

"Arnold? Perish the thought. Why do you ask?"

"I saw him the other day, at the Cold Bath in Kensington." John omitted to say that the little beast had removed the Apothecary's drawers underwater.

"How unpleasant for you."

"You don't like him, do you?"

"I can't stand the fellow, particularly after his latest exploit."

"Which was?"

The Duke coloured and momentarily lost his composure. "It was a family matter. One that I do not care to discuss."

"I'm sorry, I did not mean to intrude."

"No, of course not." The young man cleared his throat. "Well, Mr. Rawlings, can I be of any further assistance?"

This was his cue to depart and John took it. "No, your Grace, you have been most kind. However, if you should reconsider and decide to tell me who was the unidentified page-of-honour, I can assure you that you will be assisting Sir John Fielding greatly. Now I must take my leave. I ordered my coachman to return in an hour. He should be here by now."

Irish Tom may have many faults, a penchant for drinking and singing being two of them, but unpunctual he was not. The coach was drawn up outside, John's strong dark horses standing quietly, obviously having enjoyed their break as much as their driver.

"I've a mind, Sir," said Tom, as he helped the Apothecary in and pulled up the step behind him, "to go out the other way, just for the pleasure of driving over that bridge. Would you have any objection to that?"

"As long as it doesn't take us too far out of our way, no."

They swept round the house, staring at the beautiful south front, its gracious lines displaying only two towers, one on each corner. On the first floor of each tower were stone balconies, one beneath each major window, and a slight movement on one of these galleries caught the Apothecary's eye. A boy sat there, or rather lay, on a chaise, scarcely visible behind the sheltering balustrade. But at the sound of the coach he raised himself and, very briefly, peered over to see the carriage below.

It was a haunting face, even at that distance. A face dominated by enormous eyes that gazed sadly downwards, a face so thin that the skin seemed stretched to breaking point over the prominent bones. Then the boy lowered himself out of sight.

"Did you see that?" John called to Irish Tom.

"I did, Sir. Made me think of a changeling. We have lots of those in Ireland."

"Do you now?" John answered, and laughed. But inside his head the picture of the boy lingered, and the more the Apothecary thought about it the more certain he became that somewhere or other, and not so long ago at that, he had quite definitely seen the child before.

# Chapter 20

It was quite extraordinary. It was almost as if John were acting under compulsion. Ever since he had left Fishergate Place strange thoughts had flown through his mind, thoughts that he couldn't properly identify, memories that he couldn't quite grasp. Overriding all these, however, had been the fixed idea that he must visit Lady Mary Goward once more. That somehow, exerting all his powers as a healer, he must help her to speak, impress on her the need to tell him everything about her past.

Yet even while these notions overwhelmed him, the professional part of his brain, the part that controlled the apothecary who had studied diligently and for so long to gain knowledge, knew that such ideas were sheer folly, that it was highly unlikely that the widow would ever fully regain her powers after her apoplectic seizure. But still the mood was upon him, to the extent that he instructed Tom to collect Emilia and Sir Gabriel from Marybone Gardens while he picked up a hackney coach and returned to London alone, telling the driver to head towards Hyde Park and that more specific directions would be given later.

All the while he drove, John continued to mull over the situation, picturing the people involved in the mystery, certain that the answer now lay close at hand, could he but grasp the thread. Sir John had believed the children in the case held the key: Lucinda, Frederick Drummond, also called Lord Lomond, Aminta, Elizabeth Chudleigh's dead baby, and the missing black boy, if there were such a creature. But how to fit them into the puzzle and then see the final solution? And what of the Witherspoon twins? Had their sister really miscarried George Goward's child, or had the child lived and was even now lying concealed somewhere, ready to be used by its aunt and uncle as a tool for vengeance against Lady Mary?

It was as he was thinking these things, staring out of the window, gazing but not really seeing, that John suddenly came to his senses at the sudden appearance of one of the very people he had been considering. Aminta Goward, or Wilson as she preferred to be known, was walking down the street, Ebony James a few paces before her, clearing the way for his mistress. Today she was dressed and presented even more unconventionally than usual, her glorious red hair hanging straight, a simple hat topped by a bow on her head, her gown totally without hoops, blue and white, utterly artless, utterly stunning.

John couldn't help himself. He lowered the window and called out, "Miss Wilson, over here."

She looked startled, then recognised the man leaning out of the coach and dropped a demure curtsey. Acting utterly on impulse, John ordered the hackney driver to stop, then jumped out, paid him off, and joined her.

He bowed low. "May I say how delightful you look?"

Her eyes twinkled. "You may say it by all means."

"And where is Jack Morocco today?"

"He is actually working - he does occasionally, you know - giving a fencing lesson to some privileged puppy."

"You sound as if you don't approve."

"Of Jack working or the recipient of the lesson?"

"Both perhaps."

"As I told you, Jack Morocco is a free spirit and will do as he pleases when he pleases. As for the puppy, no I don't approve of those brought up with too much money and not enough hardship."

"You suffered as a child." It was a statement not a question.

"Of course, but I don't regret it. It made me so much stronger, I am more than aware of that."

"Still you must blame your father and stepmother for not wanting to take you in and bring you up."

"They are not worth the blaming," said Aminta factually.

"They are - were - far too stupid even to consider. I'm on my way to see her now," she added surprisingly.

"You mean Lady Mary?"

"Who else?"

"Then may I accompany you?"

"Of course, though first I must get flowers." She took some money from her purse. "Ebony, go and buy blooms. Don't be long and hurry back. Mr. Rawlings and I will make our way to South Audley Street."

"Yes, Ma'am," the black boy answered in a voice that made John smile. The child's original negro tones were fast disappearing beneath an accent extremely like Jack Morocco's own.

When the child had gone, John said, "I am surprised that you are calling on Lady Mary. I didn't realise you were on those terms with her."

"I am not," Aminta answered simply, "but I heard that she had been struck down and I was moved to call out of pity. I doubt she will even know who I am."

"I wonder. Will you tell her you are her late husband's daughter?"

"I might. I shall have to wait and see her condition."

"Let us hope that it has improved."

But long faces answered the door of the gracious house where Lady Mary resided when in London and, seeing them, John doubted that he and Aminta would even be given permission to enter. However, there he was to be surprised. It appeared that the sick woman's physician was forward-thinking and believed in as much stimulation as possible for those who had suffered from apoplexy - or so they were informed by a fierce looking woman who announced herself as Lady Mary's helper.

"Then we may go up?"

"Just for ten minutes. Milady is washed and ready."

And obviously bed-ridden, thought the Apothecary.

The room in which the sick woman lay was stifling, full of

the stench of decay. Casting his mind back to when he had first seen her, fat and frothy, her little-girl voice piping, her stays too tight, John was horrified by the change in Lady Mary Goward. Now she lay like a great marshmallow, pale and terrible, her face distorted, her mouth on the twist, and yet the expression in her eyes sent a shiver through him. He felt certain from the very way she looked at him, that she knew absolutely everything that was going on.

"Two visitors, Milady," said the helper loudly, as if the sufferer's hearing had also been affected.

John bowed out of sheer force of habit and Miss Wilson gave a bob of the knees. Lady Mary just stared, that same frighteningly knowing stare.

Aminta had obviously judged the situation rapidly and found the poor wretch too feeble to be told the truth about who Aminta really was. So, "I am a neighbour," she said instead. "I have brought you some flowers to cheer you. My boy will be here with them in a moment."

There was no response, just total silence and the same unflickering gaze.

"I hope you remember me, Madam," John said cheerfully, feeling utterly craven for even smiling in the presence of such affliction.

The dreadful eyes regarded him without blinking. She hates me, thought the Apothecary. She associates me with Sir John Fielding and she believes that he caused her downfall.

"Nice to have visitors," said the helper, still bellowing. "Shall we try and say something?"

The eyes moved sideways but there was no other response.

There was a sound in the hallway and Ebony James's voice rang out. "My Mistress is with Milady. These are her flowers."

"May he bring them up?" Aminta asked the helper.

"Certainly. Nice to have blooms, isn't it," she yelled into Lady Mary's ear.

Small feet pounded up the staircase and a second later the door opened and the black boy stood there, his little face grinning broadly beneath his stylish turban, his arms full of flowers.

"I'm here, Mistress," he said.

The figure in the bed heaved like a whale as Lady Mary jerked upright. John, amazed that she could have managed even that, stared at her and saw her face contort into that of a gargoyle, then heard a ghastly screeching scream come from the distorted mouth.

"No," cried the agonised woman, and sat totally straight for a moment before she fell back on her pillows, motionless.

The Apothecary ran to her side and felt for her pulse. There was none.

"Clear the room," he said to the helper. "I think Lady Mary is dead."


The fastest running servant in the house had been sent flying for a physician but even though the doctor came almost immediately, nothing could have saved her. She was dead when she hit the bed. The moment that Aminta and Ebony James had been hurried away, the Apothecary had buried his head in that billowing bosom and listened for the sound of Mary Goward's heart. There had been nothing but silence. He had looked up at the helper and shaken his head.

"She's gone?"

"I'm afraid so."

"But why?"

"A massive heart seizure, I imagine."

"But what could have caused that so suddenly?"

Again John had shaken his head but inwardly he thought he knew. Had it been the sight of a black boy of about ten years old that had frightened her, quite literally, to death? Had she thought that at long last her past had caught up with her and the day of reckoning had come?

He had stayed with the body until the physician had arrived. Had reported all that he had seen, and the measures he had used to ascertain death, then taken his leave. Now, as he descended the stairs he saw that Aminta and Ebony James awaited him in the hall, the child sobbing uncontrollably in his mistress's arms. The boy turned a large glistening eye in John's direction as he heard the Apothecary approach.

"Oh Masser, did I kill her?" His aristocratic accent had vanished again.

"Of course you didn't. She was very ill and could have gone at any time."

"But she looked at me, Masser. Oh, how she did look at me."

"What do you mean?"

"As if she knew me. But I ain't never seen her before, so how could she?"

Aminta spoke, quite firmly. "Ebony, you are to forget this whole matter and cease to upset yourself. You imagined that Lady Mary was staring at you. She had had a seizure and it had made her eyes strange. Now come along. We are going home."

"I will escort you," said John. "And then I shall make my way to Bow Street. Sir John Fielding must be informed of this latest extraordinary development."

"Tell me," asked Aminta as they stepped out into the street, "do you ever see your wife?"

"Of course I do. I was with her only this morning."

"And before then?"

"A few days ago."

She clicked her tongue against her teeth and smiled captivatingly. "You don't keep a mistress as well, do you?"

"Of course not. What a preposterous suggestion."

"Well, you would hardly have the time I suppose," she answered, and laughed so wickedly that John found himself joining in.

The court at Bow Street was just rising at the end of the day's session and John, approaching on foot, found himself swept along in the melee as those members of the *beau monde* who made it their amusement to while away an hour or two watching a blind man administer justice, poured into the street. Somewhat to his astonishment, the Apothecary noticed a familiar figure amongst them. Digby Turnbull had been in court that day. John called his name and the honest citizen turned his head.

"My dear Sir," said Digby, bowing politely, "how are you? Have you tracked down the missing Lord Lomond yet?"

The Apothecary grimaced. "Absolutely not. He and Lucinda seem to have vanished off the face of the earth. However, there has been an amazing development. Their mother is dead." And he recounted in detail the events of that afternoon.

"I can barely credit this. And you say Hannah's daughter Aminta was in the room?"

"Yes."

"Was she very upset?"

"Not at all. Obviously it was a shock but she did not grieve."

"Quite rightly, considering the way the Gowards treated her." A slow cruel smile crossed Digby's features and John realised that the man was capable of looking thoroughly evil. "So they are both gone. Hannah is avenged indeed."

He loved Aminta's mother very much, John thought. There could be no doubt of that. Only one strong emotion could provoke another of such ferocity.

Perhaps realising that he had gone too far, Turnbull's face rapidly restored to its usual blandness. "Well, I must be on my way."

"One last thing, Sir, before you go. Did you see Lord Lomond at the investiture? Personally I can't remember remarking him."

Digby grinned sheepishly. "To be quite honest with you,

Mr. Rawlings, I do not know one page-of-honour from another. The boys change, grow too old or too tall for the job, and I can never keep account of them. The only one I recognise is the Duke of Guernsey because he is the oldest and tallest and this will be his final year."

"I see. A pity. Lomond's enormous by the way, if that helps stir your memory."

"Yes, you've already told me that. But many of them are very roly-poly. Eat too much, the little devils. Ah well, sorry I can't be of assistance."

Was he telling the truth or was he covering for some reason, John wondered, and sighed as he walked into the house in Bow Street where Sir John Fielding dwelled with his family.

The Blind Beak, having just left court, was in the process of removing his formal coat and slipping into a larger, easier garment in which he could relax. He turned as John was shown into the salon by a servant.

"You have a visitor, Sir John."

The Apothecary bowed but remained motionless, wondering if the Magistrate would do his usual trick and, sure enough, after a moment or two of sniffing the atmosphere, the Blind Beak said, "Mr. Rawlings, I believe."

"That never fails to astonish me," John answered.

"It is really very simple as I have often explained. Now, Sir, take a seat. I believe you are weary. Let us have a restoring drink together."

"How did you know that? That I was tired?"

"Your voice gave it away. It lacks its usual sparkle."

"It is hardly surprising. A woman died in my presence today."

"One of your patients?"

"No, Sir, " John answered quietly. "It was Lady Mary Goward."

The Blind Beak became very still. "Is this death to be laid at my door? Did I kill her, Mr. Rawlings?"

"No, Sir, you did not. Be assured, though your questioning was hard it would not have affected anyone in a normal state of health. If Lady Mary had been fit she would have come through the interview unscathed."

The Blind Beak nodded. "I think you had better tell me everything that has happened."

"I will be delighted to do so. But before I launch into my tale may I ask you one question?"

"Certainly."

"The whispered words uttered just before George Goward was pushed. You thought they were 'What price greatness now.' Miss Witherspoon believed the key word to be 'slackness'. Can you not recall exactly what it was?"

Sir John hesitated. "It is not a question of recollection," he said slowly. "Merely that the voice dropped so low that I could no longer hear it."

"Then may I urge you once again to say whether it was the voice of a man or a woman."

The Blind Beak shook his head. "It was fluting and high, obviously disguised. Its tones were unearthly. In fact, it sounded neither male nor female."

"Oh 'Zounds," said John, and put his head in his hands, wondering exactly where this puzzle was finally going to lead him.

# Chapter 21

"I do wish, John," said Emilia, quite crossly, "that you would stop pacing about and get into bed. Has the death of Lady Mary Goward so upset you that you can't settle down to sleep?"

"It's not that," he answered. "Of course, for anyone to die in such a manner is not pleasant, but the woman herself had led a feckless life, with little concern for her offspring, so it is hardly a great loss to society."

"Then what is it that is concerning you so deeply?"

He frowned. "It's the fact that there's something I should be remembering, something that's right under my nose and yet I cannot grasp it."

"Do you mean that you know who pushed George Goward?"

"No, it's not that. It's to do with the thirteenth page boy."

"You have discovered his identity?"

"I am on the brink of it. I should have realised it by now. It's so close. Oh 'Zounds, I sometimes think that my mind is going."

Emilia laughed. "We all feel that from time to time. Come on, sweetheart, get some rest. Maybe the answer will come to you during the night."

He smiled at her. "You're so lovely. However, did I manage without you?"

"Very well, I imagine. Drawing comfort from the beautiful Coralie Clive."

"That is not kind."

"No, it wasn't very. But, annoyingly, I hear your former mistress continues to go from triumph to triumph since her sister Kitty retired."

"Then she will be achieving her life's ambition. Now don't lets talk about her any more. What's past is past."

"Yes it is." Emilia patted the bed beside her. "And at present I am missing you, so please get in."

He did so, suddenly exhausted, his entire body aching with weariness. But the second he closed his eyes he relived the dreadful moment when Lady Mary had sat bolt upright, screamed, and died. How altered she had been by her apoplexy, he thought. In the portrait painted of her by Julius Witherspoon, plump and vapid though she had looked, there had been a certain freshness and appeal about the woman. But the distorted creature lying in the bed had been transformed out of all recognition by illness.

"So changed," he muttered.

"What?" said Emilia sleepily.

"I said how changed people are by illness."

"Of course they are," she answered, almost unconscious.

"Yes," said the Apothecary in a sibilant whisper. Then he clapped his hand to his head. "That's it," he shouted. "That is it. Changed out of all recognition. Why didn't I see it before?"

"Oh, do be quiet," murmured Emilia, unable to know that in the darkness her husband was at long last smiling.


He rose at five, even before his apprentice, and walked round to the mews to wake Irish Tom, who had a room above the stables. The coachman, who had clearly had a bit of a thick night after he had brought John home, was forced to put his head into a bucket of cold water to revive himself, but finally he came to and set about getting the horses ready.

"Where are we going, Sorrh?" His accent was always very Irish when he was under pressure.

"First to Islington to see the Witherspoons, then on to Marybone."

"That is one hell of a long drive, Sorrh."

"I know, that's why we're starting early. Can you pick your way through, Tom?"

"Leave it to me, Mr. Rawlings."

"Good, then call for me at the house in ten minutes. I just want to go back and leave a message for my wife."

"I'll be there, never fear."

And Irish Tom saluted, something of the Apothecary's excitement rubbing off on him and making him suddenly cheerful.

They left exactly eleven minutes later, John pausing momentarily to put on his greatcoat for the morning was sharp with autumn cold. Tom, now wide awake and raring to go, set off at a fast trot towards Greek Street then picked his way through various lanes and alleys until he emerged in High Holbourn. From there it was a straight run down to Holbourn itself, where the equipage turned left into Hatton Garden. Now the coach headed east, passing through Clerkenwell Green and eventually joining St. John Street. Here they turned north once more, heading straight for Islington.

Even though it was still early, coaches were waiting at The Angel so that they might cross the fields in convoy and frighten off lurking highwaymen. John took this opportunity of consuming a warming brandy before he climbed into his carriage once more and headed towards the home occupied by the Witherspoon twins, his mind racing at the prospect of his theory proving correct.

Julius was at home alone, Christabel having left the house early in order to go into London for shopping.

"My dear fellow," said the painter, much surprised at the sight of the Apothecary standing on his front doorstep. "To what do we owe the honour of your visit?"

"To rather an odd request, I fear."

"Which is?"

"That I might look at the portrait of Lady Mary Goward and Frederick once more."

Julius lowered his voice. "Is it true she has died? Rumours are flying."

"Yes, it's perfectly true. I was present. It was terrible."

"The mills of God, eh?"

"What do you mean?"

"Well, if she pushed the wretched George then it's divine retribution."

"But I don't think she did," John answered, but refused to be drawn further.

The portrait was in its customary position, stacked behind a pile of others, all placed on the floor and leaning against a wall. Holding the stack while Julius heaved the picture out, John felt excitement mount within him as the artist placed it on an easel and stood back to examine it.

"It's a good likeness of her, in fact a brilliant one. But what about the boy?" the Apothecary asked.

"Poor fat Fred? Yes, I'd say it was the image of the child."

"When was it painted?"

"About four years ago."

"Making him eight."

Julius nodded. "Yes, I suppose so. He had just started at boarding school and was home for the holidays. I can distinctly remember that because it was the last time Fred was allowed back."

"What do you mean?"

"The hideous Goward announced that while his stepson remained so fat he couldn't bear to set eyes on him. Said the child made him feel physically sick. He announced that the boy was barred from the house until his looks improved."

"Bastard."

"Whoever killed that man did the world a good turn."

John nodded. "I suppose the mother did nothing to help?"

"As usual. What a fate to be born to her."

"Well, she's paid the ultimate price now and they're free of her. By the way, do you remember telling me about the black baby that she was supposed to have had?"

"Yes."

"Well," said John, "it was the sight of a black boy, about

ten years of age, that finally did for Lady Mary. She took such fright that she had a heart attack."

"So perhaps the gossip is true."

"I rather feel that it is."

Julius turned back to the portrait. "Have you seen enough? Can I take it down?"

"One minute more," John answered, and coming close to the canvas, raised his quizzing glass, peering intently at the two painted faces. Then he nodded his head. "Thank you so much. It is as I thought."

"What?"

"An idea I had. Julius, as soon as Sir John Fielding knows of it I shall feel free to tell you. But until that time I really must keep it to myself."

The little painter looked distressed. "Are you on the brink of discovery?"

"Possibly."

"Then let me beg you not to punish the perpetrator. As I said, whoever it was made the world a better place to live in when they removed George Goward from it."

"I know," said John, and sighed.


The really difficult part of the journey had begun. It was now Irish Tom's task to get them from Islington to Marybone without going back into London. Taking a circuitous route round the waterworks at The New River Head and passing the Merlin's Cave hostelry, Tom started to negotiate his way crosscountry, heading in a westerly direction and eventually, having traversed Black Mary's Hole, arriving in Lamb's Conduit Fields, close to the Foundling Hosptial. From there he continued west, crossing dangerous countryside, John at the ready with his pistol, then passing through the turnpike at Tottenham Court, then on past Farthing Pye House and finally turning north to join Love Lane.

John stuck his head out of the window. "Well done, Tom. Well driven."

"It's a good way, Sir, as long as you meet no cuthroats. But if you do, you'd be dead in the ditch and no questions asked."

"Well, we've made it safely. There are the gates of Fishergate Place."

"I hope he's in, that's all."

"You said that last time.

"That's because I'm still hoping."

But on this occasion John was to be disappointed. When the great door in the central tower opened, the footmen who answered informed him solemnly that His Grace, the Duke of Guernsey had taken a coach and gone into town.

"This is rather upsetting," John said, frowning. "You see, I am here on the business of Sir John Fielding, the Principal Magistrate. Is there no way I might be allowed in?"

"No, Sir. His Grace would not permit."

"Oh damme. Well, when may I call? When will His Grace return?"

"We do not discuss His Grace's business with strangers, Sir."

"Oh Perkins, don't be so pompous," called a female voice from somewhere in the Great Hall. "Who is there?"

The two footmen looked at one another in consternation. "It's Her Grace," whispered Perkins.

John stared, startled, thinking that he had not heard aright. "*Her* Grace?" he said. "Is that the Duke's mother?"

"His Grace's mother is dead, Sir," said the pompous Perkins. "I refer to His Grace's wife."

"Wife?" exclaimed the Apothecary. "But he's so young. I didn't even know he had one."

"Oh do stop gossiping, all of you," said the female voice, now much closer at hand. Then there was a quick light step and the two footmen bowed in unison as a young woman appeared in the doorway and gave John the most ravishing smile.

"Good day, Mr. Rawlings," she said.

It was Lucinda.

# Chapter 22

The shock was so intense that the Apothecary literally reeled against the doorpost while Irish Tom, gazing down from the coachman's box, shouted out, "So there you are you saucy minx! I wondered where you'd been hiding yourself."

Lucinda flashed her wisteria-coloured eyes in his direction. "I'm sorry, Tom." She turned back to John. "And I apologise to you as well, Mr. Rawlings. To leave you in the lurch after you had been so good to me was utterly inexcusable."

He smiled at her weakly. "May I come inside? I think it might be easier to talk."

"Of course." Lucinda turned back to the servants, who were standing agape. "Perkins, Ruff, Mr. Rawlings is a friend of mine and must be treated as such. His coachman is to be entertained in the kitchens. He and I will take champagne in the orangery."

"Very good, your Grace."

"I can't believe it," said John, following Lucinda through the Great Hall and on towards the back of the huge house where an exquisite orangery with extravagantly ornamented garden seats and tables within, had been built across its entire length.

The guinea bright hair, short still but growing longer, glistened in the light as Lucinda led the way to a cool spot and there sat down, motioning the Apothecary to do likewise.

"I am sorry to shock you like this. I still haven't got used to it myself."

"I think you had better start at the beginning." He paused, and added, "Your Grace."

"Please. I am Lucinda to you, and always will be. And I will tell you everything just as soon as the servants have gone."

For footmen were approaching, bearing trays and buckets

of ice, all of them bowing deferentially to the beautiful young Duchess and her visitor.

"And to think you were my housemaid," said John wonderingly.

Lucinda raised her glass. "I shall never forget how you took me in, Mr. Rawlings, nor Mrs. Rawlings's kindness either. If I can repay you at any time in the future, the pleasure will be mine."

They clinked glasses and drank. "Now tell me your story," the Apothecary asked.

"The early part you know. Lady Mary gave birth to me when she was fifteen, out of wedlock, a total ruination to her marriage prospects. I was immediately put out to foster parents and there I stayed until one day, during the school holidays, a brother I didn't even know I had came to join me. He had just started at the Brompton Park School but was proving to be so sickly that there was cause for concern. That was when my mother called on me to talk about him. Do you know, it was the first time I had met her in my entire life."

"Then why were you so loyal?"

Lucinda shrugged elegant shoulders. "I don't know. I think perhaps it was because she was what she was and I found it impossible to hate her."

"What about Fred? How did he feel about her?"

"Oh he loved her, poor little boy. But he loathed his stepfather and Goward detested Fred, called him a fat slug and forbade him the house. I was being educated at a girl's school but when Frederick got ill, Lady Mary made me dress as a boy and accompany him to Brompton Park. That was the way she salved her conscience."

"You know that your mother is dead?" John asked.

"Yes, Jack Morocco told Michael. It's strange, isn't it. She treated me less well than her horrible lap dogs, yet my heart was so heavy when I heard the news. How odd that invisible thread is, one longs to snap it and yet it is almost impossible to break."

"You were very good to her in so many ways, Lucinda. She deserved none of your kindness but you gave it without stint. Why, you even cleaned her gown for her when she was sick at the investiture, didn't you?" The Apothecary looked at his former servant over the rim of his glass, never taking his gaze from her face.

For the first time Lucinda's composure broke. The delicate skin flushed, the lovely eyes darkened, she looked at the floor.

"How did you know?"

"I had an inkling some while ago that the thirteenth page boy might have been you. But I didn't know for certain until last night. It was then that I realised that Frederick's appearance had altered completely through illness, and that you had gone to the investiture to keep an eye on him. Of course I saw you there, supporting your mother when she was vomitous, to use her word, but I didn't recognise you. But there were clues. Mary Ann remarked on the eye colour of the page who had seen them in. Your husband - how odd it is to use that word - knew perfectly well that you were present but lied to protect you. Somebody ran away just after Goward fell to his death. It was you, of course, hurrying to get back to my house before the alarm was raised. Then there was your absence from Nassau Street, where you should have been all along, lighting the fires and preparing for my return." John paused and drained his glass. "I rather believe, Lucinda, that you know who it was who killed your mother's husband."

She was very white but she met his eyes. "Yes, I know. But I shall never tell as long as I live."

"You don't have to. The question has already been answered."

She smiled humourlessly. "Do you want to hear the rest of my story? How I turned from a servant into a Duchess?"

"I would like to very much."

"As you probably guessed, it was Michael's half-brother,

Arnold, who raped me in my bed. Then he was foolish enough to boast of it and the Duke gave him a sound beating for his pains. Anyway, Fred was too ill to abandon in that terrible place so I ran away from your house and went to get him. I had a little money so we were able to stay at an inn for a few days, during which time I wrote to Michael at Fishergate Place. He wrote back and invited me to stay, wanting to make amends for his brother's gross treatment of me."

"Then I saw her, the most beautiful girl in the world, and I married her, not only to protect her but because I had fallen in love with her."

It was the Duke, who had approached them silently, and now stood staring at John as if he might call for him to be thrown out at any moment.

Lucinda got to her feet and flung her arms round him, then they kissed without inhibition and John was strangely touched by their youthful passion and obvious adoration of each other.

He stood up. "Good afternoon, your Grace. The Duchess is telling me all that happened after she left my house."

Michael turned to his bride. "Are you quite happy about that?"

"Oh yes, sweetheart. This man rescued me when I had run away. Then I ran away from him. I owe him an explanation. Please come and sit with us. I'll call for another glass."

She was sure of herself again and John thought how easily she had slipped into the role of peeress of the realm, then realised that her grandfather had been the Earl of Grimsby. "May I ask how you got permission to marry when you're both under twenty-one?" he said with a smile.

The Duke laughed shortly. "I'm afraid we didn't bother. Lucinda's mother was hardly likely to make any objection as she had never acknowledged the girl. My parents are dead and I have been in charge of my own destiny for several years now, so there was no one to raise a voice against my actions. We married in Marybone church where my family has a pew and I am not exactly unknown. The vicar was delighted and accepted a large fee. So who is to object?"

"Nobody really."

"Precisely." The Duke waited until another hovering servant had gone. "So, Mr. Rawlings, are you completely satisfied?"

The Apothecary nodded. "Certainly." He paused, then asked, "Where is the Earl of Lomond now? I take it he is also under this roof."

The young couple exchanged a very strange look and a clear picture came into the Apothecary's mind of a changeling, lying on a chaise on a stone balcony and peering over the balustrade at John's departing carriage.

Lucinda spoke. "Yes, Fred's here."

"Would it be possible for me to speak to him?"

The Duke answered for her. "I'm afraid Lord Lomond is ill. He is not receiving visitors."

John looked straight at Lucinda. "He has the wasting disease, doesn't he?"

She didn't answer but turned to her young husband for assurance.

The Apothecary persisted, certain now that they wouldn't ask him to leave. "It is my belief that his disease has been self inflicted. That Frederick began to fast after his stepfather banned him from the house, round about the time that his portrait was painted by Julius Witherspoon. I think that the child began by refusing to eat and soon it became such a habit with him that he could no longer stop himself. Am I right?"

The Duke answered with another question. "You know of this illness?"

"Yes, I have seen it before. Once or twice. It usually affects young women, those of a particularly brooding nature. But enough ill treatment from a brutal parent or bullying contemporary could bring it about in a boy."

"What is it called, this malaise?"

"It has no name. It is simply self-inflicted wasting disease."

"Can it be cured?" asked Lucinda.

John looked grim. "Rarely. It seems like some terrible insidious spider, wrapping its long legs round its victim and never letting go."

"Fred does have it," she answered, and started to cry, quite quietly but with enormous grief.

Her husband crossed over and put his arms round her. "She has been trying to protect Frederick from it for years, poor girl. She has coaxed him and loved him and fed him and given him all that she possibly could. But now she can do no more. Mr. Rawlings, my tragic little brother-in-law, once known as Fat Fred, weighs no more than a child of four."

"Dear God," said John, and thought to himself, for at least the hundredth time, that the Gowards, husband and wife, had indeed deserved to die.

"He's seen a physician?"

"Dr. Bolsover comes daily. He is highly respected and has treated my family for many a year. He has tried everything in his power but none of his physicks, none of his powders, can persuade Frederick to eat. He is under the crazed delusion that he still looks fat. He believes that his mother - he has no idea that the bitch has died, incidentally - will receive him at home once he is thin enough."

"God's mercy," was all the Apothecary could say.

The Duke went on, and there was a break in his voice, "The boy's arms and legs are like sticks, obscene in their thinness. His face is so hollow that his teeth look too big for him. By Christ, I tell you, Sir, that I did not kill George Goward at the investiture. But had I known then what I know now, I would have done."

"I think most present on that occasion would say the same."

Lucinda raised her tear-stained face, which had been buried in her husband's waist, where she sat and he stood.

"Michael, do you think Mr. Rawlings should visit Fred? Perhaps he could think of something, something that Dr. Bolsover might have overlooked."

The Apothecary shook his head. "If a respected physician cannot bring about a cure there is scant chance of my doing so."

"But is it worth a try?"

"I would hate to disappoint you."

"Oh please, Mr. Rawlings. Please, please, please." She was begging and it was pathetic.

But still John was reluctant. "Your Grace, Lucinda, once the wasting disease has its victim in its grip, there is nothing anybody can do."

"Do it to please her," whispered the Duke.

"Very well, if you insist. But I have no medical bag with me. This was a call on behalf of the Public Office. I simply had to check that my theory was correct. That you, Lucinda, were the thirteenth page boy."

"But how did you know I would be at Fishergate Place?"

"I didn't. But I did glimpse Frederick as I left the other day, though I didn't make the connection that it was him until last night. And I knew that wherever he was, you would be close at hand."

"Was he on the balcony?"

"Yes."

"He loves it out there, poor lost soul. Oh, Mr. Rawlings, he is so very frail. Please will you see him?"

"Of course. But Lucinda, don't expect anything. I am not a miracle worker."

And it would take that indeed, John thought as he stepped out onto the balcony and saw all that was left of Fat Fred. A changeling, a waif, a skeletal thing, turned its poor head with effort and he recognised the great sad eyes of the page-of-honour who had directed him at the investiture. But

Frederick was worse, far far worse, than he had been on that occasion. At the ceremony he had been thin and spindly, now he was emaciated to a degree beyond anything the Apothecary had ever seen before. It was repulsive, revolting, yet pitiful.

Involuntarily, John shook his head. "God help him," he said.

The boy attempted a smile, a terrible sight to see.

"Oh my dear," cried Lucinda, rushing to her brother's side and gathering him into her arms. "This is Mr. Rawlings. He is going to help you."

John turned to the Duke, who had followed him out onto the balcony. "I can't," he murmured. "Nobody could. The child is on the point of death."

"It will break Lucinda's heart."

"All you can do is ease his passing. What has Dr. Bolsover prescribed for him?"

"His physicks and powders are all on a tray in the bedroom. Please feel free to look."

It was a good selection and the Duke's assertion that the physician was excellent was certainly confirmed in John's eyes. There was a decoction of Carduus Benedictus, better known as Blessed Thistle, often used as an attempted cure for wasting disease. As was the powdered dried root of Autumn Gentian, which restored the appetite. There was also, and this was what John had been looking for, some opium powder, a concentrated form of the milky juice of the white poppy. These grains were expensive, having to be imported from the Far East, and, as the Apothecary knew only too well, there was a roaring trade in illegal importation for no apothecary worth the name would sell this to anyone who requested it, prescribing it to known patients only.

He turned to Guernsey. "If your brother-in-law sinks any lower give him one grain of this and send for the physician immediately."

"Is there no hope for him?"

"None. He has gone too far down the road to death ever to return."

Lucinda called from the balcony. "Mr. Rawlings, please. Fred is having some sort of convulsion."

He was there in a stride, as was the Duke.

The elfin creature lay in his sister's arms like a shrivelled leaf, shaking so violently that his big teeth rattled in his sunken mouth, his twig-thin arms and legs flailing.

"You must eat something," Lucinda cried out, and burst into tears.

He looked at her with enormous sadness, continuing to shake, but seemingly incapable of speech. John knelt at the boy's side, reaching for his pulse, feeling totally inadequate, knowing that there was nothing he could do to help, that the poor devil had grown too weak to sustain life much longer.

"He has deteriorated alarmingly since the investiture," he murmured in Lucinda's ear. "He is beyond my skill."

"He has eaten virtually nothing since then," she answered.

The Apothecary looked at his former servant with a steady gaze. "Guilt?"

Lucinda turned her head away and did not answer, and John was terribly aware of her husband coming to stand close by as if to protect her.

"Well?" he persisted.

"I shall never betray him," Lucinda replied, and with those words said it all.

The Apothecary got to his feet and went into the bedroom. There he mixed several grains of opium powder with barley water. Then he returned to where the boy still threshed, though more feebly now.

"Let him have this. It will help him to relax."

He passed Lucinda the glass, catching the Duke's eye as he did so. Guernsey asked a silent question and John nodded.

"Come Fred," said his sister, "drink this like a good boy."

He gulped a little, even a mouthful more than John had anticipated. Then, after a while, he grew still. But before he fell asleep, Frederick gave a small wry smile. "What price fatness now?" he whispered, then snuggled close into Lucinda's arms and closed his eyes.

# *Chapter 23*

The silence in Sir John Fielding's salon was profound, everyone sitting so still that nothing moved except for the swirls of blue smoke rising from Joe Jago's pipe. The Blind Beak, as was his way, was motionless, and John, quite exhausted by the early start to the day and all that had taken place, hardly had the energy to raise his glass of punch to his lips, an unusual state for him. Yet despite the quiet there was a strange feeling in the air, a feeling almost of unease, and it was Sir John Fielding who finally voiced the reason for it.

"It is rare," he said, "to come across a murderous child."

"I never have," responded Joe. "Not since I've been in your employ, Sir."

"I did once before," the Blind Beak continued. "In a way a similar tale. A girl of fourteen, abused by her filthy goat of a father, stabbed him through the heart."

"Was she brought to justice for such a killing?" asked John.

"She was. But my brother, Henry, had his methods and made sure that she did not get the rope. Pleading mitigation, he arranged for her to be transported to the colonies where she made a new and good life for herself."

"Something poor Frederick will never do."

"You say he died just after you left the house?"

"Yes, a rider caught up with the coach and informed me. The pathetic child went in his sleep, which I admit I induced with opium. Apparently his sister held him till the end."

"And it was definitely he who pushed George Goward?"

"There can be no doubt. Lucinda uttered the phrase, 'I will never betray him,' and that told me everything. Just before he slept, Frederick said, 'What price fatness now?' I think, Sir John, that that must have been the phrase you overheard."

"Yes," answered the Blind Beak, "that makes complete

sense. It also explains why the voice had that unearthly quality to it. It was a boy's."

"And why the shoes that Jack Morocco glimpsed were so small."

"It strikes me," said Joe Jago, puffing away, "that one or more of those pages must have seen something."

"I always believed there to be a conspiracy of silence," Sir John answered. "And I've been proved right. It's quite understandable. If the other pages knew anything of poor Lomond's background, none would betray him."

"Sir," said John Rawlings urgently, "are you going to make this situation public?"

The Beak was quiet, weighing the matter up, then he said, "No, I think it better not to do so. It can be announced by the Public Office that a mistake was made, that the victim slipped and the whole thing was a tragic accident. I believe that sad sister of young Frederick's has suffered enough."

"To say nothing of Aminta Wilson, Goward's daughter. Let it all be forgotten out of Christian charity."

"Quite right," said Joe Jago, who seemed to have mellowed somewhat since his fleeting encounter with Elizabeth Chudleigh. "What's done is done."

The Apothecary sighed deeply and finally managed to gather sufficient strength to raise his glass. "Sir John, I thank you with all my heart for what you have just said. If you had seen the lad, had seen to what he was reduced by the cruel attitude of his stepfather, then you would know as clearly as I that no blame can be attached to him. It was he who was the victim, not his cruel torturer."

"Thank God he died when he did," said Joe Jago, turning his light blue eyes on John in a long deep look.

"He had suffered enough for two lifetimes. Believe me, death came as his friend," the Apothecary answered slowly.

And with those words, uttered in the seclusion of Sir John Fielding's private quarters, the story of poor Frederick Drummond, Earl of Lomond, came at last to its tragic end.

# Chapter 24

The box at the Theatre Royal, Drury Lane, was quite the centre of attention. To start with it contained two extremely attractive women, both dressed to the hilt, though one did appear to be rounding to a child. Secondly, it had been secured by none other than that outrageous personality Jack Morocco, tonight clad from head to toe in crimson and gold, a black boy dressed like a little peacock beside him. As an added attraction there was the strangely dwarfish yet brilliant portrait painter, Julius Witherspoon, in the company. The other two men were not known to the *beau monde*, though the smaller, darker, of the two had a purple and silver suit on that was the envy of many, while the larger had such a jolly visage and booming laugh that he seemed to be worth examination. All in all, they were a young and glamorous party quizzing glasses flashed in their direction from the moment they entered their loge.

There being only six adults present, everyone had a chair except Ebony James, who stood between his master's knees, excitedly leaning over the parapet.

"No noise from you once it starts," said Jack Morocco severely. "When I go to the play I go to listen."

"You do realise that Coralie Clive is in this?" Emilia asked John with a certain acerbity.

"I have not come to see her. I have come to support Aminta," he answered firmly.

For Jack Morocco's mistress, obviously with an eye to her future, knowing that it could not lie with her flamboyant lover, had achieved her ambition and had been given a small part in this night's production of *The Merchant of Venice* in which the great David Garrick was to play Shylock to Coralie's Portia, a part in which her sister, Kitty, had excelled.

"None the less, you must be curious."

"Leave it, Emilia. My relationship with Coralie ended years ago, as well you know."

His wife relapsed into silence, only for Samuel's voice to soar above the others. Leaning close to Christabel Witherspoon's ear, he said in a loud whisper, "John and Coralie Clive were very close at one time you know." He winked at her. "Very close indeed."

Julius chimed in. "I am about to paint her portrait. David Garrick has asked me to do so."

With a concerted effort, the Apothecary changed the subject. "Such a shame that the Duke and Duchess of Guernsey are still in mourning. I am sure they would have liked to join us."

Fortunately for him Jack Morocco took up the theme and the conversation steered away from the beautiful actress with whom John had once been in love, so long ago now that it almost seemed like another lifetime.

"A very rum business that, her brother catching a wasting disease. I've never heard of such a thing before."

"It does happen," said John, "though more often to girls. But he had been teased so long by his stepfather about being fat, that the boy renounced food almost entirely."

"So he starved himself to death?"

"Yes."

"It was round about the time he died that the Public Office announced there had been a mistake, that George Goward's death was an accident after all." The negro's huge dark eyes turned on John and the Apothecary saw the gleam of intelligence in them. "So I couldn't have seen those feet after all."

"No," said John, "it must have been something else."

The black buck held his gaze steadfastly. "So it must," he said.

The elfin Christabel steered the conversation away. "Julius and I have decided to leave Islington and move closer to town. He is getting so busy that the travelling is becoming a nuisance, while I ..." She smiled at Samuel in a secretive way.

"... find that my interests are being drawn more and more towards London."

Emilia nudged John violently in the ribs and he jumped a little. "Wedding?" she whispered. He shrugged his shoulders to show that he didn't know and felt a positive rush of relief when the curtain went up and the theatre fell as silent as it ever did, which wasn't greatly, as the play began.

It was a superb performance, moving and profound, Garrick bringing to Shylock a depth of meaning that the Apothecary had never seen in the character before, while Coralie radiated charm as a truly delightful Portia. But in a strange way he was as glad to see the end of the show as he had been the beginning. Watching Coralie, remembering all her delightful idosyncracies, the way she had held him when they made love, the sweep of her black hair against his skin, was still painful after all this time, despite the fact that he had loved two women, Emilia and Elizabeth, since. So it was in a mood of introspection and soul searching that John Rawlings left Drury Lane that night.

The crowd outside jostled for chairs and hackneys and so it was in this melee that the Apothecary found himself pushed against someone and turned to apologise to them.

"Why, it's Mr. Rawlings," said a familiar voice, and John saw that Digby Turnbull stood bowing before him.

"Mr. Turnbull, how very nice to meet you again. Were you in the audience? Did you see Aminta?"

"Not only that. I have called on her and suggested that as I was so devoted to her mother and have no family of my own, I might act as an honorary uncle."

"And she agreed?"

"Of course she did. I'm on my way to see her now, as I expect are you."

"Indeed."

Digby hesitated, then said, "Mr. Rawlings, I shall be at St. James's Palace tomorrow night in my quarters there. I wonder if you would do me the great favour of calling on me.

There is something I have to ask you and this is neither the time nor the place."

The Apothecary smiled half-heartedly, positive that whatever the honest citizen wanted to know was bound to prove difficult to answer. "Yes, of course," he found himself replying.

"Excellent. Shall we say eight o'clock? I expect you'll want to dine with your wife and I cannot invite her on this occasion as the matter is confidential."

John's heart sank further. "I'll be there," he said.

There was a roar from the stage door as the first of the actors appeared, Aminta amongst them. Hearing the cheers, Digby Turnbull bowed and hurried away, and the Apothecary went to join the rest of his party.

Jack Morocco, as usual, had bought flowers in plentitude which he insisted on presenting to all the actresses as they emerged into the night, regardless of whether he knew them or not. The largest bouquet went to Aminta, but the second, somewhat to John's chagrin, was reserved for Coralie Clive, who swept out of the theatre on the arm of a nobleman and graciously received them from the bowing blackman's hands. There was a cry from a group of blades, who rushed forward in a body and lifted the actress shoulder high, carrying her through the crowd as if she were a goddess. Smiling, she looked down at her many admirers and just for a moment, John saw her emerald green eyes rest on him. He bowed low, despite the fact that Emilia was standing beside him, and Coralie blew a kiss in his general direction before she was whisked away.

"Well," said Emilia.

"Well what?"

"She obviously hasn't forgotten you."

"Well, I've forgotten her," lied John, and taking his wife by the arm led her away to join the others for supper.


That night St. James's Palace seemed more full of shadows

than ever before. As on the last occasion, John was granted admittance by a faceless sentry who seemed tall as a giant in that uncertain darkness, then made his way nervously across a courtyard lit only by flickering torches to the one place from which light shone, the private quarters of Digby Turnbull. On this occasion, however, though the interior was cheerful and a fire roared in the grate, the atmosphere seemed sombre, as if Digby's pensive mood was imprinting itself on his surroundings.

"Well, Sir," said John, when the preliminary small talk was over and done, "what is it that you want to say to me?"

The servant of the crown looked grim. "My friend, I don't know quite how to put this but I feel that there has been a cover-up of some kind and it is perturbing me enormously."

The Apothecary put on his blank face. "I'm afraid I don't quite follow you."

"I think you do, Sir."

"Could you explain further."

They were fencing verbally with one another and both of them knew it.

"I refer to the strange statement issued from Bow Street. The one in which it said that a mistake had been made in the case of Sir George Goward and that the affair was now closed. Come, Sir, come. Anyone with an ounce of intelligence must question that and ask themselves why that statement was made."

"I see," said John.

"What?"

"That you would query what was said. Others, Jack Morocco for instance, have asked in a subtle way, more by means of a look or a raised brow than a direct question. All of them, even if only half aware of the truth, seem to have decided to let the matter rest however."

"If that is a criticism of me, then I can only say that I have an enquiring mind which will not be satisfied until it knows the full story."

"Then look no further than a tragic child, Sir. A boy so undermined by his stepfather that he starved himself to death because of it. And think that if you were that little fellow, sick and weak with dieting, and that villainous creature stood almost on top of you on a steep staircase where you had been placed as part of your duty, would you not extend your wizened arms and give him the push that would bring about his death."

"You speak of one of the pages-of-honour?" asked Digby, aghast.

"I do indeed. Frederick Drummond, Earl of Lomond, son of the vacuous Lady Mary Goward. A child so injured by life that all must be forgiven him. He has paid for his sin - though I prefer to think of it as an act of justice - with his own life. So Sir John Fielding, great humanitarian that he is, made the conscious decision to draw a veil over the whole sorry incident for the sake of the boy's sister Lucinda, who has also known more misery in her young life than most of us do who live to old age."

"I am frankly astounded," said Digby Turnbull.

"And you will astound me," answered John, "if you do anything about this. For I will seriously have misjudged your character, Sir, and in that I should be most disappointed."

Digby poured out two glasses of claret. "I propose a toast, Sir. A toast to Sir John Fielding, the blind magistrate who sees all. May his clarity of vision last for ever."

"I'll gladly drink to that," answered the Apothecary. He turned to his host. "Sir, I have a mind to see that staircase once again if you would be so kind as to permit me. It will probably be the last time I set foot in this ancient palace and I would like to make the most of the opportunity."

"Then see it you shall," Digby replied, very cheerful now that the truth had been told him.

They crossed the courtyard together and went in through a side door. To the left lay the long reception room, to the right the two staircases, everything most dim in the light of the few candles that were lit. Walking slowly, John advanced to the spot where George Goward had lain dying, then he looked up to the point from which he had been pushed. Just for a moment he thought that a face, the face of a sad little changeling, looked back down at him through the wrought iron balusters, that something moved in the blackness. Then the Apothecary realised that it must be a trick of what little light there was, and turned away to join Digby Turnbull who had already vanished into the darkness.

# *Historical Note*

John Rawlings, Apothecary, was a real person. He was born circa 1731, though his actual parentage is somewhat shrouded in mystery. He was made Free of the Worshipful Society of Apothecaries on 13th March, 1755, giving his address as 2, Nassau Street, Soho. This links him with H.D. Rawlings Ltd. who were based at the same address over a hundred years later. Rawlings were spruce and ginger beer manufacturers and in later years made soda and tonic waters. Their ancient soda syphons are now collectors items and can only be found in antique shops. I am very proud to own one which was presented to me by my French fan club, based at the College La Millaire at Thionville.

John Fielding, the Blind Beak, received his knighthood in 1761. It is not on record where this ceremony actually took place and his name does not appear on the St. James's Palace list. However, this doesn't necessarily rule out the fact that the solemnities *could* have taken place there so the matter remains unproved. For the sake of my story I decided to place him at that most exciting of venues. If the facts are different, then I apologise to Sir John, who, I feel certain, wouldn't mind at all.

Miss Elizabeth Chudleigh was the eighteenth century's most celebrated bigamist. Brought up by her mother in very poor circumstances in Devonshire, Elizabeth's face was most definitely her fortune and her first serious love affair took place when she was fifteen years old. She almost married the Duke of Hamilton but an interfering aunt intercepted their correspondence and the relationship broke up. She married the Hon. Augustus Hervey privately on 4th August, 1744, the service conducted by the rector of Lainston, Mr. Amis. Both of them returned to their jobs, he as a lieutenant in the navy, she as Maid-of-Honour to Augusta, Princess of Wales and the marriage was kept secret. However, when Augustus returned to England in October, 1746, the inevitable happened and next year Elizabeth was secretly delivered of a son. He was put out to foster in Chelsea and died shortly after. By this time, Elizabeth and Augustus had split up and she preferred to conduct her life as Miss Chudleigh until, in 1759, her husband drew near the title of Earl of Bristol owing to the failing health of his brother. She now thought it sensible to establish the fact that she was married to the heir and, quite literally, forced Mr. Amis, lying on his deathbed, to enter her marriage in the register book. She shortly afterwards became the mistress of Evelyn Pierrepoint, Duke of Kingston. and her affair with him became a matter of notoriety when on 4th June, 1760, she gave a splendid ball in honour of the birthday of the Prince of Wales, soon to be George III. Meanwhile her husband, anxious to be rid of her, announced that he was suing for divorce but she refused to admit that a marriage had ever taken place. She countersued, denying everything, but was very disturbed when she had to take an oath declaring that she was a spinster. However, typically, she did. The court found for her and on the 8th March, 1769, she bigamously married the Duke of Kingston. She was presented as Duchess to the King and Queen, who wore her favours, as did the officers of state. However, her real husband, very bitter by now, renewed his matrimonial case in 1773. Fortunately for the Duke he died in that same year. In the terms of his will, the poor old fellow left her all his property for life and his entire fortune on the condition that she remained a widow, the reason for this restriction being her weakness for any adventurer who flattered her.

Elizabeth went abroad but finding some difficulty in obtaining money, threatened her English banker in Rome with a pistol. He paid up. When she returned to this country, trouble lay in wait. The late Duke's nephew laid a charge of bigamy against her and she was found guilty. Her real husband, who was by now Earl of Bristol, was also gunning for her, still wanting divorce. Elizabeth fled and never returned to England again. She died in Paris in 1788 at the age of sixty-eight.

If readers think that the character of Jack Morocco is far fetched, then let them turn their attention to Julius Soubise, the beloved black boy of the Duchess of Queensberry, upon whom the character is based. Soubise's exploits were amazing and, I quote '(he) became one of the most conspicuous fops of the town. He frequented the Opera, and the other theatres; sported a fine horse and groom in Hyde Park; became a member of many fashionable clubs, and made a figure.' He also had a wonderful life style, including a beautiful mistress, an apartment full of hothouse flowers and extravagant dinner parties complete with claret and champagne. Eventually he overstepped the mark and was hustled abroad by the Duchess for seducing a maid in sordid circumstances. He died in a riding accident in India as dramatically as he had lived.

The study of the black population in eighteenth century England is absolutely fascinating and I would recommend anyone interested to read *Black England* by Gretchen Gerzina. From abject slaves to pampered pets, this book tells it all and is essential reading for serious students. My thanks to John Oram for giving me a copy and drawing my attention to the role of negroes in our historic society.

The Pandemonium Club actually existed, its membership consisting of bright sparks and wits of the day. However, its initiation ceremony has not been passed down to us and I have therefore borrowed the rites of the Humbug Club, which was formed later in the eighteenth century, too far removed in time for John Rawlings to have been a member. The President of the Humbugs signed himself Humbugallo Rex, and Screech, the owl, countersigned all documents as Secretary. What really happened at Pandemonium ceremonies, I leave to the imagination of the reader!